# Kissing her was madness.

Colin swore to himself he didn't know why he was doing it—except that it seemed right and natural.

That she considered herself too good for him hit his pride and made him a little crazed, as did the fact he was attracted to her. In so many ways she was such a country mouse. Obstinate, fearful, defiant . . . headstrong, intelligent, forthright—and a surprisingly good kisser.

Her lips melded against his. Her mouth was still closed, a sign she'd not been kissed often. Yet something about her attracted him.

He had an overwhelming need to make mind-numbing love to her right on the floor. He pressed. She did not resist. He touched her lips with his tongue—

The spell broke. For both of them.

She stared at him, her razor-sharp gray-green eyes wide in surprise. "Why did you do that?"

"Why did you let me?"

"I didn't 'let you,' " she responded. "You took."

He had. And wouldn't mind taking again.

*Avon Books by*
**Cathy Maxwell**

# CATHY MAXWELL

## The Seduction of an ENGLISH LADY

AVON BOOKS
An Imprint of HarperCollins*Publishers*

AVON BOOKS
*An Imprint of* HarperCollins*Publishers*
10 East 53rd Street
New York, New York 10022-5299

Copyright © 2004 by Cathy Maxwell
ISBN: 0-06-009297-1
www.avonromance.com

First Avon Books paperback printing: January 2004
First Avon Books special printing: September 2003

Avon Trademark Reg. U.S. Pat. Off. and in Other Countries, Marca Registrada, Hecho en U.S.A.
HarperCollins® is a registered trademark of HarperCollins Publishers Inc.

Printed in the U.S.A.

10  9  8  7  6  5  4

*For Jean Duguid,*
*my other mother*

Nestled in the very heart of England, where the Hodder and Ribble rivers meet, is a valley so green and unspoiled, it sparkles like a gem of the realm.

Here, in the ancient hunting forests, once home to wolves, wild boar, and witches, or by village greens bordered by bubbling brooks and stone-built cottages and guarded by the ruins of Norman keeps, life has its own pace. There are those who will never leave, not even the boundaries of their own village.

And then there are those who, even if they travel afar, **must return. . . .**

# Chapter One

*Lancashire, England*
*April 5, 1816*

The faint scratch at the front-door keyhole caught Lady Rosalyn's attention as she passed through the center hall on the way to her front parlor. She paused, listening.

There it was again . . . as if someone were trying to unlock the door, which was not locked.

Rosalyn had just left her companion, Covey, as she was finishing her breakfast in the back morning room. Cook was in the kitchen and Bridget, the maid, was upstairs gathering the laundry. The other member of their small household, Old John, Cook's husband and the gardener, never used the front door, nor did any of them, Rosalyn herself included. The front door was for company, and she wasn't expecting any.

She put her hand around the brass candlestick sitting on a table by the door.

Whoever was there realized the door was unlocked. The handle turned.

She lifted the candlestick over her head. The stub of the candle in the stick fell out, bouncing off her shoulder and onto the floor. She would usually chase it down—there wasn't enough money to waste anything, including candle stubs, in her household—but this time, she had other concerns.

The door started to open. A swirl of damp, chilly air swept around her skirts. She mustered her courage, held her breath, ready to swing—and stopped.

It was no disreputable rogue who stood in her doorway, rather a well-dressed gentleman. He had to remove his hat and duck to come in her narrow door without bumping his head. His shoulders were so broad that he temporarily blocked out the light of the first good sunny spring day they'd had in April.

The gentleman looked startled to see her. There was a day's growth of stubble on his jaw. Buff leather breeches hugged horseman's thighs, and his marine blue coat was cut to perfection. He was a Corinthian, a Fashionable.

What was he doing at Maiden Hill?

His gaze followed up her arms to the candlestick she wielded with wicked intent. He held up a hand, warding her off. "I'm sorry. I see I've startled you."

Rosalyn had two instantaneous thoughts: the first, that she'd never met this gentleman before, and the second, that in spite of a shadow of unshaven whiskers, he had to be the most undeniably handsome man she'd ever laid eyes on. The mud splattering his boots, the tangled curls of his dark hair, and the loose, devil-may-care knot in his neck cloth told her she was right in thinking he was not from the Valley. He'd apparently been riding hard and for some distance.

Suddenly self-conscious of her own countrymade dress in a serviceable gray broadcloth, she demanded, "Who are you?"

"I'm the new owner of this house. I say, do you mind putting down that candlestick. You look ready to crack my skull with it."

"The new owner—?" Rosalyn started to lower the candlestick and then raised it back up again as her common sense rejected his claim. He couldn't be the owner—*she* was! "Leave now peacefully before I-I—" She hesitated, at a loss for words. Before she did *what* to such a giant?

4

Nor was he afraid. "Before you beat me around the ears until I'm bloody?" he suggested helpfully, his tone amused. "Or grab me by the scruff of the neck and toss me out?"

Rosalyn didn't answer. She couldn't. The rich, deep masculinity of his voice sparked something inside her she'd thought long dead or at least put in its proper place—a very definite interest in the opposite sex.

He took the candlestick from her hands and smiled. She was blinded into dizziness. No man should have a smile so devastating.

Then he brought her to her senses by asking, "So, are you one of the servants?"

Rosalyn didn't know if she could believe her ears. Yes, she was wearing the dress she reserved for household tasks and one, like most of her wardrobe, that was long out of fashion. And, *yes*, this morning, she'd done little more than toss her hair up in a quick knot at the nape of her neck and fasten it in place with a pin or two. *Still*, his question was a douse of cold reality. His appeal evaporated.

"I beg *your* pardon," she countered with every ounce of aristocratic hauteur bred into her. "*Who* are *you*?"

His brows rose as he realized his mistake. He

5

set the candlestick on the side table before saying, "Colin Mandland, *Colonel* Colin Mandland."

She knew the surname. Reverend Mandland was the vicar of St. Mary Magdalene's Church. "Have we met before?"

"I don't know. Are you going to tell me who *you* are?"

The abrupt response from someone who had just walked into her house set Rosalyn's back up. "I am the woman who *owns* this house. Not you. Now, sir, I will ask you to take yourself and your rude manners elsewhere. If you don't, I will take action." She reached out to close the door, irritated enough to push even a big ox like himself out of the way if necessary, but he blocked the door's closing with his arm, his next words stopping her cold.

"I bought this house from Lord Woodford. I even have a key." He held it up for her to see.

Rosalyn froze at the mention of her cousin George. She met Colonel Mandland's gaze, praying he was jesting. He wasn't. She took the key, wanting to touch it to prove it was real.

Alarm ripped through her. She dropped her hand from the door. "George wouldn't? . . . At least, not without saying something—?"

Colonel Mandland's expression turned sympathetic. He reached inside his coat and pulled out several folded documents. "Lord Woodford should have written you. I purchased the house a day and a half ago from him, but we've been talking for at least a week or more." He held out the papers to prove his claim.

"You purcha—" Rosalyn shook her head, still unable to wrap her mind around his words. "From my cousin George?" She took the documents from the gentleman and stepped around him so she could take advantage of the morning light.

Outside, there was a vehicle Rosalyn recognized from her London days—a crane-necked phaeton, the dangerous sporting vehicle preferred by the Prince Regent and his set. The wheels were red with yellow spokes, and the paint was fresh and new.

Rosalyn had never seen one in these parts because they were dangerous for the local roads. The harness of the rig lay on the seat, along with the driving whip. The horse that had been attached was happily munching his way through the spring-tender plants of her flower beds.

He wasn't particularly handsome, or young, horseflesh. The animal would have been better suited to drawing a brewer's dray than a fashionable rig. "Please," she murmured, "the land-scaping."

Colonel Mandland stepped outside. "Oscar, go on out."

Oscar looked up, the leaves and roots of a sweet pea sticking every which way out of his mouth. He had to be at least sixteen hands tall. A giant of a horse for a giant of a master.

"Go on!" the colonel commanded.

Oscar grumbled his disapproval, sounding like nothing more than a disgruntled old man. He then lumbered out onto her yard, which Rosalyn did not think a better solution. She would have preferred Colonel Mandland tying the beast up.

But Rosalyn had more pressing worries than her lawn at the moment. She quickly scanned the cramped writing on the documents. They were exactly what the colonel had said, a bill of sale deeding Maiden Hill, Clitheroe, Lancashire—her home for these last four years and more—over to one Colin Thomas Mandland for the sum of five thousand and eighty pounds. The documents were signed "Woodford," the title her cousin had inherited from her father.

Five thousand and eighty pounds? Had George

taken leave of his senses? Was that all this estate meant to him?

Rosalyn's mind went numb. When she could finally focus, it was on the colonel's horse bending down on his knees preparing to roll on top of her prized bed of forget-me-nots, phlox, and daisies, which were just beginning to bud. . . .

"Covey!" She wasn't worried about flowers right now. Instead, she spun around, leaving the door open as she raced toward the morning room.

Rosalyn had only taken a few steps when Mrs. Susan Covington, a good-natured widow some forty years older than herself, came out from her breakfast, tucking a stray gray curl neatly under her lace cap. Decades ago Covey's husband had been Rosalyn's father's tutor at nearby Stoneyhurst School. When Mr. Covington had married, her father had thought so much of his former tutor that he'd let the newlyweds live at Maiden Hill. The house was as much Covey's home as it was Rosalyn's, perhaps even more.

And Covey was very dear to Rosalyn. Since Rosalyn had moved to Maiden Hill, Covey had fulfilled the role of mother, tutor, confidante. She had become the caring family Rosalyn didn't

Cathy Maxwell

have. "My dear, why are you bellowing?"

"George sold Maiden Hill! Right out from under us!" Rosalyn held out the documents, her hands shaking. "This is beyond all reason. The least he could have done was tell us. I mean, the man he sold the house to, Mr . . . Mr. . . ." She was so troubled that her mind went blank.

"Colonel Mandland," he reminded her discreetly from his post by the door. He stood a respectful distance, but she sensed he was anxious to move into the house, to take it over.

"*Colonel* Mandland," she ungracefully corrected herself and gave the man her back. His startling good looks had soured in her mind. And why not? He had come to throw her out of her home.

"Mandland? After Reverend Mandland?" Covey asked.

"He's my brother," the colonel offered helpfully.

"Ah, yes, I see a faint resemblance. And I remember you growing up," Covey said. "Colin, right?"

"Yes, ma'am."

"A hell-raiser, weren't you, Colin?" she said with her customary frankness.

He didn't deny it. "I was different than my brother."

"Aye, but I remember you. Everyone said you would come to a bad end, but my Alfred said you had a fine mind. We were all pleased when Father Ruley took you in hand and purchased your colors."

"The military has been very good to me," he responded.

"Obviously. You've grown some," the older woman agreed.

Rosalyn cut through the "pleasantries." "Covey, please. We have a crisis here. I shall have George's head on a platter for this. To think he didn't say a word, not even a letter—"

"Letter?" Covey's eyes widened. "A letter came. I paid the frank." She covered her mouth with her hands. "Did I not tell you?"

"There was a letter from George?" Rosalyn demanded. "When, Covey? And where is it?" Her tone was sharper than she intended, but lately Covey had started forgetting all sorts of things, usually small details or matters that Rosalyn and the servants could manage—but this! George never wrote unless he wanted something, something that usually boded ill for Rosalyn.

"I put a letter in the pocket of my apron," Covey said, acting on the motions as she spoke.

"The one you wore yesterday?" Rosalyn asked.

"No, yes . . . I'm not certain. Shall I have Bridget check?"

She spoke to the air, because Rosalyn was already on her way up the stairs, clutching the signed deed in her hand. Covey's room was the third door on the left. This room, like all of them at Maiden Hill, was sparsely furnished with discarded pieces collected over the decades from the other estates the earl of Woodford owned. Maiden Hill was neither a large nor important piece of property, but Rosalyn had assumed that George had *some* sense of family responsibility. More the fool her!

Rosalyn hurried to the ancient wardrobe and threw open the doors. Covey always wore aprons around home with deep pockets. She said this helped her not to forget where she put things like her spectacles or embroidery silks. Rosalyn wondered why *she* hadn't been at home when the letter had been delivered, and then remembered her meeting with the Ladies' Social Circle. They were planning charity baskets to give out to the needy of the parish, in addition to a spring dance.

"Covey was wearing her green? . . ." Rosalyn ran her hands over the assortment of aprons and didn't discover a letter.

She turned, struggling with panic. Her gaze fell on the book on Covey's bedside table, and she saw the letter marking a place between the pages.

Flying across the room, Rosalyn pulled the letter out and broke the hastily made wax seal. George's handwriting was little more than an indecipherable scrawl. She stared at it until she could understand he'd spent the first portion of the letter on endless excuses, all of them having to do with gambling debts. Then, in the last paragraph, he wrote that he'd been forced to sell Maiden Hill, since it was the only estate unentailed. She was directed to travel to Cornwall to take up residence with their great-aunt Agatha.

For a second, Rosalyn felt as if she'd turned into cold stone, the letter in one hand, Colonel Mandland's deed in the other. This was the bleakest moment of her life. Worse even than her mother's betrayal and her father's death.

She had no home . . . and she could do nothing about it.

She looked at the letter's date. George had written it *last week*. Certainly, he'd had time to travel to Clitheroe and personally explain the situation. As she was the daughter of the man whose death had given him the title, it would have been the honorable thing for George to have done—and she would have had the opportunity to talk him out of this tragic error.

Rosalyn wadded George's letter up in one fist. The man was a drunkard who didn't deserve the noble title of Woodford. She wished she could throw the letter in the fire and the deed to the estate along with it!

How dare George lose family assets to the gambling table? At the very least, he should have fobbed off his debtors like any other gentleman of consequence. But no! George was probably in so deep he'd had the choice between selling Maiden Hill or flying to the Continent, the fate of those who couldn't meet their obligations and didn't want to be thrown into debtor's prison.

Not for the first time did she wonder why she hadn't been born a man. Then she would have had her father's title and control of her own fate.

Of course, there had been a time in England when no one would have dared throw a nobleman into prison for debt! Days when merchants had been only too happy to extend credit to the titled. After all, title should have privilege, and there were some things more important than money!

Rosalyn caught herself up short in her mental tirade. Yes, those days of rank meaning privilege were over. She knew that all too well. The good merchants of Clitheroe extended her credit, but she had to be careful with her pennies lest she overextend herself. Her pride did not want anyone to know just how far she, a daughter of the proud house of Woodford, had fallen.

And yet, she sensed they all knew.

Tears burned her eyes, but she forced them back. The earl of Woodford's daughter did not cry—no matter what life handed her.

Instead, she did what she always did in times of misfortune: She considered what she *could* do, then attempted to make the best decision. George had blithely written orders telling her to move in with Aunt Agatha but had not provided the funds to do so. She thought of her precious hoard of coins. There was not enough to pay for a seat on the post, let alone hire a coach.

And she would write and tell George so. The opportunity for action gave Rosalyn courage. This was George's problem and he must solve it. She would not go to Aunt Agatha's docilely. She'd lived with the old tartar once before. A more petulant, difficult woman didn't walk the face of the earth. Nor could Rosalyn leave Covey behind to live on parish charity—however, if Rosalyn had been a burden to Aunt Agatha, Covey would be even more so.

Rosalyn looked down at the deed in her right hand. How she wished she'd had the funds to purchase Maiden Hill for her own. If she owned it, she would never let it go. . . .

The random thought took shape in her mind, and Rosalyn knew what she had to do.

Colin had never felt so awkward in his life. He'd driven all night from London, spurred on by the pride of ownership. He remembered Maiden Hill from his childhood. He'd always admired the house, even during his early, misspent youth. Now it was his.

He had expected the house to be occupied. Woodford had told him the estate had been maintained and there were obligations outstanding to the servants that Colin would have to settle. It hadn't mattered. Colin wanted the estate.

However, this Rosalyn was anything but a servant, and he sensed matters were going to be very sticky—especially if there were a good number of people in the Valley who, like Mrs.

Covington, remembered him from the days before Father Ruley had straightened him up.

"Lady Rosalyn is very upset," Covey confided.

"I noticed," he answered. So, she was *Lady* Rosalyn. This mess was getting worse by the minute. He cast an anxious eye on the staircase. Most of his hard-earned fortune was tied up in that deed, and he wanted it back the moment she came down the stairs. He also yearned to walk through the house, to inspect every nook and cranny. This was *his* house, a symbol of all he'd been working toward. He was a landowner.

"How is your husband?" he asked Mrs. Covington.

Her expression saddened. "Alfred passed away a month before my lady arrived at Maiden Hill. Her presence helped me with my loss. I hope I haven't done anything terribly wrong by forgetting the letter?"

"It was bad news no matter when it was received," he assured her.

She relaxed slightly. "Yes, you are right. Perhaps you would like to wait in the sitting room?" she suggested, as if remembering her social duties.

"I'll wait here," Colin answered.

His brother would be surprised Colin owned

Maiden Hill. He would be surprised Colin had
returned from France. Colin was not the best cor-
respondent, although his brother, like all true
clergymen, had written faithfully at least once a
month.

Shifting his weight, Colin noticed signs of age
and wear in the tight hallway. The tile in one
corner was cracked and loose. The walls needed
painting, and there was a water mark on the
ceiling.

"Your brother is a fine man," Covey said.

"He is."

"He has a fine family, too."

"Yes."

"My favorite is Emma. Such a sweet child . . .
but then there is the new baby, too."

"Another baby?" Colin shook his head. "How
many do they have?" Of course, Matt had written about the children, but only just this moment
had they become real.

"Five, I believe. All handsome children."

*Five.* Colin swallowed his opinion. At one
time, Matt had been as ambitious as himself.
Matt's goal had been to ascend in the hierarchy
of the Church, a vocation for which he'd been
well suited. However, once he'd met Valerie, his
aspirations had melted away, and he had, appar-

ently, settled for a country parish and a horde of children.

It was too bad, really. Matt could have been a bishop.

"Lady Rosalyn," he said, "she is *what* to Woodford?"

"Oh, they are cousins. Lord Woodford doesn't write very often. I should have known the letter was important. I know I meant to give it to her. It seems of late I'd forget my head if it wasn't attached."

To that pronouncement, Colin had no opinion. However, Lady Rosalyn was a different story.

She was Quality. A true pearl of the first water, in spite of the fact that she appeared to be one of those who didn't seem to care how she presented herself. Her dress was more suited to a chambermaid than a lady, and her hairstyle was too tight and dowdy for her age. Her hair was a dark brown, and her nose straight and aristocratic. He had no doubt all the Valley matrons, as he and his mates used to refer to the wives of the gentry, basked in her reflected haughtiness.

As if his thoughts had conjured her, there was a rustle of movement from the top of the stairs. Colin looked up expectantly and watched Lady

Rosalyn walk down the stairs. He noticed two things—one, she held his deed in her hand, and the second, she had trim ankles. He suspected she was all leg.

He liked long legs, but usually on younger and more attractive women. It wasn't as if Lady Rosalyn was ugly—she was far from that—however, there was something determinedly spinsterish about her. *She'd* placed herself on the shelf, not the world, and far be it for him to argue with her.

Still, he did notice that for such a rigid, conventional woman, she had surprisingly lush, full lips. They might or might not be kissable. He couldn't tell because, at the moment, they were pressed together in anger.

As she reached the bottom stair, he saw that, in addition to the deed, she also held a crumpled letter. The correspondence from Woodford. Colin could have cursed the man, not only for his unfeeling incompetence but also for placing the mess in Colin's lap.

"Lady Rosalyn, I know this is difficult—" Colin started.

Her angry gaze swept past him and went straight out the door. "Your horse is in my perennial bed again," she interrupted as if he'd not spoken at all.

Colin turned, and, sure enough, Oscar was stomping all through the overturned earth, rooting with his nose for any shoots of green. Colin went out the door onto the front step. "Oscar, get out of there!"

The huge chestnut twitched an ear in Colin's direction and then had the audacity to pretend he hadn't heard as he kept rooting through the earth.

Colin turned to Lady Rosalyn. "Usually he is better mannered—" He stopped. This was no time to lie. "No, that's not true. Oscar has the manners of a cow."

"He looks a bit like a cow," she observed icily.

"He's good-sized and fairly ugly," Colin answered, struggling to keep his own anger in check. "But he carried me well into French cannons and I forgive him much."

For the first time since coming downstairs, Lady Rosalyn looked at him. Her eyes were a grayish green. Hostile eyes without guile framed by feminine, long black lashes.

"I don't care if Wellington himself rode your horse to drive Napoleon out of France," she said. "I-want-him-*out*-of-my-flower-bed."

Her imperiousness sliced through him. No one talked down to Colin. Not anymore.

"Do you mean *my* flower bed?" he countered. "I know you are unhappy, Lady Rosalyn, but with all due respect, the deed says it all belongs to me now, and if Oscar wants to graze there, I give him leave to do so. We've traveled a long way together to arrive here."

He anticipated a spate of temper. Or even feminine tears.

He hadn't foreseen her slamming the door in his face.

The key in the inside lock turned. He was shut out.

Colin stood in disbelief. She'd locked him out with his own key—*and* she had the deed. She could sign it or cross things out and it would take him ages to regather the witnesses and correct it.

*Bloody hell.*

"Lady Rosalyn, open this door."

For the past decade, whenever Colin had given an order, it had been instantly obeyed. His men had known better than to defy him.

Lady Rosalyn's answer was obstinate silence.

# Chapter Two

"What did you do after she slammed the door in your face?" his brother, the good Reverend Matthew Mandland, asked.

They stood by the hearth in the all-too-cozy cottage that served as rectory for St. Mary Magdalene's Church. The rugs were worn and the furniture, past its prime, but one knew this was a home.

Of course, there was no privacy in the small sitting room. Matt's wife, Valerie, had ignored any of Colin's hints that he wished to talk to her husband alone. She rocked the latest addition to the family—a baby girl named Sarah—while five-year-old Joseph charged through the room chasing his four-year-old sister, Emma, the one Mrs. Covington liked so much. The twosome disappeared in the kitchen only to turn and run back out again.

To top it all off, Colin's night of travel and the euphoria of buying Maiden Hill were catching up with him. "What did I do?" he repeated, trying to hear himself think. "Well, since she had taken the key from me, I ordered her to open the door. She ignored me. I pounded on the door, but she would not let me in. Finally, I shouted at her and, frankly, made a fool of myself. Unfortunately, she had time to lock or bar all the doors to the house."

Valerie shook her head. "Nothing ever comes of losing one's temper, Colin. You of all people should know that."

Colin bit his tongue and an urge to strangle her. Funny how he could have been away for a little over a decade, mastered his way to the top of his field, led men on the battlefield, and received commendations from Wellington himself, but when he returned to his family they talked to him as if he'd never left. They assumed he was the same wild seventeen-year-old of their memory.

He'd noticed *they'd* changed.

Couldn't they see the same in him?

He picked up the poker and, resisting the urge

to smash something with it, stirred the peat embers in the hearth. In a low voice intended for his brother alone, he said, "I've traveled all night, spent the better part of three hours cooling my heels on the porch of *my* house, and still don't have the deed. I could hire a solicitor, but there must be a better way to get the damn deed back."

"Lady Rosalyn doesn't have to do anything she doesn't want to do," Val answered patly. "And, please, watch your language." She gave a pointed look at the children present.

Matt agreed. "Lady Rosalyn has the run of the Valley. *We* do exactly as *she* wishes."

"What the bloody hell does that mean?" Colin demanded.

"Colin, the *children*," Val said. "Here, Joseph, Emma, run outside and play."

Waiting until the little ones left the room, Colin frowned an apology to his sister-in-law. "Sorry. Forgot myself." He took a step closer to his brother. "What does *that* mean?" he demanded.

Matt reached for his tobacco on the mantel and began filling his pipe. Colin wondered irritably when his brother had turned so pokey, or did marriage do that to a man?

At last, Matt said, "We call Lady Rosalyn the Velvet Hammer. Few gainsay her. She is the power behind our humble little society. Until she came along, we were a bit of a boring lot."

"Don't misunderstand him," Val hurried to add. "Lady Rosalyn does many good works, but she does things *her* way. We've all found it easier to go along. Of course, Mrs. Lovejoyce and her friends would like to dethrone her, but Lady Loftus adores her. For right now, Lady Rosalyn is in control of who does what and when."

"Even of you, Val?" Colin couldn't resist the dig.

His sister-in-law answered with complete honesty, "Oh, I'm not in anyone's class. Not with the parish duties and the children giving me more to think about than flower beds and dances."

"Lady Rosalyn came up from London," Matt explained. "Had a Season there or two. I don't know why she didn't marry, and, the truth be known, we gentlemen were happier before she brought her Society ways to the Valley. However, the wives are content, and that is often all that matters."

"Well, I'm not going to march to her tune," Colin replied. "And as for doing things a certain way, I'm accustomed to doing things *my* way."

"Exactly," his brother agreed, lighting his pipe. "That's why the two of you have a conflict."

"We have a conflict because she wants to keep *my* house," Colin stated, perturbed neither one of them seemed particularly upset by Lady Rosalyn's flat-out larceny.

"Yes," Val agreed, rising from her chair, Sarah asleep in her arms. "But you must have some empathy for the woman. Her life hasn't been easy."

"So hard she needs to keep things that don't belong to her?" Colin wondered aloud.

"Hard enough that we should have more Christian understanding," Val answered. "Isn't that right, Matthew?"

Matt answered by raising his eyebrows, a noncommittal sign if ever there was one.

"How hard can it be to be born titled?" Colin countered. "If she'd been a cobbler's son, she would have known a hard life. Matt and I have had to fight and scrape for everything we have."

"Ah, but you have always known love," Val soothed, as if it explained everything. She lowered the sleeping baby into her cradle.

*Love?*

Colin rolled his eyes. What was it with women? They believed *everything* poets scribbled.

Val caught his look. She stood with an impatient sound. "It's true, Colin. Love is a valued commodity and one Christ taught. I firmly believe the lack of it is what is wrong with much of the world—including Napoleon's problems."

He opened his mouth to protest. He'd met Napoleon. A lack of love was not his problem—but Val shushed him with a wave of her hand. "Lady Rosalyn has spent most of her life orphaned and being handed off from one relative to another. Her mother created a terrible scandal by running away with her riding instructor, and her father drank himself to death of a lonely heart—"

"Is this what Lady Rosalyn told you?" Colin asked skeptically. The proud woman he'd met today did not strike him as the sort to exchange personal confidences.

"This is what we *all* know," Val declared. "The deacon's wife, Mrs. Phillips, knew someone in London who knew *of* Lady Rosalyn's parents and, well, the information is very reliable."

"Rumor often is," Colin murmured, tongue in cheek.

Val ignored him. "Maiden Hill is what Lady Rosalyn considers her first real home. She confided that to me once herself. You can't expect her to give it up easily."

Colin did feel a bit of sympathy. He knew how

important home was, and he hated the fact that he was a soft touch for such a story.

He forced himself to be hard. The house was his. "She is her cousin's obligation. He's the head of the family. Woodford will take care of her."

"He's not done a good job of the matter so far, has he?" Val flashed back.

"Where do women find their logic?" Colin demanded in exasperation. "And what do you want me to do? Give her the house? Lose all my money and ignore *my* dreams?" He turned to his brother. "You remember Father Ruley's plans for us?" The aging cleric had been a distant relative, as well as their generous benefactor. He'd financed both their educations and had held high hopes for both of them. He'd once done the same for their father and had been disappointed. "Look at us now. You are a country vicar and I'm—" He broke off, so frustrated that words failed him.

"A colonel," Matt finished. "'Tis no small feat."

"You think?" Colin said, unable to keep the self-derision out of his voice. "I'm not knighted, brother. I should have been for my service to my country, but I wasn't."

"A knighthood?" Val echoed. "You did aim high."

"And why not?" Colin asked. "Any other man who had served as I had, who had endeavored, risked, and accomplished what I did would have been knighted."

"Then why aren't you?" she wondered.

"I spoke my mind," he admitted. "I said what needed to be said for the good of my men. If I saw something that was wrong, I corrected it. When the men went into battle, I didn't hide behind the lines, I marched with them. Wellington trusted me and used me well, but in the end, even he said I was my own worst enemy."

Matt met Colin's gaze with understanding. "We both have a great deal of pride for a cobbler's sons."

"Well, I'm proud of you both," Val said firmly. "You are men of integrity. I think well of you, Colin, for having courage and honesty. There was a time everyone feared you would have a noose around your neck."

"You didn't know me then, Val," he said testily.

"The family told me," she said, blithely dismissing his objection. Colin felt a touch of betrayal. From the moment Matt had met her, she had come between the two brothers. She was Matt's confidante. His helpmate. The mother of his children and his partner.

And what of their parents? When they were alive, did they think more of her than their youngest son, who had been a trial? Especially when he'd lost all good sense for a while after Belinda Lovejoyce had rejected him and married another?

"I had high spirits," Colin said soberly. "I wasn't criminal."

Val looked as if she had an opinion but was wisely keeping it to herself. She walked up to him and straightened the knot in his neck cloth. "What is important is that you have returned to the Valley. We need you here, don't we, Matthew? The children shall come to know their uncle, and we'll find you a lovely girl to marry."

Colin looked to his brother, uncomfortable because he felt Val patronized him. "Why is it that women believe the solution to most problems is marriage?"

"Because a marriage based on love is the secret to a well-lived life," his sister-in-law answered for her husband. She gave Colin a sisterly pat on the shoulder and returned to her chair, picking up her darning.

There was that word again—*love*. Val's mind only worked in one direction. Well, Colin had been in "love" before and a more uselessly extravagant, silly emotion did not exist . . .

"Loftus," Matt piped in.

"The old lord?" Colin asked. "Is he still alive? I thought he would have broken his neck over a fence years ago."

"He's alive and still hunting," Matt answered. "More than ever, in fact. Lady Loftus is so wrapped up in Valley routs and affairs she rarely nags him to take her to London anymore."

"But I'd wager he doesn't ride any better," Colin said.

"He is the bane of his horses," Matt agreed. "He is the man you need to talk to about Maiden Hill. He and Lady Loftus have sponsored Lady Rosalyn from the beginning. If anyone can negotiate a sensible arrangement to your dilemma, it is Loftus."

"You're right," Val agreed, knotting her thread and biting it off with her teeth.

At that moment, the front door burst open and Boyd and Thomas, Matt and Val's oldest children, ages ten and eight, respectively, came running into the cottage, followed by Joseph and

Emma. They'd seen the phaeton by the rectory stable and wanted to know who owned such a "rum rig."

Their boyish enthusiasm reminded Colin of himself and Matt as boys. He was also a bit startled to have before him all of these people who'd been born after he'd left for the military, people who bore a bit of a resemblance to him. Yes, he'd known they were born, but there was a great difference between reading about someone and seeing them in flesh and blood.

"Lads," Matt said, his use of the term reminding Colin so much of their father, "this is your uncle Colin. He has returned from the military."

The oldest, Boyd, was a touch reserved, but Thomas greeted him with enthusiasm and questions. In contrast with his older brother, Thomas had a bit of the devil in him, and Colin was again reminded of himself in his youth. He noticed they smelled a bit like unwashed potatoes and spring air.

Val shushed them. "Sarah's asleep and your uncle has ridden all night and is tired. There will be plenty of time for questions later. Colin, you are welcome to stay with us as long as you wish. We're crowded, but we always have room for one more." Emma had climbed into her mother's lap, and Val gave her a hug.

"On the floor in front of the fire?" he asked, remembering how he and Matt had always preferred sleeping there to sleeping in their beds.

"As a matter of fact, yes," his brother said with a smile. "Or you can squeeze in with the boys in their bed."

The boys' eyes widened. "Would you, Uncle Colin?"

"Perhaps," he hedged. "Actually, I'd like to see Loftus today, if we can."

"Right now?" his brother asked.

"Is there any time better? I want to see the matter settled quickly," Colin answered.

Matt exchanged a look with Val, who said, "I don't see why you must push this, Colin. I'd hate to see Lady Rosalyn gone from the Valley. There must be a solution."

All the boys looked up. "Lady Rosalyn can't move," Thomas declared. "What will we do for a judge on May Day? She's the only one who remembers everyone's name. Lord Loftus always calls us by the color of our hair. 'Hey, you, the yellow-haired one, you win,'" he mimicked, and his siblings laughed.

Looking over their heads, Colin said, "I can't give her the house, Val. It's mine."

For a moment, she appeared to struggle with her opinion. However, when she spoke, it was to say, "Then you'd best shave. You look like a pirate rogue. And do you have a clean shirt?"

"Yes, ma'am," he responded dutifully.

"Well, you'd best get on with it." Scooting Emma off her lap, Val rose from the chair. "I'll expect you for dinner either way. We need time to get reacquainted, don't we? And I know the children would like a ride in that fancy London vehicle of yours—if everyone's chores are done, and their hands and back behind their ears are washed."

Nephews and niece all turned pleading eyes on him, and he could only say yes. His response was greeted with cheers, before the children charged off to happily do their mother's bidding.

Colin turned to his brother. "Let's go meet with Loftus."

Within the hour, Matthew and Colin were on their way to Lord Loftus's house in Downham. Matthew rode a nag that was half lame. After all his traveling, the mighty Oscar didn't mind the slower gait, but Colin was restless. Rain was in the air. Increasingly larger clouds were drifting across the April sky, and he didn't know if it was a good omen or bad. He was exhausted and at this point running on sheer willpower. He wanted Maiden Hill, and he wanted to stake his claim now.

Val's words on behalf of Lady Rosalyn, in addition to the children's reactions, haunted him. He knew the Valley. It was a close, opinionated community. If he wasn't careful, in spite of the house being legally his, he could be the one ostracized—and he didn't want that. Riding along familiar roads, seeing the curve of Pendle Hill and other landmarks that were important to his childhood, Colin realized this was home, and he'd missed being here. He'd been gone a long time. Too long, he realized heavily.

"Did they suffer?" he said abruptly.

Matt didn't mistake his meaning. Colin asked after their parents, who had passed away from an epidemic some five years ago. "No, their deaths were peaceful, and Father passed on a mere hour after Mother, which was good. You know neither one of them would be happy without the other."

That was true. His parents had worshiped

each other. As a child, when he'd been Boyd's or Thomas's age, Colin had taken pride in his parents' obvious love for each other. "I wish I could have been here for them during that time."

His brother hesitated a beat before saying carefully, "Colin, their deaths were sudden. There is no way you could have been present. In fact, the parish is fortunate we lost so few to that fever." Matt paused. "The money you sent them over the years was appreciated. In fact, Val and I are grateful for what you've given us."

Colin dismissed his brother's gratitude with a shrug. He could have come. Maybe not when his parents had been sick, but at least once before they'd died. There had been occasions when he'd been sent to London, opportunities when he could have stolen a quick visit. He hadn't. He'd had duties and people to see who could have advanced his career.

His excuses seemed insignificant now.

They rode in silence a moment, and then Colin dared to ask, "Do you ever wonder if our father had regrets? I mean, Father Ruley had plans for him. He said Father could have done anything he wanted. Instead, because he married Mother, he had to settle on being a cobbler."

Matt gave his horse a kick. "No, he had no regrets, just as I've no regrets about marrying Val. He loved Mother very much."

"I didn't imply that you did," Colin said, feeling a niggling of guilt, because he did think exactly just such a thing.

"Oh, I don't expect you to understand, Colin. You've always been more ambitious than I... but Val is everything to me. I'm very happy."

"Good," Colin said, not understanding how such a headstrong woman like Val could make any man happy.

Matt laughed. "You were struck dumb when she lectured you on love. I wish you could have seen the look on your face. Of course, I agree with her, although I never thought of myself as a romantic."

"With five children you must be doing something right."

Colin's observation made his brother laugh, and Colin couldn't help but grin back. "I'm glad you are happy, Matt. However, you are right. I am more ambitious. I plan on marrying for all the old-fashioned reasons—wealth and connections."

Matt frowned at Colin's bald statement. "War has changed you."

"Losing my opportunity at a knighthood changed me. They titled lesser men than me, Matt. I worked for it, I deserved it, and I won't let opportunity pass me by again."

"Is that sort of mercenary view of life going to satisfy you, Colin?"

"Yes."

Matt shook his head. "It wouldn't satisfy me."

"Ah, but think of what I can do for your sons," Colin said. "I can be *their* Father Ruley."

"I want my sons to know what is truly important in life," his brother, the Reverend, answered.

Before Colin could respond, the sound of hounds barking and the blare of a hunting horn interrupted them. War-trained senses alert, Oscar stopped dead in the road, picking up his ears.

A beat later, a red fox charged through the thicket out onto the road in front of the horses. He paused, one foot poised in the air, seeming to look right at Colin.

It was a defining moment. Life was sometimes like that, moments when Colin felt a connection. He didn't know why and he didn't question. Experience had taught him to be aware of these moments, and right now, he felt incredible sympathy for the hunted.

The howling of the hounds grew louder.

"Run," Colin told the fox, and as if the creature understood, it disappeared into a nearby water ditch.

Colin moved Oscar over to where he'd last seen the fox, guarding the spot.

A blink later, a pack of brown and white hunting hounds rushed the thicket, some jumping over it, some attempting to squeeze though impossibly tight spaces. Their tongues were hanging out of the sides of their mouths, and their eyes shone with the enjoyment of the chase.

Matt's horse startled and did a little dance, almost unseating its rider.

Oscar stood his ground with relish. He'd been bred for battle, and a pack of dogs would not put him off. They'd meet his hooves. As the dogs moved toward him, he arched his neck and pawed the ground, warning them to beware.

Colin yelled at the pack, "Here now! Move on, move on." The beasts circled, wary of the warhorse, but the scent of the fox present. One came too close, and Oscar kicked out, sending the dog tumbling. The others quickly backed to the other side of the road, putting distance between themselves and the horse's vicious hooves.

"Tallyho!" a man's voice shouted a split second before a horse sailed over the thicket, landing in the road ahead of them and almost stepping on two of the hounds. The horse faltered and then righted himself.

"Damn you, damn you," the rider shouted at the dogs. "You almost got me thrown off!"

He was a portly fellow in drab squire's dress and muddy top boots. Tufts of gray hair stood out over his ears under his hat, and his face was red with exertion. As his wild-eyed horse circled, he caught sight of Colin and Matt. "Sorry!" he said to them. "Didn't know you were here. Could have jumped on you. Tally-ho'ed!"

"That you did," Colin agreed. "How are you, Lord Loftus? I see you still enjoy the hunt."

"Mandland!" Loftus exclaimed, at last having sufficient wits to recognize them. "You're home!"

"Yes, my lord. I had to return."

"And so you have!" Loftus barked back. "Looks fine as a fiddle, don't he, Reverend?" He suddenly frowned, his capricious mind changing its thought. "But demmed me! I'm looking for a fox! He ran through here somewhere. Look at the demmed dogs. Running around in circles. Bah! Couldn't find a fox if I hung the blasted beast around their necks. You two haven't seen a fox, have you?"

"No, my lord," Matt said quickly.

"I thought I saw a flash of red up the way there," Colin answered, pointing in the opposite direction, gratified by his brother's quick collusion. "Didn't you see it, Matt? Way up yonder."

"Up yonder? Not even close?" Loftus questioned. He pulled his hat off his head and beat it against his thighs at the dogs. "Why, oh, why can't you catch that blasted fox?" The hounds were apparently accustomed to and unafraid of these diatribes. They sat on their haunches and waited for his tantrum to subside, which it did, as abruptly as it had come.

Loftus smashed the hat back on his head and turned to Colin. "I've been hunting *this* fox all season. Haven't even gotten close to him!"

Colin nodded sympathetically and hoped his new furry friend had the good sense to keep himself hidden in the drainage ditch for a good long while.

"Oh, well," Loftus said, turning philosophical, "there's naught to do now. But I will catch him. One of these days. Where are you gentlemen off to?"

"We were on our way to see you," Colin answered.

Loftus's face broke out in a welcoming smile. "Good then! I'm ready to share a toddy. I'd wager you have good tales from the war. I want to hear all about it. Everything! Heard of your exploits. Made the Valley proud! Come along, come along." He didn't wait but turned his horse toward Downham. The dogs fell in behind him.

Colin flashed Matt a smile. Lady Rosalyn wasn't the only one to have Loftus's ear.

The ride didn't take long. Loftus barked out questions about Colin's war years in between snapping orders to his dogs and cursing the fox's cunning. In such fashion they arrived at Downham Manor, his lordship's ancestral seat. Stable lads came running up to collect dogs and horses.

The door opened and Harkness, Loftus's butler, stepped out to say, "My lord, you have a guest—"

"I have other guests, too!" Loftus said jovially. "Remember young Colin Mandland? Boyd the cobbler's devil-to-the-bit son? Here he is now! A war hero! Fetch us some hot toddies, and double the whiskey. Is my lady at home?"

"Yes, my lord. She is in the sitting room with—"

"Perfect! Right where I want her. She likes the Reverend and will want to see our *war* hero." Even though he was at least a foot shorter, Loftus reached up and clapped Colin on the shoulder with generous bonhomie.

"My lord," Harkness stressed, attempting to get his master's attention, "you have another guest—"

"Yes! Yes! Hop to, man. Double the whiskey!" Loftus strode through the door and stomped the mud off his boots on the black and white tiles of the marble floor. "Give Harkness your hats, gentlemen, and then follow me." He didn't wait but strutted toward the adjacent room, a cherry-panel-lined room with green velvet upholstered furniture and a cheery fire.

"Thank you, Harkness," Matt said, handing the butler his hat. "How is your wife feeling?"

"Better, thanks to the soup Mrs. Mandland sent over," Harkness said, a trace of Yorkshire in his voice. "Those lads of yours are good ones. Delivered it without spilling a drop."

"Good," Matt answered, pleased, and Colin realized that, like a military uniform, the cleric's collar allowed a man to travel through almost any walk of society, although there was a ceiling to how far a man could rise. Colin bitterly wished he'd been more politically astute and less set on leading his men well.

Nor did he have Matt's grace to accept his class.

"Harkness! Toddies!" Loftus ordered from the doorway, impatient to lead his guests in.

The butler bowed to attend his duties, leaving Matt and Colin to follow their host. They didn't go far. Lady Loftus came out into the hall. She was a petite woman, well rounded and matronly, with sparkling blue eyes and rosy cheeks. "My lord, I have urgent and important business to discuss with you—"

She pulled up short, her eyebrows rising in surprise. "Reverend Mandland," she said, her voice going up high on the last syllable. "And this must be your brother, the heroic Colonel Mandland."

Loftus grinned at Colin. "See, I told you we were all paying attention. Know everything you did against the French. Proud of you, we are."

"Yes, we are," Lady Loftus agreed, faintly sounding anything but enthusiastic or welcoming.

And then Colin understood her quandary. He looked past his hosts to inside the room.

There, rising from a chair in front of a tray of biscuits and cakes where she and Lady Loftus had apparently been having a cozy chat, was Lady Rosalyn, her expression pinched and guarded.

She was no happier to see Colin than he was to see her.

# Chapter Three

*R*osalyn rose slowly to her feet, uncertain if she was ready to confront her new nemesis, Colonel Mandland.

She'd placed the deed in a leather folder and hadn't let it go from the moment she'd entered Downham Manor. The colonel's sharp gaze went immediately to the folder. She wrapped her arms protectively around it, and the air between them crackled with the same energy that heralded a storm.

His eyes met hers. She knew he would stop at nothing to get what was his. He was that sort of man.

Well, he wasn't going to get Maiden Hill.

Lord and Lady Loftus were going through the niceties of introductions. They were such dear friends.

47

Lord Loftus was saying in his endearing, abrupt manner, "Lady Rosalyn, you know Reverend Mandland? Course you do. This is his brother. Colonel Mandland. War hero! Made us all proud in the Valley. Colonel, Lady Rosalyn tells us when to sit down and when to stand up. Can't plan anything without her. Isn't that right, Reverend?"

Not waiting for a response, Lord Loftus then did something he always did when introducing Rosalyn to eligible bachelors; knowing his tactlessly loveable character, she had not let it bother her—until now, when he leaned toward Colonel Mandland and said, "She is a catch. A prime filly. If I was single, I'd throw a rope around her. Put her in my stable!"

Rosalyn could have died from the embarrassment, and it wasn't anything she hadn't heard him say fifty times before. This time was different.

Colonel Mandland's expression may have *appeared* pleasantly composed to the others, but she caught the curl in his lips. He was laughing—at her. She could read his mind as clearly as her own, and she didn't like it one bit.

"Lady Rosalyn," the colonel murmured with a small bow.

If he thought he could toy with her, he was wrong. She had rank in this room.

Tightening her hold on the leather folder, she dared to speak up. "My lord, I beg a moment of your time alone to speak to you about business of the most urgent nature."

"Eh? Urgent?" Lord Loftus turned anxious. He glanced at his wife, who already knew some of the story and hovered worriedly nearby. "Why my dear child, you are upset. It wasn't my little comment there? My wife has always warned me to not take advantage of your good humor. You know I admire you."

"Yes, my lord, I do. And, no, I'm not upset about *anything* you could say—" Which was not true. His forward comments grated her nerves to no end. Her most reassuring smile plastered on her face, she started for the door. "But please, a moment alone—"

Colonel Mandland stepped right in front of her, blocking her path.

Rosalyn pulled up short, a beat away from running into his chest. She attempted to side-step him. He followed, either because he was unafraid of challenging her in public or because he possessed the manners of a bull. She didn't know which—although she did have an opinion.

"My lord," he said in his deep, resonant voice, his hard eyes on the leather folder. "With all due respect, I, too, must beg a moment of your time. Alone."

Rosalyn's smile grew tight as she met his challenge with a steely look of her own. "But I made the request first."

"Yes, but your business involves me," Colonel Mandland answered.

"You have *no* idea what I'm going to talk about," she responded.

"On the contrary, I know *exactly* what you want to say," the colonel said. "If I were attempting to steal the deed to a man's house, I'd not want him present to refute my story either."

Rosalyn ached to punch him in his arrogant nose. She gripped the leather folder with both hands. "I have not stolen anything from you. You are attempting to steal my house from me."

"I *purchased* the house. Can't you understand that? I bought the house in good faith from your cousin, who *owned* it."

They stood toe-to-toe. She had to look up to challenge him. "And how do we know that? How do we know this deed is not a *forgery*?"

Her charge struck home. For a second, his brow darkened, and his mouth opened and shut as if words failed him.

His brother cautioned. "Colin, your temper."

"What the devil is going on here?" Lord Loftus asked his wife.

"It's very complicated," she whispered.

"Well, tell me!" her lord answered, but before she could speak, Colonel Mandland found his voice.

"I do not *steal*." He took a step forward, forcing Rosalyn to move back. "I do not *forge*." Another step. "And I do *not* lie."

Rosalyn dug in her heels. "Forge?" she queried. "Is that even a word? Or at least, in the way you mean it?"

"I just used it."

"Well, I'm not accepting it. Any more than I am accepting your taking my house."

"It is not your house."

"It is!"

"It isn't!"

She turned to the others in frustration. "Listen to him. He sounds like a schoolchild."

"I? A child?" Colonel Mandland repeated incredulously.

"Yes, you." With just the right haughty lift of

her chin, she sneered, "A *gentleman* would not be so ungracious as to publicly argue with a lady."

His eyes narrowed. "A *lady* would not pick such an argument when she knows she is *wrong*."

Rosalyn delivered her coup de grace. "What would a cobbler's son know about what a lady would or would not do?"

Her barb struck home with more force than she could have imagined. She realized too late, after her proud words had been flung out into the air, that she'd not only insulted the colonel but also his brother, and she really did respect and like the Reverend Mandland.

But instead of bluster and outrage, a deadly calm enveloped Colonel Mandland, his expression so grim, his manner so tense, that her knees began to tremble.

Perhaps she *had* gone too far.

"Colin—," his brother cautioned.

The colonel raised a hand, effectively cutting off any other words that might be said. His gaze never left Rosalyn's. "Lord Loftus, both Lady Rosalyn and I are here to ask you to settle an important matter. She has in her possession a deed proving her cousin, Lord Woodford, sold Maiden Hill and all of its furnishings to me."

"Is that true, Lady Rosalyn?" Lord Loftus asked, sounding himself a bit cowed.

Rosalyn didn't answer immediately. Anger and humiliation made speech difficult. She wanted to deny the accusation, to counter with even worse charges aimed at Colonel Mandland's upstart character. But she couldn't. The same code of honor that had guided her father now led her. She would not lie.

"Yes, I have the deed. My cousin George sold the house."

She gathered her courage and faced Lord and Lady Loftus, aware that her back was now turned to the most dangerous man of her acquaintance. "George wants Covey and I to remove ourselves to my aunt in Cornwall. I don't want to go. I'm happy here . . . and Covey has never been out of Lancashire. Maiden Hill has been her home since her marriage."

"Of course you don't want to go," Lady Loftus said, coming to Rosalyn's side. "And none of us wants you to leave. Why, I can't imagine what the Spring Cotillion would be like without you. Or the Ladies' Social Circle. You've brought so much life and joy to the Valley. We need you!"

And Rosalyn needed them, too. After years of being alone, the people in the Valley had become her family. She took the hand Lady Loftus offered and said to his lordship, "Please, help me fight my cousin for Maiden Hill. He can't sell it. He mustn't."

"He already *has* sold it," Colonel Mandland practically growled. He said to his lordship, "I am sympathetic to Lady Rosalyn's plight, but I purchased the house. I want to live there."

Lord Loftus's shoulders slumped, as if he were overwhelmed at the thought of being forced to make a decision, and Rosalyn felt a measure of hope. Certainly, he would champion her.

Then the colonel prodded, "Perhaps you should review the deed yourself, my lord."

"Yes," Loftus agreed eagerly, apparently relieved to have some direction. "Let me see it."

Rosalyn didn't want to give up her hold on the folder, but she had no choice. His lordship walked over to the window, where the light was better, and took the deed out.

"You can have it reviewed by a solicitor," the colonel suggested with such a helpful attitude that Rosalyn wanted to throttle him. "All is in order."

"Harkness, send for Shellsworth," Lord Loftus ordered the hapless butler, who was just walking in with a tray of hot toddies. The butler set the tray down on a table and hurried to do his lordship's bidding. Lord Loftus explained to Colonel Mandland, "He's a solicitor. Lives just beyond the way. Should be here in a thrice." He squinted to read the cramped handwriting on the deed.

Lady Loftus gave Rosalyn's hand a reassuring pat. "Mr. Shellsworth will know what to do."

Rosalyn attempted to smile back. She wasn't very successful. Her stomach had suddenly tied up in knots. Mr. Shellsworth's wife would be pleased to see Rosalyn gone. She had made it quite clear she envied Rosalyn's role in society.

However, Lady Loftus didn't appear to care whether or not her words brought comfort, because her gaze had gone past Rosalyn to the colonel and then back again. Her eyes widened as if she had been struck by a sudden, enlightening thought.

"What?" Rosalyn whispered, wanting to

know what her ladyship was thinking and hoping it was something that would save her home.

Lady Loftus ignored her. Instead, she asked, "Colonel Mandland, when will your wife and children arrive? Maiden Hill is such a lovely estate for a family."

*What sort of question was that?* Rosalyn wondered if her dear friend was abandoning her to Cornwall.

The colonel frowned at having his attention diverted from Lord Loftus, who now moved his lips as he attempted to read over sections of the deed. "I'm not married, my lady."

His brother was more gracious. "My wife is looking forward to helping my brother find a wife. You know what a matchmaker Val is, my lady."

"I do indeed," her ladyship answered, with a suspicious note of triumph in her voice.

Rosalyn felt a headache forming behind her eyes. Any woman who would consider marrying such a boorish brute as Colonel Mandland had to be either desperate or so old and haggard no one else would want her . . .

Her evil thoughts were interrupted by the sounds of Mr. Shellsworth's arrival in the front hall.

"At last!" Lord Loftus said with relief. "Shellsworth, get in here and read this devil of a thing!"

Mr. Shellsworth minced his way into the room. He was a thin, petite man with fastidious manners. Rosalyn could easily picture him in the powdered wig, lace, and heeled shoes of days of yore. Since that was not the fashion, he doted on wearing bright colors, as seen in his bright yellow waistcoat and spruce green jacket and trousers. He liked the starched points of his shirt collar to brush his cheeks.

When Rosalyn first moved to Maiden Hill, Mr. Shellsworth had presented himself as a suitor for her hand until he had discovered she'd had no dowry. Then he had done what every male had done before him—he'd disappeared. Last year he'd married a wealthy landowner's oldest daughter.

Rosalyn had been relieved. She could barely abide his pretentiousness, and she was not alone. He was not well liked in the Valley.

Full of his self-importance, Mr. Shellsworth practically clicked his heels as he presented himself. "Lord Loftus, Lady Loftus . . . why, Lady Rosalyn, how good to see you again." He said this last in a patronizing tone. He did not acknowledge Reverend Mandland or his brother. They were obviously beneath his notice. Instead, with his usual obnoxious flourish, he said, "My lord, what service may I perform for you today?"

"Should have been on the hunt with me," Lord Loftus said. "Almost caught that fox. Next time he won't get by my dogs!"

"Of course not, my lord," Mr. Shellsworth said. He and Lord Loftus often hunted together. The local wags said Shellsworth had his head too far up his lordship's rear to be any help on the hunt.

Lord Loftus held out the deed with distaste. "Here, look at this demmed thing and see what you make of it."

The lawyer accepted it, put his spectacles on his nose, and with a "May I?" sat down at the writing desk beside the window.

The colonel's jaw tightened. He was not pleased. Rosalyn braced herself. A show of his temper would work in her favor, but his brother touched him lightly on the arm, a signal for patience.

"My lord, while Mr. Shellsworth is considering the deed, may I have a private moment with you?" Lady Loftus asked. Without waiting for an answer, she hooked her hand in her husband's arm and drew him aside.

Rosalyn ignored their whisperings and concentrated on Mr. Shellsworth's many dramatic "hmmmms" and "ahs." Couldn't the man read without making a sound?

Mr. Shellsworth set down the contract, pulled his spectacles off his nose, and announced, "My lord, this contract is valid. Not as well written as I would have done, but legal in every respect. Lord Woodford had the power to sell Maiden Hill. It was not entailed."

"How do you know?" Rosalyn demanded.

With an arrogant shrug, the lawyer said, "I know."

He meant he had found out her family's affairs—probably while he'd been wooing her for her nonexistent money. Rosalyn was glad she had never had any inclination toward such a supercilious man. Even his hands were small . . . with stubby fingers. A shiver went through her.

But the worst part was, she was going to have to admit defeat to Colonel Mandland, a person she disliked more than the lawyer.

"There *may* be something that can be done,"

Lord Loftus said, commanding the attention of everyone in the room. "Mandland, Reverend, both of you, come to my study." He started for the door.

Mr. Shellsworth hopped to his feet. "My lord, shouldn't I go with you?"

"Yes. Come. Bring the deed," Lord Loftus threw over his shoulder, and the lawyer scurried after the gentlemen, the deed in his hand. Rosalyn bit back a whimper. She hated losing control of those papers.

The moment she was alone with Lady Loftus, she collapsed on the settee. The tray of hot toddies was close by, tempting her to drown her sorrows. "So, that is it," she said quietly. "I've lost."

"No, my dear," Lady Loftus replied, taking the seat beside her and placing a reassuring arm around Rosalyn's shoulders. "I believe my lord and I have thought of the most wonderful solution. One that will make everyone happy."

"What solution is that?"

Lady Loftus pressed her lips together and shook her head, a secretive twinkle in her eyes. "I wish I could tell, but I don't dare jinx the possibilities. Everything will be fine."

Rosalyn wasn't so certain.

* * *

Colin followed in Loftus's wake, wishing this farce were over and he could have his deed. He was tired and ready to be done with it all.

His lordship led them into a study lined with prints of prized hounds and horses. In one corner, there was even a stuffed hunt hound. Loftus noticed Colin looking at it. "His name was Theodore. Best hunt dog I ever had. Smarter than the fox. Every time. Here, sit down. I've got a proposition to make." He sat himself at the chair behind a huge desk.

The smug fop of a lawyer was the first to take his seat. As he started to sit, Colin said, "May I?" He didn't wait for permission but took the deed away and tucked it inside his jacket. At last, he had what was his. He settled in a chair his brother had pulled up for him.

Loftus propped his elbow on top of his desk. Colin was fairly certain little work was ever performed in this room. There wasn't even an inkwell. His lordship said with authority, "*I* have a brilliant idea, one that will resolve everyone's concerns—"

Colin barely listened. He had his deed. It was all he wanted. The rest were mere formalities.

"—Colonel Mandland should marry Lady Rosalyn."

It took a moment for Loftus's words to sink in, and when they did, Colin's response was a definite, "No, absolutely not."

"Now see here," Loftus said, rising to his feet. "You haven't given the matter a second's consideration."

"I don't need to," Colin said. "I've met the lady. We do not suit."

"You've only known her ten minutes."

"Ten minutes was long enough." Colin rose, using his height to an advantage. "I understand your concern, my lord. I deeply appreciate your help in seeing this deed returned to me. However, with all due respect, I must leave now. With your permission, my lord?" He couldn't wait to get out the door.

"Permission denied!" Loftus barked. He looked to Matt. "Is your brother always this abrupt?"

"I'm afraid so, my lord. He may be the youngest, but he has always been stubborn."

"What?" Colin asked Matt. "You think I should marry that woman?"

"It is a possible solution," Matt suggested.

Colin choked on a response.

Loftus slapped his hand on his desk. "Come along, Mandland! I can't see why you can't at least consider the idea. You aren't married; Lady Rosalyn isn't married. The two of you marry and everyone is happy."

"Have you not noticed?" Colin said. "The lady can barely abide me."

His lordship waved away the protest. "There are ways around that. Should be easy for a handsome buck like you."

"Then I don't like her," Colin replied ruthlessly.

"Why not? She's comely enough," Loftus said. "I think she is a demmed fine filly. All her parts in the right places. Oh, I admit she has to have her lead but, again, *you* should be able to bring her to heel."

"I don't want a wife I have to 'bring to heel,'" Colin said.

"I don't see why not?" Loftus asked. "That's the fun of it!"

"No," Colin said firmly. He took a backward step toward the door. "When I marry, it will be to someone biddable." He took another step. "Someone sweet-tempered." And then another.

"Someone who wouldn't badger me to death."
He put his hand on the door handle. "Now if you
will excuse us, my lord—?"

"Ah, I know!" Loftus trumpeted. "You need
something to sweeten the deal."

"There's nothing," Colin said, feigning a regret he didn't feel. He was not going to be bullied into marrying Lady Rosalyn. He opened the
door.

"You can't leave—not until we resolve this!"

"Good day, my lord."

"What if I offered you a seat in the Commons?"

Colin froze. He stared at Loftus, uncertain if
he'd heard correctly.

Shellsworth confirmed what had been said by
jumping to his prissy feet and whining, "My
lord, you were going to give me the Commons
seat."

Loftus ignored him. He looked to Colin. "The
Valley has a seat open. It's mine to fill. I mean,
there will be a vote, but—" He shrugged. Everyone knew he would choose the winner. "They've
been after me to fill it, but I've not found the
right man."

"*I* am the right man!" Shellsworth said. He
slammed both hands on the desk. "My lord, you
promised the seat to me."

"But I need you here. We hunt together."

"You can hunt with the colonel," the lawyer reasoned.

Loftus shook his head. "Mandland is a man of the world. A war hero. He can represent my interests in the Commons as well as you could. Maybe better. And, if Lady Rosalyn is his wife, he will have a suitable hostess to entertain in London."

"*My* wife can entertain," Shellsworth argued.

"Aye, but what is a farmer's daughter when compared to an earl's offspring?" Loftus said, as if it explained everything. "Look at what she has done to the Valley. So, what do you say, Mandland? Are you interested in a seat in the Commons?"

A seat in the Commons could lead to the knighthood that had eluded him. Or, to even higher aspirations, to possibilities that he, a cobbler's son, had not dared dream.

"You like the idea," Loftus said, accurately reading Colin's mind. He leaned across his desk. "The seat is yours if you marry Lady Rosalyn."

"*I* would have married her for that!" Shellsworth protested. "If you had said something a year ago—"

Loftus ignored him.

Colin looked to his brother. Matt raised his eyebrows, letting him know this was his decision alone. "Why?" Colin asked at last. "Why would you do this for her?"

His lordship shifted uncomfortably. "It's my way of giving her a dowry of sorts. Someone must take care of her."

Loftus didn't strike Colin as the selfless type. Seeing his doubt, his lordship confessed, "My wife dotes on her. Before Lady Rosalyn arrived, my lady was always after me to return to London. She hated the country. Dragged me back to Town every chance she could and made me miserable between times. However, since Lady Rosalyn arrived, I've been allowed to hunt to my heart's content. I want my wife happy. Besides, you *will* represent me well in the Commons. You know your place. You understand how the world works."

Colin could have confessed that he didn't believe that the purpose of the House of Commons was to represent the aristocracy. But he knew he'd be speaking to a wall. Like all nobles of Colin's acquaintance, Loftus assumed everyone would hop to his command. Colin wasn't fool enough to say anything that would cause the offer to be withdrawn.

In fact, marriage to Lady Rosalyn was suddenly sounding like a capital idea.

"I was thinking I needed a wife," Colin said, warming up to the idea. He should be able to work his way around her prickliness. Of course, once they were married, they didn't have to spend time together. He could live his own life in London, and she could manage Maiden Hill and entertain Lady Loftus.

His lordship clapped his hands together. "Good! The seat is yours, that is, once you and Lady Rosalyn are duly married—"

"But the seat should be *mine!*" Shellsworth stepped between Colin and Loftus's desk. "I've busted my back, done everything you've asked me to do with the expectation of being rewarded with that seat."

All goodwill vanished from Loftus's eye. In its place was the shadow of a vindictive temper. "Shellsworth, I've made my decision. Don't push me."

For a second, the lawyer appeared ready to fight, and then he crumpled. "Yes, my lord." He stepped out of Colin's way.

"Very well," Loftus said. "Now, mind you, Mandland, I expect you to treat our Lady Rosalyn well. I know she likes to pull on the bit, but use a gentle hand and she'll bend to you."

"I'm certain," Colin agreed. He also knew without a doubt Lady Rosalyn would not like being compared to a horse. Nor did he think she would be overjoyed at knowing they had been planning her future. "What happens if she refuses my offer? I have no control over her acceptance, and I will still want the seat."

"She won't refuse," Loftus answered.

"She might," Colin said. "She has a mind of her own."

"Then it will be your job to change it. Perk up, Mandland, she wants Maiden Hill. She wouldn't think of saying no. Come along now. Let us return to the ladies." He came out from behind his desk and walked out of the room, ready to inform Lady Rosalyn of his decision.

Matt caught Colin's arm. He whispered hurriedly, "Have you thought about this, and do you truly understand what it means?"

"I want the title," Colin answered. "The end justifies the means."

"But the end may be a long way off. In fact, until death you do part."

Colin laughed. "With Lady Rosalyn's temperament, that could be tomorrow." Gleefully ignoring the glower Shellsworth threw at his back, he reassured his brother, "Don't worry. Lady Rosalyn certainly can't be more of a trial than the French were."

"I wouldn't place a wager on that," was Matt's serious response.

# Chapter Four

Rosalyn stood the moment she heard the gentlemen outside in the hall. Lady Loftus rose with her. Rosalyn held out her hand, and her dear friend gave it a squeeze.

"Everything will be fine," her ladyship repeated, as she had continually for the past half hour or so. Rosalyn prayed she was right.

Lord Loftus was the first through the sitting room door. His smile was full of confidence, and the moment his eyes landed on his wife, he gave her a nod. Lady Loftus released her breath with a sigh of relief. "It will *all* be fine," she said with more assurance than before.

Then the Mandland brothers entered the room. Reverend Mandland appeared gravely concerned. She looked to the colonel. He was smiling.

She didn't see any sign of the deed. Her one hope was that Mr. Shellsworth still had it.

The slam of the front door broke the silence.

"What was that?" Lady Loftus asked.

"Shellsworth," her husband answered. He gave a dismissive wave. "You know his tiffs."

"He's upset? Should we talk to him?" his wife said.

"I will later," Lord Loftus said. "After he has had a chance to regain his senses."

Rosalyn's heart dropped to her feet. The lawyer would not have left if he had the deed. She had lost.

Lord Loftus looked to the colonel. "Well?" he prompted. "Get on with it."

A flicker of irritation crossed Colonel Mandland's face, so swift and brief that Rosalyn could have imagined it. Certainly, Lord Loftus didn't notice. However, having lived most of her life swallowing the will of others, Rosalyn understood immediately. The colonel was being pushed, and he was not a man who liked being pushed.

She also sensed the "push" did not bode well for her.

Lady Loftus let go of her hand and moved to stand beside her husband, leaving Rosalyn alone to face Colonel Mandland.

"You won," she said quietly.

There was a beat of silence. He said, "This isn't a situation where either of us wins. We both lose something. I lose goodwill; you lose your home."

*Yes, she did.* The thought of leaving the sweet haven of the Ribble valley almost broke her. Her throat ached as she forced back disappointment. She was a Wellborne. They were made of stern stuff. Had she not proved that over and over again?

"Life is not a fair game," she said, her voice tighter than she wished. She offered her gloved hand. "Congratulations, Colonel. Maiden Hill is a wonderful estate."

He glanced down at the proffered hand and then raised his gaze to meet hers. For the first time, she noticed his eyes weren't dark but a bluish gray, like storm clouds.

"Lady Rosalyn, will you do me the honor of being my wife?"

Rosalyn stood still, uncertain if she'd heard him correctly or if she was growing as fanciful as Covey. She gave her head a shake to startle her senses. She'd thought he'd asked her to marry him?

72

"Oh, my dear, that is so wonderful!" Lady Loftus said in ringing tones. She threw her arms around Rosalyn. "You are going to be married, married, *married!*"

He *had* proposed to her.

All her life, she had waited for a proper proposal of marriage, and now she had one—from a man she disliked and distrusted. A man who'd taken everything of value away from her.

A man her closest friends obviously felt she should accept. Lord Loftus grinned like the village fool. He'd planned this and felt he'd done her a tremendous favor.

Did everyone really know so little of her?

She glanced at Colonel Mandland and knew in an instant he expected her to throw the proposal in his face.

Rosalyn wasn't going to let him down. Gently, she eased out of Lady Loftus's teary-eyed embrace and said witheringly, "Marriage? To you?"

"Considering the other two men in the room are already married, you are left with me."

His brother said his name as if to chastise him, but Rosalyn overrode his words. "Oh, you mean they aren't taking part in the farce?"

Was it her imagination, or was there a gleam of admiration in the colonel's eyes?

Lord Loftus bullied himself right in, "My dear, is that any way to answer a man's honest proposal?"

"Honest?" Rosalyn countered. "There is not an honest word in him."

Colonel Mandland clutched his chest and pretended to be having an attack. "You wound me, my lady," he mocked. "I am devastated. I shall be forced to repair to the country and nurse my damaged heart."

Rosalyn motioned a hand in his direction, silently encouraging Lord and Lady Loftus to see for themselves what sort of man he was. "Do I need to say more?"

"Does this mean you *don't* want to marry me?" Colonel Mandland asked, tossing aside the role of wounded suitor.

"It means I would rather see you boiled in oil by wild natives," Rosalyn returned levelly.

"My dear!" Lord Loftus said, both he and his wife equally shocked by her bluntness—especially to a proposal they had obviously encouraged.

But Colonel Mandland had a different reaction. He tilted back his head and laughed. The sound of it caught Rosalyn off guard. His whole countenance was transformed. He was a handsome man to begin with, but laughter made him a god.

His brother started chuckling, too—and then both brothers were laughing.

"You know," the Reverend said, "she may be the best thing for you. I've never seen anyone so handily put you in your place."

The colonel agreed with him before addressing Rosalyn. "My lady, I don't think wild natives are going to overtake the Valley any time soon. However," he went on, sobering, "you wish to live at Maiden Hill. I hold the deed. Marriage gives you what you want. It's very simple."

"I'm no green goose," she said. "Why should you agree to a marriage that gives *me* everything and *you* nothing?"

"Oh, she is definitely on to you, Colin," Reverend Mandland said, wiping a tear from his eye.

"Nor is she afraid to ask the hard questions," his brother concurred. "I like that, Lady Rosalyn. You are right, I will receive something—"

"Don't tell her!" Lord Loftus ordered.

"His lordship has offered me a seat in the House of Commons if I marry you."

Lord Loftus groaned his frustration out loud.

"Why did you tell her that, man? No woman wants to hear something so blunt."

He was right.

When the colonel had first proposed, for one magical second, Rosalyn's heart had leaped in her chest. He was exactly the sort of man she had longed for—strong, intelligent, arrogantly confident . . . and very, very handsome.

However, life was not fairy dreams. Even the chivalrous concept of love was a fantasy. Hadn't her mother proven that?

No, better she had both feet planted firmly on the ground, and apparently the colonel harbored no romantic notions, either. She could almost forgive him the blunt honesty . . . but, oddly, not the lack of romance. "Thank you for paying the compliment of speaking to me as an equal," she said to Colonel Mandland. "Better I know now than discover after we married about Lord Loftus's bribe, however well-intentioned it was."

"We want you to be happy and stay with us," Lady Loftus said. She pulled Rosalyn closer to the colonel as if sizing them up as a couple. "You and Colonel Mandland would make a very good match."

"Yes, very good," her husband agreed. "You are both long-legged, have good wits, all your faculties. Your children would be lookers."

"My lord," Lady Loftus complained, "you are making them sound like horses."

"Well, that's how it is done," her husband said. "You wouldn't want a mismatch. The children would be ugly. And you know the Mandlands are good breeders. Look at the Reverend there."

Hot color flooded Lady Loftus's face. "I am so sorry, Reverend. My husband speaks his mind a bit too often."

"No offense taken," Reverend Mandland said with his customary courtesy, and then he added, "but your husband is right. We are good breeders."

His brother smiled in agreement, and Rosalyn had had enough. This may be some sort of a jest to them, but she had better things to do with her time and her life.

"Thank you for your—" She paused. Should she say *kind*? Not hardly. *Factitious*? More the word, but definitely undiplomatic. "—offer," she said. "Regretfully I must refuse it. Now, if you will excuse me, I need to return home to make preparations for moving my household to Cornwall. Good day to you all."

Lady Loftus made a soft moue of disappointment. Rosalyn didn't wait. She marched to the door, head high, her back straight as a poker. She may not have a home, but she still had her pride.

Harkness waited for her in the front hall with her bonnet. She tied the ribbons into a bow as he opened the door. She was just preparing to leave when she heard a step behind her.

Colonel Mandland.

He didn't speak but took her arm and led her out onto the front porch landing. Closing the door behind him, he said, "You are making a mistake."

"Because I've refused you?"

"No, because you are letting your pride get in the way of what is an opportunity for both of us. So we marry." He shrugged. "We can live separate lives. You can go on as you always have, controlling society in the Valley with an added advantage. You will also have the protection of my name."

"What do *you* receive in return?" she asked.

"I want a knighthood, Lady Rosalyn. To someone born an earl's daughter that may seem presumptuous, but it is a new age. In these modern times, a man can make something of himself if he has the right connections. The Commons seat will give me that."

His voice dropped intimately. "Marry me, my lady, and I will see you want for nothing. In fact, I'm fairly well off now, but one day, I will be a rich man. I'm intelligent and I work hard. All I own will also be my wife's."

Rosalyn was taken aback. Here was a man who didn't wait for the world to come to him. His ambition attracted her . . . almost too much. It was as if the devil knew her innermost desires and had created this man as the lure.

She took a step back. "A woman owns nothing, even in this day and age, sir. I'm sorry, I can't marry you."

"Can't? You *won't*," he corrected, his frustration obvious.

With an impatient sound, she signaled for Old John to drive the pony cart forward. This conversation was ludicrous.

"You are making a mistake," Colonel Mandland said, behind her, his voice low.

"Perhaps," she agreed and then knew she had to say something or it would all roil inside her the rest of the day. "The truth is, Colonel, I believe marriage must account for something more than unbridled ambition." Truth rang in her words, and she thought of her mother, who had been coerced to marry her father for a title and prestige and who had never found happiness. Suddenly dark memories and doubts came rolling back.

She changed the subject. "You will give me a week to pack?"

"Of course," he replied, equally stiffly.

"Thank you." She escaped to the pony cart and knew without looking back that he watched her leave.

Matt came out on the step with both of their hats. "You weren't successful."

"Yet," Colin corrected. "She's interested."

"She didn't appear that way to me," Matt said.

Colin smiled. "Then she *will* be interested," he amended. "I must give her time to grow accustomed to the idea. But she isn't indifferent, Matt."

"Brother, the woman is cold to you."

"Would you care to place a wager on it?" Colin challenged. "She'll come to her senses. She has no choice."

"They *always* have a choice," his brother answered, "and I will tell you something else I've learned from years of being married—they will always surprise you."

"She's already done that," Colin confessed. "There's more to her than meets the eye. She's an attractive package, but that wit of hers . . ." He shook his head. It had been a long time since a woman had engaged his mind as well as his body. "In the end, she'll come around to me. Whether we like it or not, there *is* something between us," he said thoughtfully.

"I saw no sign of it. But then, you always were optimistic when it came to women." Matt handed Colin his hat. "So, are you going to be camping on her doorstep?"

"*My* doorstep?" Colin corrected. They walked to their horses. "No, I think I'll have others speak for me. Right now, she'd slam the door in my face, and I can only let her get away with that once."

"So you are setting up a siege, are you?" Matt said.

Colin paused before swinging up into Oscar's saddle, and then he smiled. "Yes, I do believe I will."

With that the two brothers rode back to the parish rectory.

\* \* \*

Rosalyn found the next three days very hectic. Word traveled fast in the Valley. 'Twas said you could sneeze in the morning on one side of Clitheroe and by noon everyone would know you had a cold. She discovered firsthand the saying was true.

Within a day, her friends and neighbors had heard not only that she was leaving but also that she had refused Colonel Mandland's proposal— something that shocked and surprised them all.

"Don't you want to marry?" Mrs. Sheffield asked. She was the mill owner's wife and was one of a long line of callers. She was accompanied by her friend Mrs. Blair.

"Marriage to a stranger is an affront to the sacrament," Rosalyn replied coolly. By now, she'd had a good deal of practice at defending her position.

"He *is* very handsome," Mrs. Blair observed.

"Handsome is as handsome does," Rosalyn murmured. "Would you care for another glass of sherry?" Mrs. Blair rarely refused.

There were also those who came specifically on Colonel Mandland's behalf. Lady Loftus was a daily visitor, and once she even dragged along the colonel's sister-in-law. Mrs. Mandland was quiet and reserved. She was someone Rosalyn didn't know well but respected.

However, as Mrs. Mandland was leaving, she did say she hoped Lady Rosalyn would give her brother-in-law's proposal some consideration. "He needs a wife."

"But must it be me?" Rosalyn questioned.

Even several of Colonel Mandland's former tutors from Stoneyhurst paid her a call and offered character references.

"I thought he was considered rather headstrong in his youth?" Rosalyn said to Mr. Dalyrimple, an ancient man with rheumatism.

"A lad . . . with spirit . . . is not always . . . a bad thing," the gentleman said, groaning between words. "Without it, he would not . . . have served against the French . . . so well."

She could not argue that point.

She did, however, notice the one person who did *not* call was Colonel Mandland himself.

"It's almost as if he has sent emissaries on his behalf," she told Covey.

"Is that wrong?" Her companion sat in her favorite chair and worked on a child's dress she was smocking as a gift to a new mother in the parish.

"Not wrong, unusual. In truth, I'm a bit put

out that he hasn't called." She dropped into the chair across from Covey's. She'd spent the day packing with Bridget, and her head hurt from all the decisions that still had to be made. "Tell me, Covey, you haven't said anything. Do you truly not mind moving?"

For the briefest second, Covey's needle hesitated. She lowered her embroidery to her lap. "I think I'd best go up to my room and lay down." She rose and took several stiff steps forward.

Rosalyn came to her feet, too. "That's not an answer. I wish to know."

Her friend drew a deep breath and released it before saying, "I understand that you have little choice in the matter, and my place, now with Alfred gone, is beside you. I can't let you go off to Cornwall alone, can I?"

"I wish you'd been my mother."

Rosalyn's words were impulsive but heartfelt. Covey looked surprised, and then tears welled in her eyes. "My dear child, I wish I had been your mother, too. Then I would have seen that you had received all the love you deserved."

"It wasn't that bad," Rosalyn demurred, her pride once again pulling her back.

"No," Covey agreed with the understanding Rosalyn valued in her. Her friend understood all too well. She didn't know how. Covey never asked questions, and yet she knew.

"Good night," Covey said softly and left the room.

Rosalyn returned to her chair and sat in deep thought until the candle almost burned itself out.

The next morning was cold and rainy. Rosalyn decided it was the perfect day to attack the attic. She had no idea what all was up there. Numerous trunks and miscellaneous small furniture items from different estates had been shipped to Maiden Hill over the decades and had been collecting dust. Her cousin George may not give a tinker's care, but *she* wasn't about to let something valuable to the family end up in Colonel Mandland's hands.

One trunk held moldy tack. Another contained baby clothes, folded away for the future. Rosalyn wondered who had stored those here. She ran her finger over the delicate stitching of one wee outfit, and a longing for what she did not have threatened to overwhelm her.

She shut the lid to the trunk and turned to another. There she discovered a pile of the most gaudy clothing. These must have been costumes. One dress was red, yellow, and blue stripes, with huge flounces on the shoulders and hem. She shook it out and held it up against herself. Which one of her relatives had enjoyed dressing the part of a tart? Certainly not Aunt Agatha.

The thought of the crusty old woman in such a tight, ridiculous outfit made Rosalyn laugh. The sound was rusty, even to her own ears.

A footfall on the attic steps warned her some-one was coming. Rosalyn quickly wadded up the dress and stuffed it back in the trunk. Brid-get's head popped up over the top of the steps a beat later. "Begging your pardon, my lady, but you have a visitor. It's Colonel Mandland." She whispered this last as if saying the name of a per-son of great importance.

So, at last, he had decided to come himself. Well, Rosalyn did not have time to spare. "I am not at home," she said firmly.

"But, my lady, I've already told him you are here."

"Then tell him I'm not."

"I can't do that," the maid protested. "My lady, after you are gone, he's to pay my wages. I *had* to tell him you were here." She turned and ran down the stairs before Rosalyn could object.

There was nothing else to do for it than to go

and meet him. Rosalyn wasn't about to let him think she was hiding from him.

Going downstairs, she started to brush the cobwebs off her skirts and then stopped. What did she care what he thought of her? Let him see her at her worst. She didn't even stop by her room to change her dress—although she did take a moment to glance at herself in a wall mirror and repinned her hair to tame the errant curls that were the bane of her existence.

She hated her curls. Her mother's hair had been curly. Whenever her father's family saw her curls they usually made a disparaging remark about her mother, so she'd learned to keep them hidden.

Now, looking in the mirror, she told herself that if her looking like a washerwoman didn't set him back, nothing would. She went downstairs to the sitting room.

Colonel Mandland stood with his back to the door. He held his hat in his hand and appeared to be contemplating the empty hearth. In spite of the dampness of the day and a decided chill in the room, there was no fire. There was not enough money to burn too many fires, and they preferred the cheery coziness of the back morning room.

He must not have heard her come down the stairs, and so Rosalyn had a moment to study him. In truth, the room didn't feel cold at all. His presence was enough to heat it up. Unbidden, the image of the baby clothes in the trunk rose in her mind. She had an instinctive urge to flee, but she was too late. He turned as if he'd known she was there all along.

He was wearing his best, and Rosalyn couldn't help but admire what a fine figure of a man he was. His jacket of bottle green superfine was cut with the expertise of a good tailor. His boots did gleam, and he had recently shaved. The scent of his shaving soap lured her into the room.

Why hadn't she taken a moment to change her dress?

He spoke. "I imagine my calling is a bit of a surprise to you."

"I expected you at one time or the other. There are only so many people in the Valley who either can or will speak on your behalf."

The colonel laughed, not taking offense at her skepticism. "Actually, I came because I had some questions about the house and would appreciate a tour," he said, easily making her feel foolish . . . because she had expected another motive.

"I see," she said. "A tour."

"You don't mind, do you?"

"I will have Bridget show you around."

"But I would rather have you give me the tour," he answered. He took a step toward her.

Rosalyn resisted the urge to step back. What was it about this man that made her feel edgy and anxious whenever he grew too near? His storm blue eyes seemed to see too much, their intensity disturbing to her peace.

"I am actually busy at the moment," she said. "Bridget would be a much better guide."

"Why don't you like me?" he asked.

Her heartbeat pounded in her ears. She feared he could hear and know how nervous she was. "I don't *dis*like you. I'm busy."

"Any other woman in your circumstances would be pathetically grateful for my offer."

"I'm neither pathetic nor grateful."

"I know. That's what I like about you. I understand pride. However, you have created a very difficult situation for me."

She crossed her arms protectively in front of her, uncertain where he was going with this. "I don't see how."

"Lady Rosalyn, because you have turned up your nose at my offer, I am considered a failure in the Valley. You've made an impression on everyone. No one wants you to leave, and they believe it is up to me to see that you stay. Even my niece Emma is disappointed in my efforts so far. She is quite a fan of yours."

"Emma is a good, sweet child," Rosalyn answered and then couldn't resist adding, "but what effort have you made? All I've met are your friends and former tutors."

"Would you have received me if I had come?" he asked.

"I didn't want to receive you today."

He grinned. "I know." He traced the brim of his hat with his index finger before saying slyly, "I'm not as bad as you think I am."

"I don't have any thought about you one way or the other."

"So it's my father's profession that has set you against me?"

Rosalyn felt he was trying to trap her—and he had found her weakness. She was aware of the class differences between them—aware . . . and not so aware.

He moved closer, so close she could see the flecks of blue in his eyes. "We don't suit," she said, her voice faint.

"Mmmm," was his noncommittal answer. He inched nearer, and she was reminded of standing in Lord Loftus's sitting room arguing, except this time, her knees felt a little weak, and there was a dizzy sort of humming in her ears.

"We *don't*," she reiterated, more for herself than him.

"Not at all," he agreed. His gaze dropped to her lips. He smiled. "Well, parts of us do."

Rosalyn licked suddenly dry lips. "Parts? Do what?" she asked. When he looked at her this way, it was hard to think.

"Suit," he reminded, his deep voice intimate. "Parts of us do suit. Lady Rosalyn, I learned a long time ago that lying to myself never served any purpose. I sense you hold the same belief. You may not like my lack of background or that my father was a simple cobbler. You may not even like me. But you can't deny there is something between us."

"I don't know what you are talking about," she whispered.

"Yes, you do."

Rosalyn could have ordered him out, could have informed him he was being rude or forward. That even though he hadn't touched her, he was taking liberties. But she knew such orders would fall on deaf ears.

Here was a man who made his own rules.

And she discovered it was a very attractive quality, one more potent than any other.

The next thing she knew, he leaned down and kissed her.

## Chapter Five

*K*issing her was madness.

Colin swore to himself he didn't know why he was doing it—except that it seemed right and natural.

The fact she considered herself too good for him hit his pride and made him a little crazed, as did the fact that he was attracted to her. In so many ways she was such a country mouse. Obstinate, fearful, defiant ... headstrong, intelligent, forthright ... and a surprisingly good kisser.

Her lips melded against his. Her mouth was still closed, a sign she'd not been kissed often. He could understand. Right now, she looked a fright, all covered with dust and cobwebs. Yet something about her attracted him.

He had this overwhelming need to make mind-numbing love to her right on the floor, if need be. He pressed. She did not resist. He touched her lips with his tongue . . .

The spell broke. For both of them.

Colin opened his eyes and discovered hers were wide open, too.

They stared at each other, turned cross-eyed, and broke apart.

Lady Rosalyn practically ran to the other side of the room. He brought his hand up to his mouth and realized he could still taste her. Slowly he turned, anticipating some sort of spinsterish chastisement.

Instead, she stared at him, her razor-sharp gray green eyes wide in surprise. "Why did you do that?"

"Why did you let me?"

"I didn't 'let you,'" she responded. "You took."

He had. He wouldn't mind taking again, just to see if his imagination played tricks. Pointing at her with his hat, he accused, "You didn't mind."

Her chin came up. "I was offended."

"Liar," he said without heat. He took a step forward. "Here, let me kiss you again and prove that you are not as impervious to me as you wish to pretend."

"You stay right there," she said, moving to place the settee between them. "Don't touch me. Perhaps in other places women fall into your arms, but I won't."

"Another challenge." He frowned. "How will you know what you will and won't do if we don't kiss again?"

She made an impatient sound. "This is not a game. But that is how you perceive it, isn't it? You've been biding your time, sending one person after another to plead your case. You probably think this is some jest. You believe I have no choice and you can force me to your will."

"Lady Rosalyn, I am no lothario. It is true that I sent others on my behalf. But be honest. If I'd come myself, you would have thrown me out."

"I still may," she responded coolly, and he found himself liking her. She knew how to give as good as she got. "Besides, that was not a very good kiss."

Her boast caught him up short. "It wasn't?"

She shook her head. "Inferior."

"You expected better?" he goaded.

"I've *known* better."

He almost burst out laughing. "Now that is a

lie," he said baldly. "In fact, I'd wager the deed to Maiden Hill that you have never been truly, really, *madly* kissed in your life."

"Madly kissed?" She snorted her disdain, a soft feminine sound. "What nonsense. And of course I have been kissed."

"No," he corrected, "you've been *pecked*."

"Pecked?"

"Yes, pecked," he answered knowledgeably. "You know, a closed lip, dry mouth brush on the cheek. The sort of thing a grandmother shares. Pecked."

Her nose scrunched in distaste in the most adorable manner, and he discovered for the first time she had a dimple. Only hers was not like those cheruby dimples indenting the side of rosy cheeks. No, her dimple was beneath the corner of her mouth, on the lower right side. An out-of-kilter dimple, completely unique and utterly her.

"I've been more than *pecked*," she informed him haughtily.

"I didn't find any evidence of the like."

Her brows came together. "You smash your lips against mine without warning or request and then have the audacity to complain it wasn't a proper kiss? You don't deserve a kiss of any sort."

"Now wait a minute," Colin said, holding out his hands and thoroughly enjoying himself more than he had in a very long time. "I wasn't complaining. You were."

She shook her head. "I was not."

He pressed his lips together, letting her know *he* wasn't going to argue. And her irritated response was exactly all he could have wished. She started for the door. "Our interview is at an end. Good day, Colonel—"

He hooked his hand in her arm and spun her around. Before she could protest, he kissed her, only this time, he didn't hold back.

To his surprise, neither did she.

Her lips opened to him. Her body fit his.

He put the arm of his hand holding his hat around her waist. God, how long had it been since he'd had a woman? Too long—and yet, this wasn't just lust. There was something more here. She tasted different than others, smelled different, more enticing, more appealing. Kissing her might not be enough.

And she was not indifferent to him. Oh, no, she was as hungry as he was . . .

She pushed herself out of his arms and, without missing a beat, slapped him so hard against the side of the face that he dropped his hat.

Colin had been hit harder in pub fights during his misspent youth, but this was unexpected, and she almost knocked him over.

Her eyes were bright with indignation. Her chest heaved; her color was high. She looked magnificent.

"I may have deserved that," he admitted. He bent to pick up the hat.

"Yes, you did." Her fists were still clenched at her side.

"I'm not sorry I did it, though," he confessed. " 'Twas worth the price."

Her anger abated as quickly as it had flared, and in its place was confusion. She shook her head, as if trying to clear her thinking.

In a flash of insight, he said, "It's not the kiss that upset you, was it?"

Lady Rosalyn took a step back. "I think you need to leave."

He didn't. "I threaten you now more asking questions than I did kissing you."

"I'm not threatened, Colonel Mandland, I'm annoyed. What I think and feel is none of your business."

"It is now," he answered. He tapped his thigh with his hat. "I've decided to make it my business." He started backing out the door, knowing the time to leave had come. "You are a mystery, my lady . . . and a good kisser. I shall pay a call on the morrow."

"I won't be at home," she declared, her eyes sparkling with challenge.

"Yes, you will," he assured her, "and if you aren't, I'll wait for you." He turned and walked straight out of the house, pleased to have gotten in the last word.

Outside, Oscar had waded into Lady Rosalyn's flower beds again. So much for the trick of dropping the reins on the ground and expecting him to stand still. Colin mounted and started down the drive but then stopped. He looked back at Maiden Hill.

It was a proud house. Its mistress was proud, too. He understood pride. He knew it was often a way to protect one's heart.

Perhaps this marriage thing wasn't such a bad idea after all?

He put heels to horse.

Rosalyn was furious.

How dare that arrogant military man walk into her house and manhandle her? And then pretend he knew her better than she did herself?

The worst part was that he was right. She was

afraid. She hadn't realized how afraid until he'd kissed her the second time. For one glorious moment, she had wanted to let herself believe he could care.

Then she'd remembered. She'd recalled the times she had wanted to think others cared as deeply for her as she had for them. Her first hard lesson had been the one her mother had taught her. She had thought her mother loved her, until her mother had run off with another man. She had wanted her father to love her. Instead, he'd drunk himself to death over a broken heart. His daughter's love had meant nothing to him.

Following his death had been years of being trundled off from one relative to another. "What are we going to do with poor Rosalyn?" had been the watchword.

She'd wanted to believe those aunts and cousins could care for her. She'd been starved for love in her life . . . until she'd realized that no one loves an orphan.

And so Rosalyn had learned to make her own way—until today.

Colonel Mandland's kiss did threaten her because it made her realize how much was missing in her life.

In his kiss, she could taste the one dream she'd not allowed herself to have . . . the dream of children.

Rosalyn crossed her arms, suddenly cold with apprehension. "What is it about you that frightens me so?" she asked aloud.

"About whom?" Covey said from the door. She entered the room and then stopped to look around in bewilderment. "Why, my lady, you are alone. Are you starting to talk to yourself the way I talk to myself?"

"I was reasoning something out," Rosalyn answered.

"About Colonel Mandland? Bridget told me he was here."

"You *knew* he had come to call and didn't *rescue* me?" Rosalyn demanded. "Covey, what sort of friend are you?"

"One who hoped the two of you were getting along well," she answered. "He's not a bad man. He's brave and intelligent, handsome. . . . What more could you want?"

*Love.*

The word jumped unbidden to Rosalyn's mind. He was right. Her refusal of his suit had nothing to do with him and everything to do with her own need. She wanted to be loved, and yet she feared and distrusted the passion behind desire.

There, she had admitted it. She wanted the one thing she didn't believe existed. The knowledge of how needy she was shattered her very notion of herself.

She had to think, to sort everything out. She was too vulnerable, and with vulnerability came pain. She knew that. She started walking out of the room.

"My dear, are you all right?" Covey asked, taking a step after her.

Rosalyn held up a hand to ward her off. "I'm fine. I need to finish the attic. I must go." At the door, she stopped. "Please, don't leave me alone with him. Not any more." She didn't wait for a response but practically ran for the stairs.

A few minutes later, in the loneliness of the attic, she stood in front of a dusty mirror propped against the wall and saw a stranger reflected there.

Slowly, she removed the pins from her hair. The curls she took such pains to hide sprang out in joyful abandon at finally being set free.

Tears welled in her eyes as she looked into her mother's face, the one she tried to hide. Her father had blamed his drinking on how much she resembled the woman who had betrayed his love. Her aunts and cousins had all remarked on how unfortunate it was she had her mother's overtly sensual looks. Her mother. The candler's daughter who had captured the heart of an earl, an earl foolish enough to marry her.

Of course, her father's relatives had not been surprised when the lovely Ariette had run away with someone as common as a riding instructor. Hadn't she been common herself?

"I'm not common," Rosalyn said to the reflection. "I'm not."

As she forced back her tears, her eyes burned. She repinned her hair tighter than ever and lifted her chin. "I am Rosalyn Wellborne, daughter of the earl of Woodford. I am not common."

And she almost believed it. But that night, she didn't sleep well. She dreamed of babies. Beautiful, round, laughing babies. They seemed to fall from the sky into her arms, and they all had storm blue eyes, dark hair, and slashing eyebrows.

They were all miniature Colonel Mandlands.

She woke, her heart pounding in her chest . . . and prayed she would never have another nightmare like that one.

So when he presented himself on her doorstep the very next morning, she was not happy.

Colin knew better than to wait until he was announced. He followed the maid into the sitting room, where Lady Rosalyn sat on the floor in front of a huge open trunk before the hearth. "I'm not receiving callers" were the first words out of her mouth, even before his name was announced. She didn't even bother to look up at him.

He waved Bridget out of the room saying, "Hello, how are you?"

Lady Rosalyn frowned her response. She was again dressed for a day of cleaning and work. He rather liked her industriousness. In the military, he had become accustomed to and admired ladies who could adapt to their surroundings. Lady Rosalyn would have made a good military wife, although she would have to do something about her clothes. She'd also have to stop pulling her hair back so tight that it pulled at her brow line.

Today she had added a scarf, so she reminded him of nothing less than a burgher's wife gleaning wheat sheaves from the fields.

No, he amended to himself, she was prettier than any burgher's wife could even think of being, scarf or no.

She was packing small articles from the sitting room into the open trunk. In spite of a bit of a chill, spring was in the air and the windows were open.

Colin didn't wait for her to invite him to sit. He knew she wouldn't. He pulled up a chair by the trunk and seated himself.

"I'm very busy," she said pointedly.

"I won't disturb you. In fact, I'll help." He picked up a porcelain shepherdess from a side table and offered it to her.

"Some sorts of help one doesn't need," she answered, but she took the figurine from him.

"What nonsense. Everyone needs help."

Wrapping the figure in a soft rag, she murmured, "I'd like to help you out. The door, that is," she added so he could not mistake her intentions.

"You are prickly this morning. You must not have slept well."

Her glance flew to his in alarm, as if she was afraid he knew something she did not want him to know.

"What?" he asked.

She frowned and dropped her gaze to the task at hand. "Nothing."

Colin rested his elbows on his knees. "Well, it must have been something. You looked as if I had read your mind."

"It was nothing," she said with the right amount of testiness, and he knew she lied.

"Did you dream about me?"

The rag-wrapped figurine slipped from her hand into the trunk. There was a small, foreboding breaking sound. With a soft cry, she pulled the shepherdess back out and unwrapped it.

"I broke the staff." She raised distressed eyes to Colin. "It's Covey's. Her husband gave it to her as a wedding gift. She's always doted on it."

At that moment, there was a sound in the hall, and then Mrs. Covington appeared. She wore one of her lace caps and an apron with a streak of dust, a sign she had also been packing. "Bridget said we had company," she said pleasantly. "How good it is to see you again, Colonel."

Colin came to his feet and made a small bow. "Thank you, Mrs. Covington. I don't know if you will be so happy once you know what I've done." Colin didn't know why he was taking the blame, but it felt right. "I broke this shepherdess piece." He swooped the porcelain out of Lady Rosalyn's hands.

"I broke her little crook," he said, walking up to the older woman.

Mrs. Covington took the figurine out of his hands and, taking a moment to reach into her apron pocket and put her spectacles on the end of her nose, she inspected the damage. Her fingers trembled as they lightly touched the beloved item. "It's not such a bad break." She drew a breath and said, "Perhaps it can be repaired."

"Yes," he agreed.

She smiled, but the expression didn't reach her watery eyes. She handed the shepherdess back to him. "On another thought, perhaps she should stay here. Alfred gave her to me when we first moved in to Maiden Hill. We barely had a shilling to our name, and he knew I'd secretly coveted this piece, which set in Highson's shop. I was so surprised by the present." Mrs. Covington walked over to set the figure back on the mantel. "Here, this is her home. Perhaps she should stay? You would not mind, would you, Colonel Mandland?"

"I'd be honored," Colin said, knowing without looking that Mrs. Covington's words were like darts to Lady Rosalyn's heart. He looked back at her and was surprised to see he was wrong.

She sat unmoving by the trunk, but her face carried no expression. No regret, no sadness, no emotional turbulence of any sort.

And yet he *knew* she felt keenly.

Lady Rosalyn rose. "How kind of you, sir," she said quietly. "Covey, I must help Bridget. Would you be so kind as to entertain our guest."

She didn't wait for an answer but walked out of the room as if her knees were frozen.

There was a beat of silence, then Mrs. Covington said, "My lady broke the figurine."

"I thought to spare her, and it was my fault."

"You can't protect her." Mrs. Covington turned the shepherdess on the mantel so she could look out the window. "No one is harder on my lady than she is on herself. But I think you understand how that is? Are you not the same way?"

He was. One of the reasons he had taken risks in battle, leading his men himself and always volunteering for the difficult assignments, was that he didn't want anyone to think later that he had not carried his own weight. It was a point of honor to him.

"I believe Lady Rosalyn was upset because she knows how much the piece means to you," he said.

Mrs. Covington made a *shush* of aggravation. "She means more than a piece of pottery, and she knows that. She's also rarely clumsy. What did you say to her before the figurine broke?"

"I'd asked her if she'd dreamed about me."

A light came on in the older woman's eyes. "What was her answer? She was very out of sorts this morning."

"She didn't answer. The porcelain slipped from her hand."

"That *is* an answer," Mrs. Covington said, her face a wreath of smiles. "My dear, dear colonel. You are an answer to my most secret prayers." She took his hand. "I know you seek your own gain, but my lady is a wonderful woman. She has so much love inside her, and yet she holds it back. Please, save her."

Colin shifted uncomfortably. He had never been one to play Lancelot. Sir Galahad, yes. "Our marriage would be a good investment for us both."

Mrs. Covington frowned. "Bah to investments!" She released his hand. "Perhaps you *aren't* the right man," she said, her voice more disdainful than anything Lady Rosalyn could have used. "Good day, sir." She turned and walked out of the room.

He stood there, alone, puzzled over how he'd ended up that way. He looked to the shepherdess. "Did you understand any of that?"

Her painted smile mocked him.

Colin knew when he'd been dismissed. He left, but as he mounted Oscar, he knew he would be back.

Rosalyn assumed she'd not have to deal with Colonel Mandland again. He was gone, probably for good. Men were not known for courting difficult women—and she had been difficult. She could tell, because Covey pointedly did not mention his name again.

Then Rosalyn surprised herself, because she was the one to say his name. She couldn't help herself. Over dinner, she said, "The colonel's horse has ruined the rosebushes. Do you think he will notice?"

"A few men dote on flowers," Covey answered.

"He doesn't strike me as the type."

A sly smile appeared in Covey's eyes. "I think you are right."

So Colonel Mandland surprised them both the next afternoon when he arrived with a rosebush.

"Where did you get this?" Rosalyn asked.

"Aren't you going to say thank you?" he prompted.

"Thank you," she said, still stunned. The plant was healthy, although dearly needing to be planted. And it dawned on Rosalyn that no one had given her a gift in a very, very long time.

"I must confess, Val suggested the gift," he said. "I told her Oscar has eaten a good number of your flowers, and he and I should make amends before you send us out the door."

It was on the tip of her tongue to remind him she had done exactly that more than once . . . but the tart words died in her throat. A gift. And such a thoughtful one . . . "Do you know what color it is?"

"The roses?" He smiled. "Red."

Even Covey was impressed, and the colonel knew he'd done well.

"We should plant it now," he said. "If planted this early in the spring, Val said it could bloom this summer. I actually know very little about flowers except that Oscar seems to have quite a taste for them."

The minute he talked about planting, it struck Rosalyn what his motive might be. He probably thought she would want to stay at Maiden Hill and see the roses bloom. Clever, clever Colonel Mandland . . . because he was right.

"We could plant it right outside this window," he suggested. "That way the shepherdess can oversee its growing."

Covey glanced at Rosalyn, who couldn't help but smile. Who would have thought a gentleman could be so fanciful? Or successfully woo two women at once.

"Yes," Rosalyn agreed. "We should plant it there."

Old John was called in to supervise the planting. He was happy to have a new rose. The four of them—John, the colonel, Covey, and Rosalyn—had a little planting ceremony, which ended in laughter.

No mention was made of the upcoming move . . . and there was more than one moment when Rosalyn felt in perfect accord with Colonel Mandland. More than one moment when their eyes met. More than one moment when they exchanged asides for their benefit alone.

At one point, they could hear Lord Loftus's hunting dogs barking and baying in the distance in pursuit of "his" fox. "The man is possessed," the colonel murmured, and Rosalyn was startled because she'd just had the same thought.

It was on the tip of Rosalyn's tongue to invite him to stay for dinner, and yet she was shy. As it was, he took his leave, making a grand show of ordering Oscar not to nibble on the rose's tender leaves.

Rosalyn went into the house but stood in the sitting room window and watched him ride out of sight.

That night, she dreamed of babies again . . . and she was afraid. This was the sort of obsession for one person that had claimed her father's sanity and life. In the darkest hours of the night, Rosalyn lay awake, staring at the ceiling, and she knew she must do all to protect her heart.

# Chapter Six

The next day was Sunday, and a more perfect spring day would have been hard to find. Who could avoid attending church on such a lovely morning?

Rosalyn was kneeling in prayer before the Sunday service when the hairs tingled on the back of her neck.

Colonel Mandland had arrived.

She couldn't resist stealing a look at the door, and she hoped no one noticed; if they did, she would be embarrassed. Her days as a green girl were gone. A woman should be more sophisticated in her interest . . .

He caught her looking at him and grinned.

Hot color flooded her cheeks. She knew everyone must have seen him smile at her. She bowed her head and forced herself to return to her prayers . . . until he slipped into the pew beside her.

He was a big man and took up most of the narrow space. If they hadn't seen him smile at her, then certainly, everyone in the church noticed him sitting beside her. Rosalyn could feel their speculation, and she could catch the barest hint of whispered comments travel through the congregation. Some were probably laughing at her, while others would suggest it was a pity Lord Loftus had to buy her a husband. Or that she was brazenly throwing herself at the colonel.

It was the pity that hit her hardest. Wellbornes had no use for pity. She could recall her father saying that.

Colonel Mandland leaned close to her bonnet. "I almost didn't recognize you without a dust rag in your hands."

If he'd meant it as a compliment or a joke, she didn't take it as such. She was too conscious that everyone watched them.

He knew immediately he had upset her. "I was jesting."

She ignored him, keeping her eyes on the pew ahead. She didn't like the awkwardness of being singled out. It reminded her of the days when she'd had to move into a new household where everyone, including herself and the servants, wondered what her status was.

Before Colonel Mandland, everyone respected her. Now, considering the number of stares and nudges she saw in the sanctuary, she wasn't so certain.

Covey had no such insecurities. She leaned around Rosalyn and welcomed him with a smile.

The service started. This was good. Rosalyn could pretend Colonel Mandland wasn't standing by her side—except that he wanted to share her prayer book, a gesture almost more intimate than a kiss.

Reverend Mandland liked singing. He incorporated it in the worship service, usually before the sermon. He had a strong, fine voice, and the parish enjoyed singing with him.

Colonel Mandland was not as gifted as his brother. Yes, his voice was strong, but off key. Still, he sang with enthusiasm and knew the hymns by heart.

If no one had noticed them before, they certainly couldn't have avoided noticing them now.

Perhaps if she and Colonel Mandland had been a love match, Rosalyn could have handled all the attention. She would have looked up at him with adoring eyes and thought his flat-noted singing endearing.

Instead, she wished he would mouth the words the way she did so as not to draw undue notice.

She barely heard the sermon, which seemed to be a homily directed at the colonel about how one should have a better goal in life than ambition.

Meanwhile, inside herself, she struggled with what seemed to be a thousand demons. She was too conscious of him, of his thigh that brushed against hers, of his arm that bumped hers, of the scent of him, of the sound of his breathing, of every detail and nuance.

Colonel Mandland's mercenary pursuit for her hand and the Commons seat was threatening her sanity. She longed for the days—a mere week ago—when her life had been orderly and exactly as she had arranged it.

Was it the incense in the church or his presence that made her a bit dizzy?

When the service came to an end, she wanted to shoot out of her seat—except he was blocking her exit. Nor was he in a hurry to leave. He took his time, greeting the other members of the church, giving the impression to one and all that they were decidedly a couple.

Rosalyn wondered what he would do if she were to climb over the pew trying to get around him. It wasn't fair of him to threaten her this way. A call at Maiden Hill was one thing. Being courted in public was another. She was too old for such nonsense. She keenly felt her age when she caught sight of a number of children avidly watching her, as if she was going to be the topic of many a table conversation in the evening.

Consequently, when the colonel did turn his attention to her, she was definitely cold to him. "You're upset," he observed, unrepentant.

"I'm ready to go home. If you would please excuse me?"

He didn't move, and at that moment, Mr. and Mrs. Blair walked up to wish them well. Mrs. Blair pretended to converse with Covey, but Rosalyn noticed that her beady eyes didn't miss a thing. So, when Colonel Mandland—*finally!*—stepped out of the pew into the narrow aisle and placed his hand possessively on Rosalyn's elbow, she had to pull away. She didn't want to give the gossips any more fodder than they already had.

Colonel Mandland got the hint, and his reaction was stronger than the time she'd slapped him. He understood, and he was offended. She could tell by the sudden tension in his body. The smile on his face became more pronounced and less genuine. He knew she did not want to be in public with him. Not until she'd had a chance to sort out her feelings.

The wall went up between them, and this time, it was made of bricks.

She wanted to say *good*.

Instead, she slipped by him, waited for Covey, and, taking her friend's arm, walked out of the sanctuary. She could feel him watching her leave, and she sensed his silent command for her to turn around and come back right that minute.

In the vestibule, Rosalyn stepped aside to let Covey pass first out the door. Only then, a heartbeat before she followed, did she look back to Colonel Mandland.

Their gazes met—and then *he* turned away.

She went outside.

Covey waited, anxious to keep Rosalyn a moment before mingling with the other parishioners who were visiting and enjoying the lovely weather. "What was that about?"

"What was what about?" Rosalyn said. She smiled at Mrs. Sheffield and Mrs. Blair, who stood perhaps ten feet from them, their heads together in gossip.

"Did you truly mean to cut Colonel Mandland in front of those biddies?" Covey asked.

Rosalyn looked at her. "Colonel Mandland is presumptuous. He makes his own bed."

"He'd like to make yours," Covey responded, surprising Rosalyn with her bluntness.

She blinked a moment, a rush of undefined feelings circulating through her at the thought of being in that man's bed. "He wants the Commons seat," she reminded herself. "He cares not a whit for me."

"You can make him care."

"No," Rosalyn replied, more to herself than Covey. Knowing she sounded abrupt to her friend, she attempted to explain all the reasons she'd thought of through sleepless nights. "I know there are those who feel every woman should be married, no matter what the cost. But, Covey, my pride is the only legacy my father gave me. I'll not sacrifice it. I'll not sell myself to marriage."

Covey placed a gloved hand on Rosalyn's arm. "I had thought, especially after yesterday, that you were not adverse to his suit."

"Do you believe me so shallow as to fall in his arms for no other reason than because he is handsome, charming, and brought me flowers?"

Rosalyn shook her head. "My father courted my mother. He did everything for her, and in the end, it meant nothing."

"You can't judge marriage from what your parents had. Alfred and I—"

"Alfred and you were the exception, not the rule. My cousins all married well, and there is not one of them who can abide their husbands. I used to listen to my aunts vent their frustrations over the treatment they received from *their* husbands. Yes, Lord and Lady Loftus seem a good match, but look at the others. Mr. and Mrs. Blair speak civilly only in church. The Lovejoyces are famous for their battles. Covey, the list goes on and on."

Rosalyn tried to explain herself and the feelings she'd rooted out the night before. "I want more." There, she'd said it. "I'm not certain what more is. Perhaps this is a legacy from my mother. My father's title wasn't enough. It couldn't keep her by his side. Sometimes I wish I'd met that riding instructor. Perhaps I would understand why she hurt so many people—all in the name of love."

"Oh, my lady, who knows why we hurt others? But we all do, often unintentionally."

"I don't, Covey. *I don't.*"

"Then your rudeness to Colonel Mandland a few moments ago was intentional?"

Rosalyn flinched, as if her friend had poked her in the back. There were times Covey knew how to make her point too well. "There is nothing between the colonel and me for which I must apologize. I did what I must."

Rosalyn didn't wait for an answer but walked over to say hello to Lady Loftus, who was talking to Mrs. Shellsworth, the lawyer's wife.

Lavonia Shellsworth was reed thin, with a long neck and a chirpy laugh. As Rosalyn walked up, she was chirping over something Lady Loftus had said.

Her ladyship stretched a hand out to Rosalyn. "Isn't it a glorious day? Spring is my favorite season of the year."

"Oh, I do love it too," Mrs. Shellsworth pronounced, as if Lady Loftus had just solved a mystery of the universe.

Lady Loftus smiled, but the look in her eyes was one of pleasant dislike. She changed the subject. "Lady Rosalyn, I noticed Colonel Mandland by your side during the service." She raised her eyebrows knowingly. "I've heard he's been paying marked attention to you."

Before Rosalyn could answer, Mrs. Shellsworth

said, "If his attentions toward you are so marked, Lady Rosalyn, then what is he doing over there, keeping company with Belinda Lovejoyce?"

"Belinda Lovejoyce—?" Rosalyn repeated and turned in the direction Mrs. Shellsworth had indicated. She did not recognize the petite, buxom blonde Colonel Mandland was speaking to under the flowering cherry tree at the edge of the parish graveyard along the church walk. The woman stood close to him, too close. She seemed to enjoy peeking up at him through dark, full lashes . . . and he seemed to enjoy her attention.

With a woman's power of intuition, Rosalyn knew the blonde and the colonel were not strangers. Jealousy stabbed through her with a force that was staggering.

"Weren't Colonel Mandland and Belinda Lovejoyce promised to each other at one time?" Mrs. Shellsworth asked.

Lady Loftus hurried to say, "That was *years* ago. And do you not remember, Mrs. Shellsworth, that Belinda Lovejoyce left the colonel? She married another man. What was his name? Regis? He was from Preston."

Belinda Lovejoyce Regis had complete command of Colonel Mandland, and she was everything Rosalyn wasn't, including wealthy. The strand of pearls around her neck may or may not be real, but Rosalyn could tell the dress had come from London.

"She has a husband," Lady Loftus warned Rosalyn quietly, as if wanting to bolster her spirits. "You need not worry."

"Oh, did I not mention the news?" Mrs. Shellsworth chimed in happily. "Belinda is a widow. Her husband died last year, and she is just out of mourning. She's returned home to her parents' house. I heard from her mother she was most anxious to see Colonel Mandland, and I can understand why. He's come a long way from the Colin we used to know."

Rosalyn looked in surprise. Of course Lavonia Shellsworth would have known him. He was one of them. She was the outsider.

Mrs. Shellsworth smiled slyly. "I wonder if Belinda is wishing she'd not been so hasty to marry money. Her husband was twenty years older with a wart on the end of his nose."

At that moment, Colonel Mandland glanced over and saw Rosalyn and the other two watching them. She was embarrassed, until with a cynical lift of his eyebrow, Colonel Mandland deliberately gave her his back.

"Oh dear," Mrs. Shellsworth said without sympathy. "Did he just cut you, Lady Rosalyn?"

"I must be going now," Rosalyn said to Lady Loftus. Her knees felt shaky, and she didn't like how important Colonel Mandland's presence had become in her life.

"I thought things were going so well," Lady Loftus worried.

"There is nothing to go well," Rosalyn answered. "Now, if you will excuse me?" She started off to find Covey.

"Well, I suppose the Commons seat is still available, isn't it?" Mrs. Shellsworth said as Rosalyn left.

Covey was a short distance away, talking to some friends. The after-church crowd had thinned considerably.

"Are we ready to go?" she asked as Rosalyn approached.

"Will you be seeing Colonel Mandland this afternoon?" one of Covey's friends asked Rosalyn with avid curiosity. Oh, yes, everyone in Clitheroe fished for gossip.

"No," Rosalyn replied firmly, taking Covey's arm and guiding the older woman to where Old John waited with the pony cart.

"Things are not good?" Covey asked.

What could Rosalyn say? "Things are as they should be."

It was the right answer.

"Well, I hear Cornwall is pleasant country," Covey said sadly.

"I'm sorry. Maybe I'm too old to marry." Or too stubborn, or set in her ways . . . or too proud.

Covey took a seat in the cart opposite Rosalyn's, her expression sad and thoughtful. They were well on their way home before she said, "You're right. It is probably for the best."

It *was* for the best, Rosalyn reminded herself. Colonel Mandland was *too* male, *too* bold, *too* aggressive for her tastes.

He was also too busy listening to Belinda Lovejoyce's prattle to even glance back in Rosalyn's direction.

She knew because she *had* looked back.

Out of the corner of his eye, Colin watched the High-and-Mighty-*Princess* Rosalyn leave, and he was damn angry. She had the ability to make him feel lower than the grit beneath her feet.

And he didn't know why.

Women liked him. Without vanity, he admitted it was his looks *and* his ambition. He was a man who had accomplished much and would accomplish more—something *she* didn't deem to notice.

The last woman who had made him feel that way was Belinda Lovejoyce, and right now, she appeared to eat him up with a spoon. She was in the market for a new husband, and now Colin met her standards.

There had been a time when he would have done anything for Belinda. Not any more. He wasn't even the same person as the reckless youth who'd believed the only value any woman possessed was her looks.

He needed more now. Someone who shared his sense of humor. Someone who had intelligence. Someone who understood traits like honesty, bravery, loyalty.

Belinda didn't have any idea what loyalty meant. She spoke of her deceased husband with derision. More than once she dropped sly hints that he'd been too old to satisfy her in bed. Otherwise, according to her, she would have given him a child and not found herself bullied out of his estate by his children from a previous marriage.

Well, Colin was not going to be her bedmate now. He was not second best. But he smiled and listened to her and, as soon as Lady Rosalyn left, he excused himself from Belinda.

"Are you coming home?" Matt asked as he walked up to Colin.

"I think I might go for a ride. Clear my brain a bit. Soak in the pointed message my brother sent me in his sermon."

Matt laughed. "At least one person was listening. We'll see you at dinner at half past three?"

Colin nodded.

"Don't be late, or Val will take you to task." Matt set off for the rectory but turned and walked backward to say, "Your singing is improving, Colin. You almost had *some* of the right notes."

"Go to the devil," Colin replied without heat.

Matt laughed and Colin realized it was good to be home.

A half hour later, he had Oscar saddled. He set off on the road to Chatburn. Being Sunday, there was not much traffic, so Colin let Oscar have his lead before jumping a hedgerow and taking off at a full gallop across a farmer's unplowed field.

As they headed into the forest, Colin pulled Oscar up short when he heard the tiresome sound of howling hounds. Obviously, Loftus had no respect for the Sabbath.

Oscar's ears pricked up. He had to have heard

the dogs, but it did not explain why he suddenly did a prancing dance—until the fox skulked out from a hollow log that served as a bridge across a shallow stream.

Once again, Colin and the fox confronted each other.

"Run, my little friend," he advised the animal. "They are on their way."

The fox appeared to release a weary sigh before splashing down the middle of the stream. Colin watched him go and then guided Oscar in the direction of the hounds.

A moment later, he caught sight of the dogs coming up and over a bluff, Lord Loftus and another rider charging after them.

Keen on the scent, the dogs raced past Oscar toward the woods. Colin was fairly certain his friend the fox would make another escape. He waited for Loftus, who reined to a stop when he saw him. The rider was Shellsworth. Colin didn't like seeing him with Loftus.

"Oh, Mandland!" Loftus's face was red with exertion. "Did you see the damn fox?"

"I thought I caught a glimpse of one running north across the farmer's field on the other side of the woods there."

"Drat! Damn dogs are going the wrong way!"

"I hear your marriage plans are not going well," Shellsworth said.

"You know women," Colin answered with a shrug. "They are capricious by nature."

The lawyer smiled, the expression ugly. "I'm certain you are enough of a lapdog to trip along at her feet anyway—"

"Shellsworth, shut up!" Loftus said. "Mandland will call you out and then I'll lose a lawyer because the colonel will make mincemeat out of you. There would be nothing left. Not even your boots." He looked to Colin. "You handle our Lady Rosalyn. You know what *I* want. I know what *you* want."

"Yes, my lord," Colin answered.

"The fox ran across the farmer's field?" Loftus asked, bringing his mind back to the more important matter.

"He was heading toward Barley Booth," Colin said helpfully.

"Good man," Loftus said. "Come along, Shellsworth. Let's see if your nag can run."

"But, my lord," Shellsworth said. "Look at the dogs. They are milling around the stream and not crossing."

"Damn fool hounds! Can't sniff anything," Loftus declared. "Didn't you hear Mandland?" He rode off. The hounds and Shellsworth had no choice but to follow him.

Colin watched them disappear from sight. "What do you think, Oscar?" he asked. "Do you think I should dance to Lady Rosalyn's tune, or should I be the one playing the fiddle?"

Oscar grumbled a response.

"I know. I'd best get home, too, or I'll be late for dinner, and I have no desire to cross swords with my sister-in-law."

He didn't even need to prompt the horse, who happily turned on his own and headed back to the stables.

Colonel Mandland did not call the next day, or the next.

Rosalyn wondered if he was biding his time again the way he had in the beginning. She didn't think so.

Lady Loftus called on Monday, but she left angry because Rosalyn refused to discuss the matter. After her failed visit, no one called. Rosalyn understood how Valley society worked. She was not falling into Colonel Mandland's arms as they wished, so she was being given a cold shoulder.

In the end, the decision to leave was taken out of her hands. Her cousin George did send money to travel to Cornwall, although it was less than necessary. Rosalyn would have to supplement it with her meager savings.

When George's letter and money arrived, Covey became very quiet and distracted.

"You don't have to leave," Rosalyn told her. "Certainly, someone in Clitheroe or the Valley would take you in."

"No, no. My place is with you," Covey insisted, and Rosalyn was selfish enough not to push the matter.

The next morning, Rosalyn drove the pony cart through town. She saw Colonel Mandland speaking to Mr. Jeffries, the banker, in front of the White Lion public house. The two of them were involved in an earnest discussion. She wondered what scheme the colonel was cooking up now. She expected him to ignore her. After all, wasn't that what he was doing . . . when he wasn't pursuing the Beautiful Belinda?

So she was surprised when, as she drove by, he stopped the conversation and nodded to her. She pretended not to notice. She didn't know why she pretended this, except that it was easier than to acknowledge him.

And was it her imagination, or did she sense him watching her as she drove out of sight? She didn't have the courage to look back and check. However, halfway home, she stopped the cart. She was still trembling just from that one "almost" close encounter with him.

What in the world was the matter with her? She barely knew the man, and yet he consumed her rational thoughts. Or *was* she turning into a spinster maid who giggled around men? What would she be like after a few years with Aunt Agatha?

Rosalyn came face-to-face with her deepest fear. She wasn't pretty enough or clever enough or anything enough for a man like Colonel Mandland. Forget the Commons seat. *She wanted to be chosen for herself,* and she should know better. The world didn't work that way. People used people—just like her mother had used her father.

She didn't want to be either a user or the used.

"So, Aunt Agatha it is," she told the cart pony. The animal didn't care. He sighed, a sign he was ready to go home. She picked up the reins and honored his wish.

Drizzle was starting to come down by the time she returned to the house. John met her to unharness the cob. She went in to find Covey. The time for procrastination was past. The sooner they left, the sooner they could move forward with their lives.

But Covey was not in the sitting room or the morning room. Rosalyn went upstairs and knocked on her companion's door. There was no answer. She opened the door and found the room empty.

Down in the kitchen, she found Bridget helping Cook with dinner. "Have either of you seen Covey?"

"No, my lady," Cook answered.

Rosalyn went outside. John hadn't seen her either, and she was nowhere to be found on the immediate grounds. Rosalyn grew worried. This was not like Covey at all—except for the one time she had fallen, grown confused, and wandered off. John reminded Rosalyn of it.

"Hitch up the cart again," she answered. "Perhaps she walked to town." But then, why wouldn't Rosalyn have seen her on the road?

Rosalyn fetched a shawl and one for Covey. She noticed what she hadn't seen earlier in

Covey's room—her friend's lace cap was on the bedside table, and her good bonnet was missing from the wardrobe. Perhaps she had gone to visit friends ... but Covey never went anywhere alone.

Evening was drawing near. If they didn't hurry and find her, they could lose her in darkness. Bridget volunteered to run over to the neighboring houses. Cook would stay and keep watch at home in case Covey returned.

"John and I will drive back into town," Rosalyn said. There were only so many places Covey could wander.

They rode into Clitheroe, past the Norman keep, and down the street. Shops were closed, both sides deserted. People had gone in, out of the damp. Candles were being lit, and their soft glow marked how late the hour was growing. The fog was rolling in, drifting along the ground. Rosalyn could only hope Covey was someplace safe.

"There she is, my lady," John said. "Over there in the churchyard. I thought she might go there."

"Amongst the graves?" Rosalyn craned and saw Covey on her knees. "What is she doing?"

"Her husband, my lady," John reminded her. "He's buried over yonder, right where she is."

Rosalyn could barely wait for the cart to stop before she hopped out and, carrying the extra shawl, ran to her friend's side.

Covey didn't act like she heard Rosalyn approach. She sat silent, looking more drawn and older than she ever had before. Her bonnet shielded her face from the rain, but her body trembled with cold. Rosalyn put the shawl around Covey's shoulders, and the woman stirred.

"I would have brought you here if you had asked," Rosalyn said softly.

Covey raised worried eyes. Rosalyn was relieved she seemed aware of her presence and this wasn't another "episode." "I don't want to leave him," Covey whispered. "I'm trying to be brave the way he would want me to be, but I've never left the Valley. My whole life has been here. And I don't want to leave *him*."

Rosalyn sank to the wet earth beside Covey and put her arms around her. Covey felt so frail. She would never survive the move to Cornwall. She'd die away from the beauty of the Valley.

And Rosalyn knew what she must do.

"We won't leave," she promised Covey. "Now, come, get into the cart with John."

Covey grasped Rosalyn's arm, holding her down. "Don't marry for me. Don't marry a man you do not love. I told your mother that, but she didn't listen. I tried to warn her. I did."

Rosalyn pulled back in surprise. "Covey, you've never said anything of this to me before. I didn't think you even knew my mother."

"I told you I understood why you couldn't marry Colonel Mandland. Look at the pain your father suffered. You are very much like him. You feel things too deeply."

The chill was no longer from the cold. "Please, don't say that."

Tears welled in Covey's eyes. "Don't be bitter. That's why I never told you I knew her until now. She wanted to do what was right. She tried."

"Some would say my mother didn't have a heart," Rosalyn said tensely. "If she did, I was never in it."

"You poor child. I wish she'd made different choices. Our choices are our destiny. Rosalyn, don't marry for me or Maiden Hill. Marry for love."

"What if there is no one out there for me to

love?" The question was haunting. "Perhaps I was meant to be alone. Perhaps I *want* to be alone."

"No one wants to be alone, Rosalyn. No one."

The truth of Covey's words hit Rosalyn hard.

"Come, Covey, let me help you to the cart. We need to get you home and get you warm."

Covey glanced around, as if just realizing how late it was. The mist was turning into a soft rain. "I didn't mean to worry you. The church is only a stretch of the leg, you know."

"I know, and I'm impressed you can walk here, but next time, ask me, and we will use the cart." Her friend was so weak that Rosalyn could have carried her in her arms. John met them halfway. "Please take her home and have Cook put some hot broth in her."

"Yes, my lady."

"Aren't you coming?" Covey asked.

"John will bring the cart back for me later. To the rectory, John."

"Yes, my lady."

"Rosalyn—"

Rosalyn shushed her. "'Tis my decision to make. Now go home and, John, hurry back."

She didn't wait to argue but pulled her shawl up over her head and crossed the road, heading for St. Mary Magdalene's rectory.

At the front gate, she hesitated before lifting the latch and going to the door. Light shone from the windows, and there were the sounds of voices and laughter, as though the Mandlands' children were highly enjoying themselves.

Before she lost her courage, Rosalyn hurried up the front walk and knocked on the door.

Seconds passed like hours. She heard footsteps approach, a man's deep voice telling Joseph to leave Emma alone, and then the door opened and Colonel Mandland himself stood there.

He held a baby in his arms.

For a moment, Rosalyn couldn't speak.

Inside, a fire burned in the hearth, and the room smelled of the sausages they must have cooked for dinner. Colonel Mandland did not wear a coat, and his shirt was open at the neck.

"My lady," he said, a touch surprised. He shifted the baby's weight to rest on his hip. "Here, come in out of the rain."

She didn't move. She didn't dare go farther. Instead, she hovered in the doorway, uncertain. The cozy, cheerful atmosphere of the sitting room was too much of a contrast to the cold night. It made her realize how empty her own life was. Reaching out, she touched the baby's precious, perfectly formed fingers. The child's skin was smoother than the finest velvet.

She looked up at the colonel and said, "Is your offer of marriage still available?"

# Chapter Seven

$C$olin wasn't certain he'd heard Lady Rosalyn correctly. "You want to marry me?" he repeated dumbly. Everything about her since last Sunday had told him louder than words he was well beneath her notice.

Her expression pale and defiant, she nodded.

Her hair, usually pulled back so tightly, was now windblown and curling in the mist-dampened air. She pulled her shawl closer around her shoulders.

"Come in and let's discuss the matter," he answered, opening the door wider.

She shook her head. "No, I'm—" She frowned. "John will be coming for me. I don't want him to wait." She paused a beat and asked, "Are you afraid to tell me you have changed your mind? I know Belinda Lovejoyce has returned to the Valley. They say you were close." Her words suddenly came tumbling out of her mouth. "But she married another. I think you should remember that."

Was she truly as nervous as she sounded, or was the night air too much for her?

Colin decided to find out.

He turned to the children, who, quietly, for once, watched the little drama unfold. "Boyd, come take Sarah. I need to speak to Lady Rosalyn a moment alone."

"Yes, Uncle," Boyd said. "Hello, my lady," he said shyly, as he took the baby from Colin.

"Hello, Boyd," she answered.

Her acknowledgement opened the gate for the others. Emma stood and waved, as did Joseph. Lady Rosalyn waved back. Even bold Thomas seemed shy.

"Watch the others until I return," Colin told Boyd. "I'll only be outside." He came out on the step, closing the door behind him. "Little pitchers have big ears," he explained as he took her arm by the elbow and walked to the shelter of an oak some five feet from the cottage. "I've learned that the hard way. If Thomas uses one more swear word and tells his mother he learned it from his uncle, Val will evict me with her broom."

She made no response. Not even a smile. Her head was bowed and her gait stiff.

Colin said, "The Clitheroe gossips never forget a thing, do they?"

"Why should they?"

"Belinda Lovejoyce Whatever-Her-Last-Name-is-Now was many years ago," he confessed.

"She's still very lovely."

He stopped. They were in the shelter of the oak's branches. It was still too early in the spring for leaves. "Lady Rosalyn, you aren't jealous, are you?"

That got her attention. She raised her head and frowned. The high planes of her cheeks and the tilt of her nose were clear to see in the light from the house. The rest of her face was in shadows. "Yes."

Her simple response could have knocked him over. Not for the first time did he wonder what kind of woman she was. There was honor and loyalty and a blunt honesty that he'd never found in anyone else.

His own qualities were put to the test when she asked tightly, "Perhaps you are still attracted to her? She obviously has eyes for you."

"She has eyes for any man with money. Her father is not pleased she has returned home with creditors. However, she played me for a fool once. There will not be a second time."

Lady Rosalyn nodded, barely acknowledging his remarks.

Frustrated, Colin stabbed his fingers through his hair and said, "What is this about? You've made it very clear you were not interested in my suit from the moment we met, and then now you show up on my doorstep asking me to marry you?"

"You snubbed me, too. At church, in the yard. We are even."

"If we are keeping score."

"Aren't we?"

Colin pulled back. The woman had a mind as sharp as a barrister's. "I was angry."

"You haven't paid a call since Saturday," she said.

"You have been as prickly as that rosebush we planted and very clear in your intentions to throw my suit back in my face."

"My pride is my gravest fault." Her voice sounded strained, as if she wanted to cry and couldn't.

He understood. The walls she had erected around herself wouldn't let her.

"Have you ever been in love?" he asked abruptly, wanting to know who had destroyed her trust.

His question appeared to startle her. "Why do you ask?"

"It's a fair question. You know a bit of my past, and if you don't, Mrs. Blair and Mrs. Sheffield will happily give you details."

"Actually, Lavonia Shellsworth enjoys chronicling your life."

"Lavonia?" He made a disgusted sound. "She had her nose into everyone's business even when she was Emma's age, and half of what she knows isn't true but the product of a bored imagination."

Lady Rosalyn choked on what sounded like laughter. Colin capitalized on it. "What is the matter? Do you think I shouldn't be so blunt? 'Tis nothing you haven't thought yourself," he challenged.

"But I would not speak the words aloud."

"Maybe you should."

She took a step back. He pushed on. "You don't because you are a single woman. Society frowns on outspokenness in those without husbands to defend them. But a married woman has complete *freedom*."

He knew the power behind that last word, and he could feel her response to it. He pressed, "So, I repeat my earlier question—have you ever been in love?"

"No." She drew a breath and released it. "Pity, isn't it? I once fancied a young man when I lived with my aunt Maribeth. Her husband is a Russian count. The young man I admired was the one they had chosen for the oldest daughter."

"A chinless daughter with protruding teeth and a squint, no doubt."

He caught the flash of her smile. She looked away, covering her mouth with her hand a moment to hide it. "My cousin had a beautiful singing voice."

"People who squint often do. Helps them hit the high notes."

Now she did laugh, and he grinned, pleased with himself. Her laughter always sounded a bit rough to him, as if she'd not exercised it enough.

"You've lived with numerous relatives in your life, haven't you?"

Her laughter died. "I had no choice. Because of Covey's presence, Maiden Hill is the first place where I've been"—she hesitated slightly, and then said softly—"*free* to be out from the rules of others."

"And allowed to care for yourself."

"Yes."

He nodded. He understood. "So what became of the young man you fancied?"

"He married my cousin, and then I was moved to my aunt Agatha's." She shivered. "The woman's a dragon."

"She's the one Woodford wants to ship you off to."

"Yes." The curt word cut through the night, and she seemed to think she should soften it. "It's not my relatives' faults. It is awkward having an orphan in the midst at any age."

"I don't agree. In my family, the door is open for everyone. Of course, I'm having to sleep on the floor, but only because I can't stand Boyd's snores and the way Thomas's feet smell."

She laughed again, and he thought making her laugh could become quite addictive. "Of course, I'm not a beautiful, unmarried woman amongst relatives who squint," he hazarded.

"I'm not beautiful," she said flatly. "Nor do you need to flatter me. I can catalog my faults."

"Name one," he said, wondering what she would say. From the way she usually wore her hair all pulled back, he sensed she was not pleased with it.

"My lips are too large," she answered.

*Her lips were kissable.* "Who told you that? Aunt Agatha?"

"No one told me. I have a mirror."

"I see," Colin said. "But no *man* has told you this?"

She made an impatient sound. "That isn't proper talk between a man and a woman."

Colin could have told her it was the best sort of talk, and yet he was secretly pleased. She was untouched physically and mentally. The possessiveness he'd begun feeling toward her grew a bit more.

"There was another gentleman in London during my first Season," she said. "He paid me marked attention even after my aunt Grace told him my circumstances."

"What happened to him?" Colin asked, uncomfortable with the niggling of jealousy. He'd noticed her voice had softened at the mention of this man.

"He married another one of my cousins. In the end, he said we did not suit. I went through another Season with two of my younger cousins, but I didn't take."

"But your heart," he pressed. "Has no one ever touched your heart?" Damn, when had he started sounding like a poet?

She moved deeper into the tree's shadows. She did not answer his question. Instead, she said, "You have not given up on the Commons seat, have you?"

In fact, no, he hadn't, and he hadn't given up on her. He had been letting her cool her heels. His pride had been wounded by her coldness, especially in the church, where all had been witness. He would not have let her leave for Cornwall without one more attempt. He had been biding his time. "I'd *hoped* you would come to me," he answered.

There was a beat of silence, and then she said, "I'm here."

"Why?"

"Does it matter? Ours will be a marriage of convenience. Who cares about our motives?"

"I do." And he discovered in truth he did. He

took a step toward her. "You've worked so hard to ensure I knew my motives were repugnant to you." *And that I was socially inferior.*

"It doesn't seem right to be so cold about marriage."

"Marriage should be thought of in the cold light of day. It is a major change in our lives. Now you appear on my doorstep in the night and *you* are the one to make *me* an offer. Asking why you've had a change of mind seems a very sensible question."

He expected her to balk at his demand like any high-strung mare. He wouldn't have been surprised if she'd stormed off.

She did inch away from him as if tempted to run, but then she planted her feet firmly on the ground and said, "Covey. I'm here because of Covey. She can't leave. She's spent over forty years of her life at Maiden Hill. She has no children or family. Her memories are all she has now. I found her tonight at the grave of her husband, and I realized just exactly how much I was asking her to sacrifice for my pride. She'd not last in Cornwall. She'll die, and I've learned she's all I have. She's the only person in the world who has ever given a care to what I genuinely needed

or genuinely believed. I can't let anything happen to her. She's too valuable . . . too precious."
She lifted her chin in that resolute way of hers that he was starting to anticipate, daring him to contradict her.

"Then answer the question I asked earlier."

"I thought I had. Or else I've forgotten the questions," she said irritably. "What do you think I'm evading?"

"Has your heart ever been involved before?"

"*No.*"

Colin smiled, pleased. "A straight answer. That wasn't difficult, was it?"

"Men are vain," she answered, accurately pinning him.

"Yes, we are," he said. This was a battle of wills. Rosalyn Wellborne challenged him like no other. "We shall do well, Rosalyn," he said. Her name alone, without the affectations of a courtesy title, rolled off his tongue like music.

"We shall live separate lives," she informed him. "Isn't that what you said? Separate."

Ah, yes, leave it to Rosalyn to dictate the terms. "Don't worry. Arranged marriages are often the best."

She frowned. "My mother's was an arranged

marriage. It was a disaster." There was a wealth of unspoken pain in her words. This was the first time she'd let him have even a glimpse of her true self.

He remembered the story Val had told him. "What happened?" he asked, wanting to hear the tale from her.

Immediately, she backed away. "All I ask is that you are discreet in satisfying your desires," she said with high-handed authority. "Belinda Lovejoyce would not be discreet."

"Wait a minute. We will have a marriage of convenience, but not one 'in name only.'"

"What's the difference?" she asked, alarmed.

"Sex."

He could feel the heat of her blush even in the dark. "Why?" she begged, and he almost pitied her.

"I want children," he said.

She pulled her crossed arms closer to her body. "I do too," she whispered so softly that he could have mistaken her words.

"There's only one way to have children," he told her. He reached out and touched her arm. She stiffened but did not move away. Gently, he stroked his fingers back and forth on her arm, not threatening her but not leaving her either.

"We may not be as bad for each other as you anticipate."

He could almost hear her heart pounding against her chest. She was either afraid or attracted. He took another step toward her. She didn't move. A part of him warned this was madness and he should leave well enough alone.

He couldn't.

Her gaze came up to meet his. Her eyes were shiny in the dark. Carefully, he brought a hand up to brush the softness of her cheek. He wondered how long her hair was. Did it reach midway down her back? Did it curl on the ends? What did it smell like?

He leaned closer for a sniff. She tensed. "This isn't wise," she said.

"The marriage? Or that I have an urge to seal our troth with a kiss?"

"Both."

For a moment they stood, frozen in desire . . . and then she started to break away, but Colin wouldn't let her.

He caught her arm. "Rosalyn, you had a reason for coming here. I have a reason for wanting to marry you. But there is also this attraction between us. It is not such a bad thing between a man and a woman."

"You don't know," she said, and at last he heard the fear in her voice. "People hurt those who care for them."

"I won't harm you."

"I won't let you," she countered. She brought her hands up to his chest to push him away, but she stopped. For a second, her right hand rested over his heart. It was as if she'd felt its beat and could not move.

"See?" he said gently. "I'm flesh and blood. I have dreams, desires, hungers . . . just like you. Trust me, Rosalyn. Trust me even a little."

He would have kissed her then, but as he bent down, she slipped out of his arms as smoothly as if she'd been turned to mist.

She moved beyond the sheltering protection of the tree. The fog drifted around the hem of her skirts. "We'll have children," she said, "but not until I'm ready."

"Of course—"

"No easy promise. I must have your word."

Colin felt a flash of temper. "Why? So you can make me jig to your tune?"

"You want the Commons seat. Is this so much to ask?"

No, what he really wanted was her. He could

face that now. He wanted to be in her. To feel, taste, touch, and experience every inch of her.

He was also aware that the price she asked might be higher than he was willing to pay. The devil with it. "When do we marry?" he demanded.

"You haven't promised."

"To what? To not force myself upon you? Very well, I promise. I've never forced myself on a woman in my life. I won't start with my wife."

His words didn't seem to satisfy her, but what choice did she have? "I don't care when we marry," she said. "You decide, and you'll have to tell George, too. I'm certain he will be irritated that you did not ask him first . . . if he remembers my name."

"I'll handle him," Colin assured her. "I'll tell him that when I took possession of Maiden Hill, its occupant took possession of my heart."

"He won't believe that," she said flatly, and he realized that her dowdy, sparrow-colored wardrobe and pulled-back hair was a picture of how she saw herself. And he didn't understand why.

Of course, tonight her hair wasn't straight and flat. The mist brought out curls, springy, tight curls.

"Let's elope," he suggested unexpectedly.

"What?" She practically stumbled backward.

"Elope," he said gently, following her. In fact, the more he thought of it, the more he liked the idea.

"Have you taken leave of your senses?" she demanded, moving around the tree away from him.

Colin stopped. "Possibly." He held out his hands. "But why not? We're not far from the Scottish border. We could be there by morning."

"Think of the scandal." She tucked her arms in to hold her shawl tight. "People like us don't elope."

"People like us do whatever we wish. Besides, it wouldn't be scandalous. It would be *romantic.* There would be people who would be surprised, but haven't you ever wanted to shock people, even once in your life?"

"People won't be shocked. They will think we are foolish."

"Then let's *be* foolish," he urged her.

"What of your brother?"

Now there she had him. Matt wouldn't be pleased. Colin knew it. Matt would want the banns announced and a respectful period observed before a wedding.

Whereas Colin was the opposite. He answered to no one. And he liked the idea of eloping. It was daring, bold, and immediate. If they waited for a church wedding, Rosalyn might come to her senses and refuse him.

"Matt will understand," he decided.

"It's a foolish idea, and I've never done anything foolish," she vowed.

"More the pity you," he said. "As for me, I've done many foolish things, but this may be the wisest thing I've ever done."

"To elope?" she demanded incredulously, but he sensed she could be persuaded when she asked, "How can you say that?"

"Rosalyn," Colin chided, "think about it. The gossips' tongues will wag whatever we do. Let's give them something to talk about. Let's send them into a tizzy of gossip. After this, anything we do will not be a surprise to them. Besides, my back is starting to ache from sleeping on my brother's floor. I want to be at Maiden Hill, in my own bed."

Still she shook her head, but he sensed her indecision. From a distance came the sound of a horse's hooves. "That must be John," she said. "He's here to take me home." She took a step toward the road, but Colin hurried to stop her. He caught her hand and laced his fingers in hers.

"I'll come for you in three hours," he said. "By morning, you can be a new person. Mrs. Colin Mandland."

"I like my own name. I like my title," she said a bit desperately.

"Yours is a courtesy title," he averred. "In time, I will earn a new title for you, one that is yours alone." He played on her ambition. He was excited about the adventure.

"I—" she started, but Colin cut her off by placing his fingers over her lips.

"No, for once, Rosalyn, be daring. Don't worry about what people think. You came to me tonight. You want this marriage. There is no reason to hesitate."

Her wide eyes studied him, and he felt this moment was magic. This moment would determine his destiny.

"Rosalyn, for once, do what is unexpected."

His words found their mark. That adorable chin of hers came up, and he knew he had her. He removed his fingers and she said, "I will be waiting for you at Maiden Hill."

"That's the spirit," he said. "Pack light," he ordered in a low voice.

She nodded and started for the servant and cart waiting for her. At the gate, she turned. "Midnight?"

"It's the best time for all new endeavors," he assured her.

She hurried to the cart. Colin watched her leave. She pulled her shawl up over her head, the gesture both elegant and feminine.

"Good night, my lady," he whispered. The thought struck him that he seemed doomed to be attracted to women who had ice for their hearts and ambition in their veins.

But this time, he was getting what *he* wanted, and he wasn't one to overly worry himself about the future. Instead, he did something he hadn't done since boyhood—he rolled a somersault, right there in the grass of his sister-in-law's garden.

The front door flew open. His nephews and niece crowded the doorway.

"Uncle," Emma said, "did you fall down?"

He sat up and laughed. "No, sweetling, I never fall down. Never ever." Then he entertained them even more by doing a cartwheel, and they all tumbled out of the door to play with him.

Colin couldn't wait until midnight. He was going to be a Member of Parliament.

And there was something else to be gained, too, something of almost equal importance—he was going to make love to Lady Rosalyn.

He stood on his hands, and the children clapped.

# Chapter Eight

$S$itting in the pony cart, having a moment of panic, Rosalyn heard children's laughter floating on the mist. She looked back at the rectory and wondered if her imagination was playing tricks on her. *What in God's name had she agreed to?*

On the one hand, she was greatly relieved she would not be leaving Maiden Hill. On the other, not only was she marrying Colonel Mandland but she was also *eloping*. She could hear her aunts' voices now.

"Colonel Mandland seems a nice fellow," John observed, a mouthful of conversation for the usually silent gardener.

"Ummhmmm," Rosalyn answered.

She knew all the servants were curious as to

what the status was between her and the colonel. When Covey had returned alone this evening, there had probably been a good deal of speculation.

Was there no place safe from gossip? And what would happen on the morrow when everyone learned she had run away?

Rosalyn paused, struck by the realization that ever since her father's death, she had wanted to do exactly that—run away. After all, wasn't that what her mother had done?

John turned the cart onto Maiden Hill's drive, and Rosalyn was struck by what a bravely foolhardy thing she was about to do.

And deep inside she discovered, if the truth be known, that he was right: she rather liked it.

Well, there *was* still the pesky problem of tying herself to Colonel Mandland for the rest of her life . . . but he wasn't such a bad sort. In fact, he seemed able to understand her when she didn't always understand herself. What had he whispered? *"For once, do what is unexpected."*

John pulled the cob to a halt in front of the door and Rosalyn climbed out of the cart, feeling herself a changed woman from the one who had left the house mere hours ago.

"Thank you, John," she said.

"Cook put Mrs. Covington to bed. She's sitting up with her."

"I knew all would be taken care of." She took a step toward the house, and then stopped. "In fact, John, thank you for all that you've done for me over the years."

John ducked his head, embarrassed. She reached out and gave his hand a pat. "Go on, put the pony up and seek your bed."

She hurried into the house. A candle had been left burning by the door for her. She picked it up and climbed the stairs. Her first stop was Covey's room. Cook sat in a chair beside the bed, quietly snoring. Covey's tired, frail figure was under the covers.

Gently, Rosalyn woke Cook. "How is she?" Rosalyn asked the servant.

"I gave her a drop of laudanum. This is the first time she didn't fight me over it, and she went to sleep like a child."

"Good. Thank you, Cook. Why don't you go on to your bed now? John should be finished with the pony."

"Yes, my lady." Cook raised her bulk out of the chair. She shuffled toward the door, but then stopped. "He's a good man, Colin Mandland is," she said almost defensively. "He'll treat you well, and he isn't hard on the eyes. Then Mrs. Covington can stay because this is her home. It's where she belongs." And then, knowing she'd overstepped the class boundaries between them, she added, "Begging your pardon, my lady."

Rosalyn sat in the chair Cook had vacated. The seat was still warm. "No offense is taken, Cook. I know you care for Covey as much as I do."

"I care for you, too, my lady." She ducked her head as if she'd said too much, dipped a hasty curtsey, and left the room.

Rosalyn sat in the silence a moment before turning to Covey. "I'm going to do it," she said to her friend. "You rest easy and well. I will take care of both of us." She hesitated a beat and then added, "Cook is right. He's not such a bad man. Perhaps he's not like your Alfred, but he isn't like Father either . . . or that riding instructor. Did you know, I used to believe I didn't know the riding instructor, but yesterday, a memory came to me, and I knew I had met him. I liked him very much as a child, until mother ran away with him. He was a nice man. Not as handsome as Colonel Mandland, but attractive enough in his own way." She would never have admitted such a thing a few weeks ago. It would have been disloyal to her father.

But she found the ability to tell Covey now. Perhaps because she was sleeping? Rosalyn didn't know. She only knew that at this moment, it didn't hurt to remember the past.

And why not? She was creating a future.

Rising, she leaned over and kissed Covey's brow. "Sleep well. Tomorrow everything will be fine," she promised and tiptoed from the room.

Packing didn't take long; choosing what to wear to elope did.

This would be the first trip in her memory where she wasn't being passed off from one relative to another. She caught a glimpse of her face in the mirror and was struck at how much younger she looked. Of course, after spending so much time in the mist, her hair was a mess . . . but it did look better worn looser and without so much restraint.

She was also tired of the drab colors of her wardrobe. Brown was not a happy color. She searched through her clothes and settled on a forest green day dress with a matching pelisse. The dress had a matching high-brimmed bonnet with lace trim. It was the most fashionable thing she owned.

Her portmanteau packed, she sat on the edge of her bed and waited. The minutes passed slowly. She looked out the window into the night. The moon had finally managed to escape the clouds, and there was a soft, silvery light on the landscape below. Even the fog had returned to its lair. She wondered fancifully if Colonel Mandland would climb the trellis to her window. The picture in her mind amused her. . . .

Something woke Rosalyn. It sounded like rain. She sat up, frowning at finding herself dressed and even wearing her bonnet. Then she groggily remembered she was eloping. Rain would not make an elopement easy. Or was she dreaming? She could see the moon. There would be no moon if there was rain. Then why did she think it was—?

A shower of pebbles hit the window. She got up and hurried over. Colonel Mandland stood in the drive. His beast of a horse, hooked up to that ridiculously flimsy phaeton, was grazing on her shrubs—again.

She opened the window.

"What are you doing up there?" he demanded. "I've been knocking at the door for almost an hour. Or were you expecting something dramatic, like my climbing the trellis to your window?"

She realized with a start she had been dreaming of just such a thing. What was wrong with her? She never dreamed, and yet, ever since this man had entered her life, she'd had the strangest, most vivid dreams.

"You did, didn't you?" he accused. "Well, I'm not. The thing is flimsy, and I detest heights. Besides, we're both beyond that. There is no angry papa to watch out for."

"How do you know so much about elopements?" she asked, still cranky from just waking.

"Rumor. Now hurry. I want to be in Scotland by first light."

Definitely not the way to start an elopement. They sounded more like they were already married. Rosalyn yawned. "Perhaps we could wait until morning." Perhaps marrying him was not the best move. In the light of day, she could think better.

"All right," he said irritably. "I'll climb up to the window. But if the trellis breaks, I'll bust my bum." He started toward the wall when, with a flash of irritation, she felt guilty.

"No, I'll be down," she said and slammed the window shut. The candle had practically burned down to the stub. She picked it up with one hand, hoisted her bag with the other, and stomped downstairs. She opened the front door. The colonel stood right there, leaning a shoulder against the doorjamb. He really was very handsome.

"Let's go," he said.

"I need to write a note to Covey," Rosalyn suddenly remembered.

"Couldn't you have done that while you were waiting for me to come?"

"Are you always this peevish?" she threw over her shoulder as she carried the candle into the sitting room to the secretary by the window. Paper and ink were in a drawer.

"Yes," he answered, "when I have someplace to go. I'm anxious to get on with it."

"My bag is by the door." She sat down and dipped pen in ink, but the words didn't flow easily. There was so much to explain. When Covey went to bed, Rosalyn was barely speaking to Colonel Mandland, and now she was *eloping* with him. How to make sense of all that had transpired?

"We can't take all of whatever you have in this bag," he said from the doorway.

"We must," Rosalyn answered. "I only packed the barest of essentials."

He held up the bag and then pretended it weighed a hundred stone. She frowned. "It's not that much. Put it under my feet if need be."

"There is no 'under your feet,'" he answered. "The phaeton is not designed to carry luggage."

She'd seen it out the window hitched up to his horse but just now realized the import. "You must be jesting. We can't drive to Scotland in that vehicle."

"We are."

"It's night. You'll run us off the road in that thing."

He made an impatient sound. "I drove from London to Lancashire at night. I can certainly take us a few hours up to Scotland." He came into the room and dropped the bag on the settee. "We can leave this behind. We'll be back before you need it."

Rosalyn sighed. His high-handedness didn't sit well, but she was in no mood to argue. She had to finish her note.

He crossed over to the desk. "What have you written so far?"

Like a schoolchild hiding something she didn't want the tutor to see, Rosalyn covered her words with her hand. "I've said I hope I didn't alarm her, but I've eloped with you. Now, will you please let me finish?"

He reached down, shooed her hand off the note, and said, "Let me have the pen."

"Why?"

"I have something to write, too."

"But I've not finished."

"Yes, you have. You've said what is important." He took the pen without asking, slipping it neatly out of her fingers. Dipping the pen in ink, he scribbled something across the bottom of her carefully worded note and stabbed the pen back in the inkwell. "Now come." He took her arm.

Rosalyn held back. "What did you say?" She glanced at the note. His bold handwriting was easy to read, even by the flickering candle.

*I'll take good care of her—*

*M.*

No one, not even her father, had wanted to take care of her.

For one complete moment, she would have followed him anywhere—even in a phaeton. She blew out the candle. "Let's go."

Outside, he helped her up on to the seat. The back wheels had to be close to a ridiculously eight feet high. She felt as if she could be tipped forward and tumbled out of the seat. Holding on to the side with both hands to keep her balance, she said, "I thought you didn't like heights?"

"I don't," he answered, climbing up with one big step and taking the reins and whip. His horse flattened his ears in protest. He would prefer eating plants. However, a crack of the whip over his head and he set off smartly.

Colonel Mandland was right. There wasn't any storage room for luggage, and if there had been, the way the wheels bounced over the rough road would have tossed anything to the wayside. She was torn between holding on to her seat or her bonnet.

"Do you have any idea where you are going?" she asked as he turned off the Market Road.

"I know exactly where I'm going. I traveled all these roads as a lad."

"You went all the way to Scotland?" she asked skeptically.

He shot her a glance that told her louder than words how much he appreciated her doubts.

Still, she had to suggest, "I think you should slow down."

"Don't worry. I'm quite a hand with the reins. We'll be in Scotland before you can blink."

"If we don't break our necks," she muttered, and he laughed.

"Then we'll go happy," he pronounced.

Rosalyn wasn't ready to "go" at all, and yet, it was rather exhilarating. No one was on the roads. They were all at home in their beds, and she could imagine herself and the colonel the only ones alive.

An owl swooped down from a tree and glided across their path. Moonlight silvered his wings, and he appeared almost bewitched.

"Your horse doesn't seem to tire," she observed after they had traveled a while at a bruising pace.

"Oscar," he answered.

"I beg your pardon?"

"His name is Oscar. I bought him for ten pounds from a Portuguese peasant, and he is the most noble horse I've ever met . . . when he isn't smashing your plants, that is."

"He hasn't touched the rose you gave me," she said.

Colonel Mandland smiled at her. "Give him time."

She yawned. The fresh night air was making

her wish for her bed, but she didn't dare close her eyes while riding in the phaeton.

He answered her yawn with one of his own. "Don't go to sleep on me," she warned. "We'll end up in a ditch."

"I won't fall asleep. I used to like night marches the best. You move quickly because you don't have to worry about the enemy."

She glanced at him. He was watching Oscar and the road ahead. In spite of his rank, she sometimes forgot he was a fighter. "How ironic that one brother went into the Church and another into war."

"Not ironic at all," the colonel said easily. "Matt fights for souls and I fought for England."

"And now you wish to be in the Commons."

"Of course." He gave her a smile and said, "They won't let me in the House of Lords."

"They let in George. What a pity."

He laughingly agreed with her, and then he yawned again before turning onto a side road even narrower than the one they'd been taking. "Are you certain this is safe?" she asked, nervous about the ruts the wheels bounced over.

"It's safe. Besides," he continued, "this is the night before our wedding. Nothing will go wrong."

"I would feel more confident if you would slow down, even a bit."

"You worry too much," he answered and snapped the whip again for Oscar to pick up the pace. For a while they rode in companionable silence until they drove over a bridge and came to a fork in the road. He started one way, and then changed his mind. "This isn't the right direction," he said, using his body weight to control the phaeton as they took the corner at a sharp angle.

Rosalyn wanted to close her eyes. "We are going to break our necks."

"You're safe," he insisted, even as they must have hit a stone in the road. It was enough to throw the lightweight vehicle off balance. There was a sick cracking sound, and the phaeton careened crazily, leaning to Rosalyn's side, and nearly plummeting into a ditch.

Colonel Mandland threw an arm around her to keep her from being thrown out of the vehicle while he struggled to rein Oscar to a halt. It demanded all of his skill as a driver. To his credit, they didn't flip over.

The horse didn't seem the least bit disconcerted by the accident. He came to a halt, waited a moment, and started munching on weeds by the side of the road.

"Are you all right?" the colonel demanded.

Rosalyn pushed the now crushed brim of her bonnet back. "Yes, I'm fine. What about your-self?"

He dismissed her question with a wave and hopped out of the phaeton. Turning, he placed his hands around her waist and swung her down as if she were lighter than a bed pillow.

The ground was muddy here. The damp oozed up into her kid slippers. She should have worn her walking shoes.

Colonel Mandland went around to inspect the damage. "One of the wheel spokes is broken." He swore softly.

"We'll have to return to Clitheroe," she said. "Perhaps a farmer will pass by here in the morning."

"Oh, no," Colonel Mandland said. "We are on our way to Scotland, and to Scotland we will go."

"But how will we get there?"

"Oscar," he said, starting to unhitch the horse.

"We can't *both* ride him," she protested.

The colonel laughed. "Look at his back. It's nothing to him to carry us." Having unhar-nessed the horse, he pushed the phaeton out of the ditch and into a thicket. He pulled a knife from his boot and began cutting branches to hide the vehicle. "So that it is here when I return for it," he explained.

"Perhaps this is an omen," Rosalyn said. "Perhaps we shouldn't elope."

"That's nonsense," Colin replied, catching Oscar and starting to create a halter and reins for him.

"No, it's common sense," she argued.

"Perhaps it is a test of our determination and will," he responded. He looked at her. "Rosalyn, did I not promise you an adventure? Well, here it is." He led the horse back to the bridge so he could use the stone railing to mount the beast bareback. He trotted up to Rosalyn. "Let me have your hand."

"You can't expect me to ride without a saddle. My dress—?"

"The Scots won't care what you look like," the colonel assured her. "And I don't like that hat much anyway."

She opened her mouth to contradict him about the hat, but before she could say anything, he reached down, took her arm, and pulled her up onto the horse in front of him. She sat sidesaddle, her legs over his.

Looking into her astonished gaze, he said, "We're off." Oscar started down the road.

For a fearful moment, Rosalyn was certain she was going to be bounced off the horse. She used to ride all the time as a child, but she hadn't been on a horse's back for at least five years.

Colonel Mandland was completely at ease on horseback. His strong arms kept her in place, and his muscular legs provided the extra width she needed to keep her seat without a saddle. The warmth of his body staved off the chill of the spring night.

Slowly, she began to relax. "How far do we have left to go?"

"Three hours, maybe a bit more."

"Are you always so tenacious at getting what you want?"

His lips curved into a confident smile. "Yes."

"And you want this marriage for the Commons seat?"

"You keep mentioning that." He glanced down at her as if trying to read her thoughts. For once, the darkness helped her hide from him. "I want this marriage, period," he said simply. "And you're right. Once I make up my mind, I do get what I want—usually. We'd walk to Scotland if that was the only way."

Part of her was alarmed by such steadfast single-mindedness. Another was secretly pleased.

There was something powerful about a man who went after what he wanted . . . and right now, she sensed he wanted her.

They rode in silence, each keeping their own counsel. At one point he said her name.

"Yes?" she answered.

"I was worried you'd gone to sleep."

"I'm here." She didn't know why, but her response seemed to please him.

Shortly after dawn, they rode past the marker on the road separating England from Scotland. Within minutes, Colonel Mandland guided a tired Oscar into the yard of a wayside inn. There was a rushing stream beside the yard, and three brown-and-white dogs ran up, yapping a greeting.

The colonel dismounted first, and then, placing his hands on her waist, helped her down. Her legs almost buckled under her from the hours of riding. Fortunately, he had anticipated the possibility and steadied her with a hand on her elbow.

The day promised to be a clear one. The dawn of her wedding day.

Suddenly nervous, she looked down at her dress and pelisse, both hopelessly ruined, and she was certain the crushed brim of her hat gave her a comic appearance.

"You look fine," he said.

Rosalyn glanced up at him sharply. "You're jesting."

"No, I'm not," he said. "We've dashed up here in record time, ridden all night, and almost broken our necks. Considering all that, you look marvelous."

Rosalyn didn't know if he was teasing or serious. "You look like you need a shave."

He laughed, not taking any offense. "I imagine I do."

A stable hand came lumbering out, yawning, leading three horses. Rosalyn had to yawn in answer, and she caught the colonel stifling one too. She couldn't wait to go to sleep.

The lad took one look at the two of them, their clothes and their horse, and frowned. He tied the horses to a post and would have turned on his heel to go back in the stable except for the colonel stopping him.

"Here, lad," he called to him. "Rub this horse down and feed him well. He's done his duty for the day." He flipped a coin in the air with one hand. Before the coin landed back in his palm, the boy was in front of him, ready to take Oscar's reins.

The colonel pressed the coin in the boy's

hand. "There will be more if he is well taken care of."

"Yes, sir," the stable lad said and pulled his forelock.

"Shall we?" the colonel said, offering Rosalyn his arm. "The place looks decent enough. All the shutters are on their hinges."

She placed her hand in the crook of his elbow and let him lead her toward the inn's door. "I just realized," she said, "that I don't know your prospects. You own Maiden Hill, but will we be scrimping and saving, or are you wealthy?"

He stopped, and her first thought was she had offended. Instead, he studied her a moment and said, "I like the practicality of your mind. It is a good quality in a woman."

Rosalyn didn't know whether to be flattered or insulted. Perhaps this was why she'd never had an offer before. She was too "practical." The word made her feel frumpy. But then, practical women married for security—and what was she doing?

"So, do you have an answer?" she prodded.

"I'm not as wealthy as I'm going to be," he assured her, opening the door, "*after* I marry you."

She didn't know if this was more of his flattery or a statement of fact. She really knew very little about him. A wiser woman would run now.

But it was too late. She was committed. She'd said she'd do it, and so she would.

They stepped into an open tap room filled with trestle tables. The fire was cold in the hearth, and the air smelled of stale ale. This was a man's place, although a young woman with shaggy yellow hair was wiping down tables. On the other side of the room were stairs that presumably led up to the guest rooms. The walls were yellow with smoke and age.

A short, thin man with a big nose and eyebrows that looked like caterpillars came out from behind the bar. His shirt was clean. "May I help you?" he asked in a soft Scots accent.

"We've come to marry," the colonel said grandly. "I know this isn't Gretna, but do you have a parson?"

The innkeeper looked over Colonel Mandland, with his roguish growth of whiskers and travel-stained clothes, and Rosalyn, with her now shabby bonnet, and he must have thought them a pair escaped from an asylum. However, he generously kept his opinion to himself.

"You can marry here. The parson is a patron of ours, but you may have a wee bit of a wait."

"We can't wait," the colonel said, hanging his hat, which was almost the worse for wear as her own, on a peg. "We want to be married this morning. The sooner, the better."

The innkeeper raised his bushy eyebrows, and his gaze dropped to Rosalyn's belly. She caught the implication and felt herself blushing.

"Well, you can marry whenever you want," the innkeeper said, "but first, you'll need to wake the parson." He stepped aside and nodded to a pair of boots coming out from under a table by the wall.

From the other end of those boots, as if to punctuate the innkeeper's words, came a rumbling snore accented by whiskey fumes. The parson wasn't just asleep. He was dead drunk.

# Chapter Nine

*What else could go wrong?*

Colin wanted to grab the parson by his boots and pull him out from under the table, except he was afraid of what he'd find. The temper he tried to keep always in check threatened to ignite.

And then Rosalyn started laughing. It was a giggle at first, but it built quickly into a merry, tinkling sound.

He turned, fascinated by the music of it. He was also stunned to realize that he wanted to marry. He wanted to marry *her*.

The realization almost sent him flying for the safety of the front door.

She met his gaze, her eyes animated and alive. "I'm sorry," she managed at last. "But the Fates are against us. I mean, who would have thought the parson would be drunk? Especially at this hour of the morning?" She almost doubled over, unable to control herself.

"I'm certain Matt wouldn't be surprised," Colin answered, and he started to chuckle himself. "Of course, he'll be angry enough about the elopement. We must never tell him about the parson."

She sobered. "Your brother doesn't know you eloped?"

A sharp stab of guilt pricked Colin's conscience. "The subject didn't come up."

"You didn't tell him?"

"Some things are better left unsaid," he hedged.

"I thought you were close."

This was the Rosalyn he knew, the woman who turned into a terrier when she had her mind wrapped around an idea. "We are, as long as what I do is what he approves of. Innkeeper, do you have a bucket of water?" Colin said, changing the subject. "And hot coffee or strong tea?"

"He always likes a nip of the dog that bit him to bring him back to his senses," the innkeeper explained.

"Then bring me a tankard of that," Colin ordered.

"You can't give the man more drink," Rosalyn protested.

"Why not? He's already had more than his share," Colin answered and, lifting the parson's leg, unceremoniously dragged him out from under the table.

"He's in no shape to conduct a service," she predicted.

"We can get him in shape." Colin knelt down, lifted the parson's head, and started rolling it back and forth between his hands. The man didn't even blink.

Rosalyn crossed her arms. "You were saying about your brother?" she asked

Colin frowned at her, a word to the wise that this was not the time to question him. He'd been up all night and was not pleased to have a sodden parson on his hands.

She frowned right back, and suddenly the innkeeper, who was walking over with a tankard of ale, started laughing. "Are you sure the two of you aren't already married? You bicker just like my wife and myself."

"You don't get along?" Rosalyn asked, her eyes

widening in mortification at the innkeeper's blunt remark.

"We get along fine," the innkeeper soothed in his slight brogue. "She has her way of doing things, I have mine." He lowered his voice to admit, "The truth is, she often knows better than I."

"But you can't be happy if you argue," Rosalyn said.

"Arguing can be the best part of a marriage," he answered. "We agree on everything important, and the little things don't matter if you get along in the bedroom." He waggled his bushy eyebrows for emphasis. Holding up his ring finger to display a gold band, he said, "Twenty-two years, and every night is as good as the first. *That's* a good marriage."

Colin thought Rosalyn would go up in flames, she was so embarrassed.

Nor was she the only one.

The blonde who had been cleaning tables came up behind the innkeeper and cuffed him on the head. Seeing her face up close, Colin realized the woman was older than he had first thought. "Lucas, the lady doesn't want to hear you brag."

"It's not bragging when you are telling the truth," her husband answered.

"Well, if we can't bring the parson to his

senses, we'll not be married at all," Colin said. He took the tankard and dribbled a few drops onto the parson's lips when the man was in mid-snore. To Colin's surprise, his glassy eyes popped open immediately. His tongue searched out the drops.

"You have it bad, don't you, friend?" Colin murmured.

"My best customer," the innkeeper told Rosalyn.

"Sad, isn't it?" his wife echoed. She turned away to finish her cleaning, just as four gentlemen dressed for hunting came down the stairs.

The innkeeper excused himself to see to his other guests.

Colin waved his hand in front of the parson's eyes. They didn't move in one direction or the other. "Are you awake?"

"I will be with a drop or two more" was the answer. The parson sat straight up. He reached for the tankard, which Colin managed to skillfully keep away from him.

Rising, Colin said, "We need to have a wedding done, and then you can drink all you want."

"And pay off the tab from last night with your fee," the innkeeper's wife hinted. Obviously feeling a need to enlighten Rosalyn, she said, "Those gents are up here for the hunt. Hounds are being brought over. There's a party of twelve."

"Fox hunt?" Colin asked.

"Yes, sir."

"Barbaric sport," Colin answered, setting the tankard down on the table.

"Only if you are the fox," Lucas the innkeeper replied as he returned to join them. "Will you be needing a room? I have one left, and those gentlemen over there are saying they want it for this night. Turns out one of their number snores, and the others refuse to share a room with him if they don't have to."

"We'll take the room," Colin said.

"I thought you would," the innkeeper said, but Rosalyn interrupted him.

"I'm not certain." Colin could almost hear her thought process. *A room? Together? No one was saying anything about* two *rooms.* "Don't we need to get home?"

Colin bit back his first response. "I'm tired," he said simply.

She nodded. She was, too. Tired and bedraggled . . . and that was what he was gambling on.

"I want a drink," the parson said, as if his opinion mattered. He scrambled to his feet on surprisingly short legs. His head barely reached Colin's chest. He reached for the tankard.

"After the ceremony," Colin reminded him, sweeping the mug out and away from under the man's grubby fingers. "We'll take the room," he told the innkeeper.

Rosalyn told herself everything would be fine . . . including the room debate, because she didn't want to argue in front of the hunters, who were now craning their necks to see what was going on.

"A wedding," the innkeeper helpfully explained to them, and Rosalyn could have cheerfully wrung his neck. Her affairs were none of these gentlemen's business.

They made it so.

One hopped to his feet. "I say, I'll be a witness," he volunteered and crossed the room to join them. He clapped his hands together in anticipation. "This will make for a good story back in London. Galen," he introduced himself. "Lord Galen."

"Mandland," the colonel answered, "Colonel Mandland." Was it Rosalyn's imagination, or did she catch a hint of annoyance in the colonel's voice? Was she starting to know him well enough to pick up the nuances in his speech?

Lord Galen was oblivious. Two more members of their party made their way down the stairs, and he called cheerily, "Patterson, Tomblin! Look at me. I'm a witness at an elopement!"

His friends grumbled a response, obviously done in by last night's drinking and more interested in their breakfast than a wedding.

The parson took advantage of Colonel Mandland's diverted attention, snatching the tankard out of his hands and draining it dry. With a satisfied smack of his lips, he announced, "I'm ready to perform the ceremony." He sounded surprisingly sober.

Rosalyn didn't know if she wanted to go through with it. Her wedding ceremony was not a novelty for a hunting party.

Then Colonel Mandland took charge with more courage than anyone in the Valley would have had. "I appreciate your offer, my lord," he said to Lord Galen. "However, you must remember, no matter where the ceremony is performed, it is a sacred moment."

Rosalyn was touched until his lordship mugged

a face, showing his concern to his companions, who snickered.

The colonel ignored him. He motioned for the innkeeper's wife to come forward. "Will you be our other witness?"

"Yes, sir," she said, tucking her wash rag in the waist of her apron. She came to stand beside Lord Galen.

One of the hunters who sprawled at their table yawned, and Rosalyn had to stifle one herself. If she wasn't so tired, she'd march out of this farce.

The colonel looked at Rosalyn. "I know this is unusual," he said in a voice for her ears alone, "but please trust me."

Had he known she was tempted to turn tail and run? She should. A wise woman would.

She didn't. "Let's get on with it."

He rewarded her with a kiss on the forehead. "That's my girl." To the parson, he said, "We're ready."

"My throat is dry," the parson complained.

"*After* the ceremony," the colonel reiterated.

The parson frowned but reached into his dirty coat with the torn sleeves and pulled out a Book of Common Prayer.

At least the ceremony would be Anglican. Colonel Mandland noticed he held the book upside down and turned it right side up for him.

"Oh, thank you, sir," the parson said. "Thought I needed my spectacles, and I haven't seen them in a month. We would have been in trouble, wouldn't we?" he asked rhetorically, smiling at his own humor. Rosalyn took a side step to avoid his breath.

"Very well," the parson went on when he saw no one was smiling. "The fee is two guineas and my drink for the day."

"I'll pay you three guineas and a pint of stout at the end," Colonel Mandland countered. "I'll come out ahead."

The parson didn't look pleased, but he didn't argue either.

Two more members of the hunting party strolled down from upstairs. They greeted their comrades, who shushed them so they could witness the ceremony. The innkeeper poured tankards of ale for their breakfast, and the gentlemen sat down happy.

Rosalyn suddenly found herself so nervous that it was difficult to breathe. From someplace in the inn, the scents of baking bread and frying sausages being prepared for the breakfast trade drifted to her. She stood in what had been, at the beginning of the trip, her best dress. Her bonnet was a shambles, but she had not bothered to take it off. Its presence provided a modicum of respect.

Her groom didn't look much better. He was unshaven, and his dark hair was in need of a cut. His clothes would have looked better if he'd slept in them.

The parson begged her attention. "My lady, is this marriage of your own free will?"

"Why, yes," Rosalyn answered, a bit startled by the question.

"It's the law," the innkeeper's wife explained. "To prove you aren't being forced."

Rosalyn nodded, appreciating the clarification. "I'm here of my own will." Her voice didn't sound like her at all.

Colonel Mandland took her arm. She didn't know if it was because he knew she needed bolstering, or he feared she'd bolt for the door.

The parson didn't waste time on a preamble but plunged right into the heart of the matter, needing to use his finger to read the words on the page. "Marriage was instituted by God in paradise and first celebrated by Adam and Eve," he droned.

Rosalyn frowned. She'd not heard these words before.

"It was adorned and beautified by Christ at Cana," the parson "read." "And must not be entered upon for the wrong reasons—"

A flash of guilt added to her discomfort.

"—The right reasons being procreation of children, con-tin-ence," he sounded out, "and mutual society, help, and comfort."

One of the party of hunters had fallen back to sleep and had started to snore.

Colonel Mandland pulled the book out of the parson's hands. He turned several pages and said, "Start here."

"Oh, yes," the parson answered, squinting to read the words. "Good place to start."

"I thought it was," the colonel said under his breath, and then, seeing the question in Rosalyn's eyes, he confessed, "You are right. My brother *will* want to shoot me."

"Maybe we should stop here," she suggested in an equally low voice and would have pulled away, save for his hold on her arm.

"We've come too far," he answered, and Rosalyn realized he was right. She was six and twenty. The future held nothing for her except for the misery of Aunt Agatha's company. He was her only option.

"Are we ready?" the parson asked peevishly.

"We're ready," the colonel said, and Rosalyn agreed by nodding her head.

With a great show of how terribly put out he was, the parson lifted the book eye high, but paused. "You know, this is easier for me with a pint," he suggested hopefully.

"*After* the ceremony," the colonel said, and the hunting party stifled their laughter.

"Very well," the parson answered, resigned to his fate. He addressed Rosalyn, "Do you—?"

He stopped, stumped . . . and she realized he didn't know her name. "Rosalyn Clarice Wellborne."

"Yes, Rosalyn Clarice Wellborne, take this man—" He paused.

"Colin Thomas Mandland," the colonel supplied.

One of the hunters said in surprise, "Mandland? The war hero? I say, Harry, isn't Mandland the one Wellington was talking about last Wednesday—?"

The colonel shut the man up with a glare. He turned to the parson, took the book out of the drunk's hands, and, with a snap, he faced Rosalyn. "This is not how I imagined it."

"Me either," she agreed with relief and a bit of disappointment, too. They weren't going to get married. She started to move away, but he didn't release his hold. Instead, he laced his fingers in hers.

Looking directly in her eyes, the colonel said, "Repeat after me. I, Rosalyn Clarice Wellborne."

She hesitated. His gaze held hers, and she realized he was most serious. Slowly, she said, "I, Rosalyn Clarice Wellborne."

"Take you, Colin Thomas Mandland, for my lawfully wedded husband."

*Oh dear.* "Take you, Colin Thomas Mandland, for my lawfully wedded husband."

"In sickness and in health, for richer or for poorer."

These words were easy to say. "In sickness and in health, for richer or for poorer."

"To honor and obey."

She couldn't stop the smile as she said, "To honor." She dared him to ask more.

He didn't. In fact, there was a glimmer of respect in his eye as he continued, "Until death we do part."

"Until death we do part," she repeated.

He set the book aside on a table so he could take both her hands in his. "I, Colin Thomas Mandland, take you, Rosalyn Clarice, to be my wife. I will give you my name and my protection. I will honor and cherish you all the days of my life—until death we do part."

He sealed his troth with a kiss so quick that Rosalyn didn't have time to react. Lord Galen led the hunters in applause.

"There, it's done," the parson said, rubbing his hands together and practically stepping between them. "That's three guineas and a pint."

"Not until the witnesses have signed a document of some sort," the colonel answered.

In short order, a certificate was found behind the pub's counter. It was grease stained but legal enough once all names were signed.

Rosalyn moved as if she were in a dream. She was married—and not just married to anyone, but to a man whom others knew as a war hero. Wellington spoke of him. He was a man who would be sitting in the House of Commons. A man who had in the space of a minute given her his name and his prestige.

A man who had left out the promise to "love" in his marriage vow and had not asked it of her.

So great was her disappointment that she

could not smile. Before she realized what was happening, the colonel had taken her arm and, amongst the well-wishes of the hunters and the innkeeper and his wife, directed her up the stairs and to a room at the end of the hall.

He had a key in his hand, and he opened the door to a good-sized room. The window was open to let in fresh air. The sky was blue, birds were singing, and all she could see was the ancient four-poster bed dominating the middle of the chamber.

Rosalyn's feet turned to lodestones. Perhaps marriage wasn't such a good idea after all. But before she could protest, Colonel Mandland swept her up into his arms and carried her into the room.

# Chapter Ten

*R*osalyn stiffened like a board in his arms, and Colin knew he was going to have trouble coaxing her into consummating the marriage. All through the ceremony, he'd half expected her to either bolt or pass out.

She hadn't done either—yet.

He kicked shut the door, and they were alone. She stared up at him with eyes that threatened to swallow her face. She still wore that ridiculous bonnet, the brim hopelessly misshapened, and he had the urge to kiss her properly. Not the peck before strangers that he'd given her downstairs after they'd exchanged vows but the full, demanding kiss of a man who wanted to make love to her.

And he *did* want to make love to her. He was

surprised by how much. His weariness evaporated at the thought of it.

This was his wife. Someplace, deep inside him, a hardness that had carried him through life until now softened at the word *wife*.

He'd never thought he needed one. Funny, the twists life took, and he wanted to kiss her until she stopped being so foolishly defiant and realized this was an amazing moment in their lives.

He also knew ravaging her was the one thing she feared he was about to do.

So, he couldn't.

He wanted his Rosalyn willing, and he hadn't lied when he'd bragged that he'd never forced a woman. He also believed that he could bring her around—eventually.

Colin walked to the bed and tossed her on it. The ropes providing the foundation for the mattress were a bit loose and swayed gently back and forth. True to what he had anticipated, Rosalyn rolled off the other side of the bed and onto her feet. Her silly bonnet fell over her face, and she pushed it back.

"What do you think you are doing?" she said, indignation covering every single word.

"Carrying my wife over the threshold of a new life," he replied. Her face was pale, and her fists were doubled. Colin sighed. Why did he have to have married a strong-willed woman?

"It's tradition," he said. "Perhaps not in your family, but it is in mine." He shrugged out of his jacket and hung it on a chair in front of a small desk. No fire had been set for the hearth, which was fine. He'd keep Rosalyn warm, and there was a hooked rug on the floor to ward away chill.

"You see," he explained, "in the old days of the North country, there was such a thing as marriage by capture. If a man liked a woman or coveted her lands—or her sheep, mustn't forget her sheep—he would kidnap her."

"I was not kidnapped," she informed him coolly.

"No, you weren't," he agreed, tugging the knot in his neck cloth. "I'm just telling you the history." He pulled his neck cloth free. It felt good to open his shirt. He placed his hands on his hips to finish telling his story.

"Occasionally a bride, understandably, did not want to be captured and therefore refused to go peacefully with her bridegroom. She knew if she went into his house, all was lost. So, unfortunately, more than one bridegroom had to drag his wife across the threshold. Being men, it took awhile to realize it was easier just to pick her up and carry her across, and that is how the tradition was born."

He sat down in the chair and started to pull off his boots.

"What are you doing?" she demanded suspiciously.

"Getting ready for bed," he said, as if it were the most normal thing in the world to do.

She backed away into a far corner. "Our marriage is one of convenience only."

"Yes, with sex," he agreed amiably, knowing what havoc such a bald statement would have on her.

Her eyes widened to the size of saucers. "I don't want to share a bed with you."

There, she'd finally said it. He'd expected it. One thing about Rosalyn, she could be predictable. But Colin found himself wondering why she resisted his bedding her. They were attracted to each other. Even now, he could almost see her heart pounding against her chest, and the air between them was filled with the sort of tension that made for great sex.

Oh yes, she was aware of him as a man, and he certainly knew she was a woman.

He decided to ignore her declaration. He

dropped one boot to the floor and started to pull off the other, saying, "There is another reason a man carries a woman over the threshold. It's a tale my mother used to tell. She wasn't a very educated woman. When my father met her, she worked in the dairy." He stopped, suddenly seeing his mother as if he'd conjured her presence out of thin air.

"My mother had the strongest, most capable hands I've ever known," he continued softly. "She could do anything with her hands and worked alongside my father." The scent of tanning leather and the grease used to make it supple permeated the senses of his mind. It mingled with memories of the meat pies she made every other day. How strange to be thinking of that now, and yet he could not stop himself.

"Her voice was soft," he told Rosalyn, "with a lilting Yorkshire accent. When she sang, which she did all the time, it was the loveliest, most melodic sound on earth." He grinned. "Matt inherited her talent . . . but I still got a piece of her. I enjoy music. I'm not good," he admitted candidly. "Can't carry a tune, but it is as if a bit of my mother's spirit can be found in a song."

Suddenly, Colin felt very alone. What would his mother say now? Would she be proud of him? Had he been proud of her? The uncomfortable question was one he dared not answer. . . .

The overwhelming sense of loss caught him off guard. He'd loved both his parents, but in a child's selfish way, he had never looked back once he'd left home. Now he wished that they had been alive and could have been present at his marriage—although neither one would have approved of such a havey-cavey affair.

"What is the tale?" Rosalyn asked from her corner bastion, bringing him back to the present.

"The tale?" Colin repeated blankly.

"Yes, the story your mother told," she prodded. "The one about carrying the bride over the threshold?"

It took him a moment to gather his wits. "The threshold? Yes, well, she had a good story." He pulled the hem of his shirt out of his breeches. Rosalyn was listening so intently that she appeared not to notice.

He cleared his throat, as every good storyteller should, and realized this was a habit his mother had shared, too. "In my mother's family, the groom carried the bride over the threshold because it was believed that demons from a woman's family followed her."

"Demons?"

"Demons," he assured Rosalyn. "And since every man has his own demons, why would he want a wife to bring more demons into the house? So, to keep his wife's demons out, the first time the bridegroom brought his bride to his house, he picked his bride up and carried her over the threshold. The demons couldn't follow her then."

"What about the next time she had to go in the door?" Rosalyn asked, reasoning for flaws in the story, as he had anticipated she would.

"Once you carried your bride over the threshold, the demons could never follow her again. She could go back and forth as often as she liked and only needed to worry about her husband's demons."

Rosalyn considered this a moment. The out-of-kilter dimple made one of its appearances as she pursed her lips. "I've never heard such a story," she said at last.

"You're not from the North."

"My father's family should have been at one time or the other, else we'd not own Maiden Hill."

Colin grinned. "Either that or your ancestors

did their own bride capturing." He punctuated his words by pulling his shirt up over his head in one fluid movement.

Her reaction was swift and silly— Rosalyn turned her face to the wall, giving him her back. He could almost feel the heat of her embarrassment and wondered at such modesty.

"It's just my chest," he told her.

"We have a marriage of convenience," she said, as if reminding herself.

"Yes, absolutely," he agreed easily. "But that doesn't mean we have to be strangers."

"It doesn't mean I want us to be naked in front of each other either," she told the wall.

"Rosalyn, this is ridiculous," Colin said, suddenly tired. He'd woo Rosalyn later, when his wits were sharper. But for now, the bed beckoned for another reason older than time—sleep. Rosalyn could stand in the corner all day; he wanted a pillow. He lay down, discovered the bed was softer and more comfortable than he had imagined, and went to sleep.

Rosalyn heard him lay down on the bed. The air in the room closed in around her.

She didn't understand what was wrong. The sight of his stocking feet had been disconcerting and, in some way, intimate, but seeing his bare chest . . .

She'd had to turn away, or else ogle him like a cow herder. The man was all muscle. Hard and unyielding. It also looked as if he had a scar on his shoulder, a star shape of puckered, red, angry skin. She wondered what the story was there.

The silence between them stretched out. From beyond the window a bird called its mate. The door of the inn closed, and she heard the masculine voices of the hunters preparing to mount their horses. They were excited about the day's hunt.

But she heard nothing from the colonel.

She dared to glance over her shoulder. Colonel Mandland was stretched out on the bed, but she expected to catch him watching her. She had imagined his sly, slightly crooked grin as he waited for her to do what she just did—peek.

However, he wasn't even paying attention to her. He lay with a feather pillow under his head, his body on top of the covers, his back to her. He was definitely asleep.

Slowly, Rosalyn faced the bed, not knowing what to think. A part of her was disappointed. The sparring between them was done, and she discovered she actually liked matching wits with him. It had been exciting when he'd lifted her in his arms and dropped her on the bed.

And she had to confront the fact that secretly she had not been expecting a story about demons or her husband going to sleep. She'd been hoping he'd take the decision of whether to consummate the marriage out of her hands after she'd expressed a decent amount of outrage so he wouldn't see how attracted to him she was.

Now she was disappointed she wasn't going to be ravaged. The realization was profoundly deflating.

Rosalyn frowned at the sleeping man who was now her husband. A demon started to possess her—the demon of anger. How dare he fall asleep on her, when she was so tense and uncertain?

She was tempted to take off her bonnet and smash it further by clobbering him with it over and over again. Then she'd wager he'd notice her—!

The violence of her thoughts caught her off guard and increased her anger tenfold.

Over the years, she had learned to bottle her emotions, but Colonel Mandland had a way of slipping past her guard, and she didn't like it one bit.

Furthermore, if he thought she was *ever* going

to climb into bed with him after he'd ignored her and left her standing in this corner—he was wrong. She had her pride. She was the daughter of the earl of Woodford.

Rosalyn took off her bonnet and pulled off her gloves. She crossed the room and laid both on the washbasin. Although she'd dearly liked to have splashed some water on her face, there was none in the pitcher.

She caught a glimpse of herself in the mirror and almost cried out. She appeared a fright. Her cheeks were pale, and she had deep circles under her eyes from a night of travel.

No wonder he hadn't wanted to ravage her.

After taking a moment to pin her hair tighter, Rosalyn pulled the chair—piling his coat, shirt, and neck cloth over the empty washbasin—over to her side of the bed. She needed sleep, too, but she was not going to lay down on that bed.

Instead, she positioned the chair so that she could use the bed for a footstool. She slipped off her slippers, sat in the chair, propped her feet up on the bed, and tried to get comfortable enough to sleep.

It was hard. Outside the window, the inn yard's day was just getting under way, and no one attempted to keep his voice down. Furthermore, the dogs that had greeted them yapped a greeting at every new traveler. Horses whinnied, barrels were rolled, men laughed, and Rosalyn didn't see how the colonel could sleep through the racket.

She got up and closed the shutter. It helped a measure. Returning to her chair, she attempted a new position that she hadn't tried yet. Her neck was getting a crick in it. At some point, Rosalyn realized she was so tired that she almost didn't care where she slept . . . and the bed began looking very good to her.

After all, the colonel was sleeping on top of the covers. Would it be so terrible if she stayed fully clothed and slept *under* the covers? She didn't worry about her dress. It was hopelessly wrinkled by now anyway.

At that moment, Colonel Mandland stretched like a satisfied cat.

Rosalyn went tense, expecting him to wake.

He didn't. With a soft, relaxed sigh, he settled himself in more contentedly.

Rosalyn had never known jealousy the likes of which she felt watching him sleep peacefully. She almost couldn't stand it. Her body yearned for sleep. Her eyes ached.

Unable to resist, she capitulated. A woman

could only resist so much. Stealthily, she climbed onto the bed and slipped under the covers.

*The mattress felt so good beneath her tired body.* She curled up with a contented sigh—

The bed moved. He rolled toward her, and his arm draped over her waist.

Rosalyn froze, uncertain.

He didn't move closer. His breathing sounded steady. She waited. When he didn't stir, she slid a look over her shoulder.

He was asleep. Truly asleep.

She laid her head back on her pillow and didn't know whether to be relieved or offended.

In the end, she went to sleep.

Rosalyn came awake with a start, not recognizing her surroundings or remembering anything. She'd been dreaming that she had gotten married, and now, to find herself safe in bed—?

Except it wasn't her bed. And she was fully dressed.

Rosalyn sat up. Her hair was a mess. She'd gone to bed with it pinned, and now the pins were either falling out or sticking in her skull.

Looking around the room, she began to remember where she was and why.

She was married.

She turned to the other side of the bed and found it empty. The imprint of the colonel's head dented the feather pillow, but he wasn't there.

She could find enough signs of him. The room smelled of soap. The clothes she had tossed over the washbasin were gone. A razor lay beside the pitcher, and she knew he'd shaved. There was also a tub in front of the empty hearth. He'd done more than shaved, he'd bathed. Here. While she'd slept . . . he'd been naked.

Rosalyn released her breath slowly. After all, she was a married woman now.

A married woman who would dearly enjoy a bath.

She got up from the bed and crossed to the tub. Testing the water, she found it still warm. The linen towel he'd used to dry off was crumpled and hanging over the top slat of the straight-backed chair.

This was the same chair she'd dragged over to her side of the bed, and Rosalyn felt on edge. The idea that he'd moved furniture, shaved, and bathed, and she had slept through it all was disconcerting. She felt as if her privacy had been invaded and yet not. . . .

She moved to the window and opened the

shutters she'd closed earlier. All was quiet in the inn yard. It had to be close to the supper hour. Save for a dog scratching fleas and a horse tied to a post and munching hay, the place could have been deserted.

Shuttering the window, she wondered where the colonel was. She listened and could hear no sounds through the inn's thick walls. Her gaze once again fell on the bath.

Her body longed for the soothing calm of a good soak. Some people did not practice bathing. Rosalyn believed there were benefits in cleanliness, and she was both pleased and relieved the colonel agreed with her. The bar of soap he'd used was in a dish, and there were two more clean towels folded, ready and waiting for her.

She knew now what had woken her. It had been the door shutting when he'd left the room. She knew him well enough now, or at least trusted him enough, to know he'd left the water for her use. It was nice to be married to someone who anticipated your needs. And the water was very tempting.

She scratched her head where a pin had indented her skull. Warm water could soothe troubled nerves—and if she hurried, she could be done before he returned.

Rosalyn didn't waste a moment. She had to bathe. She couldn't stand being in these clothes one moment more. A quick dip in and out, she promised herself. But then she noticed tooth powder by the washbasin.

She had to stop and do her teeth. She also pulled every pin from her hair. Her teeth clean, Rosalyn threw off her clothes, keeping them close on the chair, and climbed into the tub.

The water was heaven . . . as was the fact that this was one bath she hadn't had to draw and heat for herself, which was often not the case at Maiden Hill, as Bridget went home before supper.

The hip bath had a high back, turned toward the door to avoid any drafts, and she could rest her head against the metal and relax. The tub was not overly large, but it was roomy enough for her if she bent her legs. She couldn't imagine how the colonel had gotten his big body into the tub. The thought of it made her laugh.

Picking up the soap, she started lathering. It felt so good to be clean, and she wanted that feeling all over. Her hair could use a wash. However, she would need the pitcher by the washbasin for the rinse.

With a quick glance at the still closed door, she

hopped out of the tub and, dripping wet, fetched the pitcher. She was just stepping back into the water when she heard a step outside the door.

A key was put in the lock. *The handle turned.*

Rosalyn dropped the pitcher. It hit the hard wood floor and smashed into pieces. She could have cried out loud, but the door was opening and she didn't have time to think. Instead, she dove into the tub, reaching for one of the pathetically small linen towels for cover.

# Chapter Eleven

$C$olin heard the crash inside the room and threw open the door, not knowing what to expect but ready to do battle with anyone.

He pulled up short when he saw the room was empty. The unmade bed showed signs Rosalyn had been there, but she was nowhere in sight in the room now. He looked to the window. The shutters were still closed and the room was in murky darkness. He walked over to open them.

As he threw back the shutters, his booted sole crunched something beneath. He looked down and saw the shards of the basin pitcher.

That's when he heard the sound of water swishing. Slowly, he turned to the tub, and for a moment, Colin couldn't believe his luck. He saw the movement of an arm cowering behind the high back of the bath.

Her dress draped over the chair beside the tub confirmed his suspicions—and he couldn't resist. God didn't hand him opportunities like this very often.

On catlike feet, he walked around to the front of the tub, moved her dress, and sat down.

Rosalyn sat huddled in the bath, legs longer than he had imagined pulled up to modestly hide her nakedness from his view. Her skin was wet and slippery with soap. The cleavage and soft roundness of full breasts were barely hidden behind the knees and a square of linen she hugged close to her body. He knew from sleeping beside her on the bed that her waist was trim.

It was a provocative situation.

But what robbed him of speech was her hair, which was down.

It's color wasn't drab, as he had supposed. No, her hair was the color of the deepest ale. Dark and full-bodied, with a hint of gold in its midst. And her head was covered with curls. Springy, riotous, joyful curls celebrating their freedom. They tumbled down around her shoulders to a point not far below her breasts. They made her appear younger . . . and wonderfully wicked.

Colin reached out. He couldn't help himself. She leaned away, her gray-green eyes full of distrust . . . and he realized it wasn't just her full lips that were sensual and inviting, lips that had enticed him more than once to abandon common sense and steal a kiss, but the whole package of her. His body had known better than his mind what hid beneath Rosalyn's rigidity.

"You're a bloody beauty."

He'd not realized he'd spoken aloud until her eyes flashed indignation and that stubborn chin of hers came up. "I'm not. Now, will you please remove yourself from this room."

"I can't," Colin confessed.

"Why can't you?" she demanded.

"Because these leather breeches are tight, and if I rise"—which he wanted to add he most certainly had, but he feared she wouldn't appreciate the double meaning of his words—"I will embarrass both of us."

Her anger turned to uneasiness. She was naïve, something that did not displease him. "Why would I be embarrassed?" she asked faintly, as if uncertain that she wanted to hear the answer.

"Many reasons," Colin said, not wanting to scare her off too soon. There was a mystery here, a mystery of why a woman so lush and exciting would deliberately hide her best attributes. Her actions defied everything he knew about feminine vanity.

He wondered if her nipples were large and brown or petite and pink. Either way, he didn't care. He ached to feel the weight of her breasts in his hands.

Colin leaned forward. "May I wash your back?"

"No."

He put his hand in the water. He couldn't help himself. Making slow figure eights close to her thigh, he said, "Certainly there is something I can do."

Rosalyn shook her head.

Colin circled his fingers closer until he could place them on the slick skin of her thigh. "You should finish your bath." *And let me wash you all over.* He knew such a suggestion would earn another slap.

She watched his hand and then pushed it away. "I will finish if you leave me alone."

*I can't.* He swallowed the words and asked instead, "How did the pitcher break?"

"You aren't going to leave me alone, are you?"

"Rosalyn, we're married."

"Why do you keep reminding me?"

"It is expected for me to be with you at private moments like this." *It is expected for me to pick you up out of that tub all wet and shiny and kiss you dry—*

Colin came to his feet, tossed her dress on the unmade bed, and walked over to the window. He had to put space between them. The images in his mind were too vivid for her to be safe so close to him. He looked out the window, trying to focus on anything but the woman behind him.

He was failing. He wanted to bury his nose in her hair, to drink in the scent of her with his tongue—

"I was going to wash my hair," she explained, interrupting the intensely lurid direction of his thoughts.

"What?" Colin asked, not connecting with her conversation.

"You asked how the pitcher broke?" she prompted. "I was going to wash my hair. I heard you coming and I dropped it."

Colin turned to face her. She sat as he'd left her, arms and legs protectively wrapped against him, the invader. But he understood. She was making an attempt.

"It will be hard to wash your hair now," he said.

She nodded.

"I could help you," he suggested carefully.

Her gaze slid away from his.

"I don't want to frighten you, Rosalyn. I want you to trust me. After all, we are going to be together for a very long time," he said gently.

She lowered her head, considering his words. Her glorious hair provided the curtain that hid her thoughts from him. He waited.

Silence stretched between them. She broke it by saying, "I needed something to help me rinse my hair."

"The bowl of the pitcher is still mostly intact. I could fill it with water."

"From where?"

"The bath."

Rosalyn didn't give him a yes or a no. Nor did Colin wait. He retrieved the basin from the wash stand, picked up a mostly intact piece of the pitcher's broken bowl, and sat down. He filled the bowl with water from her bath. She watched every move he made, and he was reminded of the fox Loftus was trying to capture. Neither Rosalyn nor the fox trusted him . . . and yet he had their well-being at heart. He didn't know why God had placed these two in his path. He only knew that as he'd helped the fox, he had to help Rosalyn—and he didn't know from what.

Like so many other matters in his life, he was now trusting his instinct.

The question was, could he control his own base impulses?

"Lean over," he ordered.

She looked at him. He could feel her doubts. This was not the Velvet Hammer, as those in the Valley referred to her, but a woman far too aware of her own vulnerabilities.

And then she leaned over.

He poured the water over her head. "I'm certain it's quite cool by now."

"It's fine," she murmured and brought her head up. "Could you hand me the soap?"

She kept her knees tucked, but Colin caught a glimpse of her full breast. Her nipples were pink and hard. He handed her the soap and turned in the chair so he was looking in the opposite direction.

He'd never have made it as a monk.

Resting his elbows on his knees, he listened to the sounds of her washing her hair.

A minute later, she said, "I need to rinse."

Dutifully, Colin refilled the pitcher bowl and poured water over her head twice. And one time, he really did make an attempt not to look. The sight of her wreaked too much havoc within him. It was as if he was sixteen again and not in control of his body's reactions. He was randy, anxious, and driven. If he touched her, he knew he would not stop, and again he had the vision of making love to her—

Colin set the pitcher bowl aside and stood. He focused on the door and moved purposely in its direction. "I, um, think it's best if I wait for you downstairs." Maybe then he'd be able to think again. All the blood had left his head, leaving him dizzy and far too aroused for her safety.

Her voice stopped him at the door. "You mean what you say, don't you? When you give your word, you aren't lying."

He looked to her. She'd glanced around the back of the tub to watch him. Her wet hair was slicked back, and he wondered why any man hadn't noticed exactly what a true beauty she was.

"I try. Come downstairs for dinner when you are dressed," he mumbled and then practically stumbled over his own feet, attempting to get away from her before he did something *really* foolish.

Rosalyn waited until Colonel Mandland left, shutting the door firmly behind him, before she sat back in the tub. The water was now almost cold, but she felt hot and something else . . . something she couldn't quite name. Her stomach was all twisted into knots, and every inch of her skin seemed more aware of him than any other presence on earth. Yes, she could *feel* anything and everything when she was around him, even the air.

And she knew his reaction was the same.

Those kisses they'd shared had merely been the prelude. She understood this now with an intuition as old as time.

Rosalyn rose from the tub. She wrung out the towel she had used to protect herself and dried herself off with the fresh one.

Colonel Mandland had left, but he hadn't wanted to. The thought made her smile. It also gave her a sense of power. True power.

"Colin." The sound of his name pleased her. He was her husband, and the constant core of tension in her chest, which seemed to be with her when she was around him, eased. In the mirror over the washbasin, she caught her reflection. For the first time when looking in a mirror, she smiled.

"Colin." Her husband. The man who promised to protect her.

Thoughtfully, Rosalyn began dressing. She wasn't ready to trust him completely yet, but she was coming close. He'd not lied to her or misled her once. He had kept his promises—and that was worth a great deal to her.

She started to pin her hair back up . . . and then, remembering the expression on his face when he'd first seen her curls free, she changed her mind. These weren't her mother's curls. These were *her* curls. She twisted her hair and pinned it loosely in place. The style softened her face.

She wondered what Colin would think, even as she knew the answer. Nor did wearing the green dress dampen her spirits.

He waited for her at the bottom of the stairs. She heard him before she saw him. He was whistling tunelessly—or, remembering his singing ability, she realized he might have been on tune. She paused on the landing, where she could see him. He appeared lost in thought, but the moment he heard her tread on the step, he stopped whistling and came to attention. His sharp gaze went directly to her new hairstyle. He smiled approvingly, and her heart did a funny little flip in her chest.

Colin took her arm and guided her down a

narrow hall away from the tap room. She glanced back and saw the parson in there drinking with some friends. He looked well enough along.

"I spoke for a private room for us," Colin said. "They've already set the covers out. Do you like trout?"

"Yes." Although when he was this close to her, she wasn't hungry at all.

The inn's private room overlooked a pretty little stream. The sun was setting, and the last light of the day gave the world a warm, golden glow. Covered dishes were already on a small table set for two, and the food smelled delicious. Her appetite returned.

Colin pulled the chair out for her, saying to the serving girl, "We'll serve ourselves."

The girl lit the candles, curtseyed, and left the room, closing the door behind her. They were alone.

"Do you prefer wine or cider?" Colin asked.

"Wine, if it is good."

"We'll find out," he said, showing her the bottle. "Looks French, but one never knows. I've had vinegar that was bottled as French wine."

Rosalyn didn't know what to say. He was the most handsome, worldly man of her acquaintance and the only one with the ability to make her tongue-tied.

Fortunately, Colin didn't seem to expect conversation from her. He poured their glasses and offered one to her. "To our marriage."

"May we both get what we want," she whispered.

His eyebrows rose. "What does that mean?" he asked quietly.

Rosalyn shifted uncomfortably. "You want the Commons seat."

He leaned forward, his glass still in the air, waiting to touch the brim of hers. "You keep reminding me of that. But what of you, Rosalyn? What do you want?"

His question caught her off guard. What did she want?

She'd entered into the marriage for Covey . . . or had she? Mayhap she'd always known—from the moment he'd first proposed their arrangement in Lord Loftus's sitting room—that she would end up here one way or the other.

"You've asked a difficult question," she said.

"But an important one." He clicked his glass against hers. "Drink up," he ordered.

She sipped the wine. It was surprisingly good. He served. His movements were fluid and economical. His fingers were long and tapered, his knuckles large. Capable hands. Like his mother's. Or, since he looked like he could wield a sword as easily as a serving knife—a gentleman's hands.

The trout was fresh and moist. Baby peas and carrots were also offered. Being the wife of a man of means had advantages.

"Is the hunting party still here?" she asked by way of conversation.

"They dine out tonight," he told her, refilling her wineglass. "The inn will be quiet until they return."

She nodded, conscious that meant they would *really* be alone. She drained her drink.

"Easy," he warned. "If you keep this up, I'll fear you are trying to avoid me through drink."

Rosalyn did feel a bit light-headed, but it was not an unpleasant feeling. "I never thought I would marry," she said and then wondered why she had blurted out such an admission.

"Why not?" he asked. Was he still on his first glass of wine? Or had she drunk it all?

She decided not to check. "I was fine alone," she answered blithely.

His intent blue eyes studied her a moment

over the brim of his wineglass. "I like this new style to your hair."

Her cheeks grew warm. "It's too curly," she demurred, shifting her gaze away from his.

"I think your hair is one of your best assets," he told her, his voice so warmly seductive that Rosalyn almost dropped her fork. She set it down.

"You are flattering me."

"Ummmhmmmm," he agreed.

"Men don't flatter me, not usually," she answered. "Why are you?" But she had an idea why, an image of his bare chest this morning springing to her mind.

Colin picked up her fork, speared a piece of trout, and held it up for her. She leaned forward and ate it off the tines.

"I flatter you because you are beautiful," he said. "In fact, I don't understand quite why you've wanted to hide your beauty. You're contrary to every other woman I know."

Rosalyn didn't know how to react. Defensively, she said, "When people see my hair, it reminds them of my mother."

He set down her fork and leaned his arms on the table. "What is the matter with that?"

She reached for her wineglass. "In Father's family, everything." She put her lips to her glass but didn't take a sip. If anyone should know the whole story, it was her husband. "You didn't marry that well. My grandfather was a candler in Norwich. Are you surprised?" she challenged.

"Not really," he answered. "And I'm the cobbler's son, remember. We all have to come from somewhere. It's what we do with our God-given talent that matters."

Rosalyn set down her glass. Her husband was a freethinker . . . and she liked it. "Yes," she agreed. "The story is my father saw Mother making a delivery one day and was so struck by her beauty that he followed her. From that day on, he paid court until she agreed to marry him."

"I imagine *his* family did not take the news well."

"That is an understatement. You've heard my mother ran off?"

He nodded.

Of course. That story always made the rounds. She folded her hands in her lap. "I was always reminded that my father didn't marry well. Mother disgraced not only herself but also the family. Since she wasn't there to pay for her sins, they took it out on me."

"What of your father? Didn't he protect you?"

"My father found solace in the bottle and died three years later."

"How old were you?"

"Fourteen."

"So, after that you lived with relatives?"

"One right after the other. Aunt Agatha, the one George wanted me to join in Cornwall, was my least favorite of a distasteful lot." It was Aunt Agatha who had complained the most about her hair. Rosalyn had been sixteen when she'd been sent there, a lonely girl who'd already seen more of life than she wanted. She lowered her hand to her lap. "Society can be cruel to those who don't meet expectations."

"If one lets them," Colin countered. "You're lucky you look like your mother."

No one had ever said that to her before. "What makes you say so?"

He grinned. "Because you don't look like your cousin Woodford or any of the relations I met in London from your father's side. Their noses are all twice the size of yours."

His bald statement stunned her.

"You're right. I don't. I never have." The admission was freeing. Laughter suddenly bubbled up inside her. She couldn't stop it.

Colin began laughing with her, as if he enjoyed her amusement.

She thought of her cousins, of the things that had been said to her and whispered behind her back all her life. Things that had cut her deeply. She laughed harder. And then there was her father, who'd barely recognized her presence and the things she had tried to do to make him care. Her laughter grew louder. Harder. Until suddenly, laughter turned to tears.

Rosalyn broke down. Deep, heart-wrenching sobs doubled her over. She couldn't stop them. They came from a place deep in her soul that no one had known about . . . not even herself.

The tears she had spent her life refusing to shed could not be denied now. They poured from her, steaming from her eyes and choking her throat.

She turned from Colin, embarrassed to have lost control over her senses.

But she couldn't escape him. He came around the table and knelt in front her. His arms circled her shoulders.

She tried to turn away.

He would not let her.

In the end, she didn't have the strength to fight. Not anymore.

Had it been the wine? Or the sympathetic ear that had made her break down?

She didn't know. She didn't care. She put her arms around Colin's shoulders and sobbed against his jacket like a child.

"I just wanted them to like me," she managed.

"I know," he cooed, sitting on the floor and bringing her down into his lap. He wrapped his arms around her. "We all want that."

"*They* didn't. *They* never cared." The hurt rolled through her, bringing fresh tears in its wake. She soaked his jacket and shirt with them.

Colin rocked her gently. "They are behind you now. They don't matter."

Rosalyn pulled back slightly. "But they are family." Her nose was running, and her words sounded nasally.

He shrugged. "Family can be important if they are kind and have good hearts. They can also be destructive if they don't." He pulled her cloth napkin down from the table, and she thankfully blew her nose.

"I wasn't raised to believe that," she said. "My family was all I had. I didn't even have a home to call my own, or even a trinket of my parents. George took it all."

"Yes, but he doesn't count anymore. Now you have Mrs. Covington."

"She's not really family."

"She is. Friends become the family of our choosing." He took the napkin from her, chose a clean corner, and wiped the tearstains from her cheeks. "Family is our link to ourselves," he mused, "and in a way it is a pity. I was blessed with a good one. You weren't so fortunate, but that doesn't mean you have to let them hurt you."

"All they've done is take care of me. I shouldn't be ungrateful."

"All they've done is ignore you," he contradicted. "They've made you feel an unwelcome burden. Being angry at their treatment is right and natural."

His words were cathartic. He was right. Being shuttled back and forth amongst bickering family and being criticized for her every fault had hurt. Deeply hurt.

"You've lost both your parents," he continued. "I understand your sense of loss. I miss mine. I didn't realize how much until I returned to Clitheroe and was around Matt's family. If I, an adult, find it hard being an orphan, what must you have felt?"

Rosalyn sat in the haven of his arms, but the guilt that had been her constant companion for so long refused to dissipate. She discovered she was reluctant to let it go. She'd carried it for so long, and she was accountable for some of it.

"My mother is alive," she confessed. Not even Covey knew her secret.

"I beg your pardon?" he said, leaning closer. Her voice had been so low that he'd not heard her.

"My mother is alive," she repeated.

Colin accepted the information without reaction, and she realized he didn't fully understand what she meant.

"My mother lives here, in Scotland, with her riding instructor. I've received letters from her."

Now he understood. "Have you written back?"

"*No.*" She dropped her gaze to the knot in his neck cloth. "I would *never* contact her."

"Why not?"

The question stunned her. "Because she disgraced the family. She left my father." Fresh tears threatened. She swallowed them back before adding, "She left me."

Anger mixed with shame. "They are married now. I have two sisters and a brother."

Colin reacted as if he didn't know what to do with this information.

"I wouldn't see her," Rosalyn said. At his continued silence, she emphasized, *"Ever."*

She waited, daring him to criticize her. Turning one's back on a parent was a sin. It was unnatural.

It was painful.

He must have sensed her sorrow. His hands covered hers in her lap, and he laced their fingers together.

Rosalyn looked down at their joined hands, and the hardness in her chest dissolved.

"It's all right," he said quietly. "However you choose to handle it is *your* decision and no one else's."

"Since I've moved to the Valley, she writes me every year," she said. "She wants to come see me."

"If you don't want to see her, you don't have to."

"Sometimes I wish I could see her," Rosalyn confessed. She glanced up at Colin to gauge his reaction. Anyone else of her acquaintance would have a very definite opinion about such a matter.

However, in his eyes, she saw only acceptance. Whatever decision she made *was* hers.

And in that moment, she began to fall in love.

Funny, she'd never believed it existed, and yet here it was, shimmering in front of her, more beautiful than the poets' praise, more real and vibrant. Whether she had believed in it or not, it had always existed. She'd just never seen it—before Colin.

Now, she couldn't imagine her life without it.

"Rosalyn?"

He didn't know what had happened to her. She heard his confusion in his voice. Had she changed that much? That quickly?

Yes, she had.

So she did something completely alien and radical. She kissed him.

# Chapter Twelve

*C*olin went very still, surprised by what was happening and afraid that if he moved, she'd stop.

She pressed her lips against his, tentatively at first, and then with growing ardor. His poor mouse, she still didn't know how to do a kiss right, although she was on the right path.

He released the breath he was holding and decided to show her.

Putting his arms around her, he kissed her back, urging her to open to him. Her hands slid up to his neck. When his tongue touched hers, she didn't draw away but sucked gently on it. Her breasts flattened against his chest—and every fiber in Colin's body reacted with a force that defied any law in the universe.

What had happened to his shy Rosalyn?

He didn't know. He didn't care. He wanted her. Now. On the floor, if necessary.

But that wouldn't be good. At least not for this first time. He knew better. Reluctantly, he slid her off his lap. Their lips reluctantly parted.

"We should go upstairs," he whispered.

Her answer was a moue of protest. She pulled him back to her and kissed him again, nipping his bottom lip before she did so.

Colin was amazed. There was fire in Rosalyn. Passion.

And he was exactly the man to quench her needs—but he didn't want the innkeeper or serving girl to come in and find them rolling on the floor. He stood, bringing her up with him.

Her legs didn't support her weight, and she rested against him, using the opportunity to fit her body intimately against his. She moved her hips and almost brought him to his knees.

From the moment he'd met her, even when he'd been blistering angry at her for stealing his deed, he'd wanted her. He recognized that fact now. She challenged him in a way no other woman ever had.

Was it the wine that had brought about this change?

Colin didn't know. But in case it was, he reached for the bottle. "Come," he said, taking her hand.

In the candlelight her eyes were luminous and dark. Her curls had escaped her pins, and she had the look of a woman who needed to be loved. He led her out of the room, checking first to make sure no one was in the hallway. She surprised him by slipping past him, taking his hand, and leading him toward the stairs.

Dear God, did any man ever understand women?

In front of their door, he tucked the wine bottle in the crook of his arm while his fingers fumbled with the key in the lock. The job would have been done quicker if she hadn't been kissing his neck.

Inside the room, Colin didn't waste time. He couldn't. He slammed the door shut, grabbed his wife, and gave her the kiss she'd been begging for. He held nothing back, and to his delight, she met him with an equal passion.

The wine bottle in his hand was now a nuisance as he walked his bride back toward the bed, their lips locked. A candle burned on the washbasin, probably set there by a maid, but it was enough light. They needed no more.

Colin wasn't certain what had enflamed Rosalyn's desire, but he wasn't one to question such good fortune. He set the bottle down beside the bed and turned his attention to the pleasurable task of undressing her.

Pushing her dress down around her shoulders, he kissed the satiny smooth skin of her neck and shoulders, moving himself steadily lower. Pressing his lips to the pulse point beneath her chin, he could tell her heart raced with a beat that matched his own.

Nor was she a submissive partner. She slid her hands in his jacket, sliding it down his shoulders, and tugged his shirt out of his breeches. Her deft fingers untied the knot in his neck cloth and tossed it aside.

He adored her abandoned response. Rosalyn was not one to do anything halfway, especially something like making love. He shrugged his jacket the rest of the way off and threw it to the other side of the bed.

Her hands ran up under his shirt just as he freed her breast from the confines of her chemise. She pulled his shirt up over his head. He bent her back and covered one pink, hard nipple with his mouth.

Rosalyn gasped in surprise, her body arching, as if ready to jump out of his arms.

It took all his control to stop. He looked up. "Do you not like this?"

Her mouth was open, her eyes wide with disbelief. "I've never felt anything like it."

"I'll stop—"

"Don't stop," she ordered and used both hands to bring his head back to her breast.

There were some orders a man didn't question.

He pulled her dress down over her hips, the image of her as she was in the bath never far from his mind. She began unbuttoning his breeches. Her fingers were clumsy. He didn't mind. It was exquisite torture.

Kneeling, he pushed down her chemise, petticoat, and skirts. Her legs were longer than he had anticipated, and he could barely hold himself back any longer.

He gently leaned her back on the bed. She freed one button and came down to the second. Colin feared he would die before she was done.

He took over, his fingers almost as clumsy as hers, but who could blame him?

Her skin was a pale gold in the candlelight. Her curls formed a halo around her head, and her naked body was the stuff of dreams. She still wore her stockings and garters.

She was shy but watched him intently, her

eyes trusting—and that was his undoing. The fact that she depended upon him.

He'd taken a vow to protect her. A tenderness the likes of which he'd never known welled up inside Colin. This would be no common mating. This was the joining of two people for life.

Sitting on the bed beside her, he pulled off his boots. He stood to slide his breeches down his legs. Her gaze settled on his obvious arousal, and he knew this was the first time she'd seen a naked man. "Let me have your hand."

Unquestioning, she placed her hand in his. "If I do anything to cause you distress or pain in any way," he said, "squeeze my hand and I will stop whatever I'm doing."

And then he bent down to kiss her. She was open and eager. Their tongues teased each other, while Colin ran his free hand over the curve of her hip and down the length of her thigh, marveling at the perfection of her. Pressing her back onto the bed, he settled himself between her thighs.

Instinctively, she curved to accommodate him. He prayed he didn't do the wrong thing. Lacing his fingers in hers, he raised her hands above her head, kissed her, and thrust deep.

He felt her tear.

*She was his.*

Her hand squeezed his.

He stopped. All he wanted to do was push forward, to fill her. The primal urgency to do so was astounding, and yet he forced himself to stop.

"Are you all right?" he whispered.

She swallowed and then relaxed. "I think. I don't know?"

"I won't go on if you don't want me to."

"We're not finished?"

Her question slipped past his guard. Colin chuckled—it was either that or groan—and her eyes brightened. "I felt your laughter," she said, "all the way inside me."

He dared to press deeper. She smiled, and he knew the pain was gone. He kissed her temples, her cheeks, her lips. "It will be better now," he promised.

Her fingers relaxed, and he began moving.

Nothing had ever felt as good as being inside Rosalyn. She was liquid fire. The perfect fit.

Timidly at first, and then with gathering eagerness, she met his thrusts. His last coherent thought was that he had been meant to make love to this woman.

She released her hold on his hand. Wrapping her arms around his neck, she buried her face in his shoulder and held tight.

Colin reached the point where he could not have stopped if she'd begged him to. He drove relentlessly forward. Rosalyn was whispering his name, her soft cries pushing him to completion.

He wanted to tell her it would be all right. He wanted her to know what awaited her at the end. But he couldn't speak. Dear God, he could barely think of anything save his own need—

Rosalyn tightened. She cried out, a sharp exclamation of surprise and wonder, and Colin could not stop himself. His seed shot out of him, deep within her. His senses were full of her. She was his only link to sanity and earth.

They held each other as if they feared letting go, and he knew their loving had been as intense and mighty for her as it had been for himself.

Colin rolled over on his back, bringing her with him. He never wanted to let her go. Their hearts pounded in unison. He could feel hers as clearly as his own . . . and slowly they both drifted back to reality.

Their overheated bodies began to cool. Colin

reached for the other side of the bedcover and flipped it over them. Rosalyn's head rested on his chest. Her legs entwined with his.

He traced the tilt of her nose with his finger, and she raised her head to look down at him. Her eyes were the dreamy opaqueness of a woman who had just been loved well. Her lips were swollen from his kisses. "Is it always like this?" she whispered.

"It's *never* been like this," he replied, and knew he spoke the truth.

She smiled, her expression sleepy. "We'll get to do it again?"

Beneath the covers, Colin ran his hand up the curves of her body. "Oh, yes," he promised, "again and again and again."

Colin fell asleep first. As supple and indolent as a cat, she contentedly used his body for her bed and affectionately watched his eyes close. She lay her ear against his chest and listened to the strength of his heartbeat.

For the first time in her life, she felt completely whole. She'd learned the secret of marriage. She understood why men and women searched it out. She was surprised everyone wasn't married and understood Covey's devotion to Alfred, because she now knew where she belonged—beside Colin.

With a soft sigh, she closed her eyes.

He woke her sometime in the night. She didn't know the hour, but it was dark. His fingers found her secret places, and when she was panting and needy, he entered her. This time, there was no pain, and she knew the pain was gone forever. From here on out, there would only be pleasure.

They didn't bother to get out of bed or even dress the next day. Colin told her that he had hired the stable lads to fetch his phaeton with the broken wheel. It arrived that afternoon, and they watched from behind the shuttered windows as it was unloaded. Seeing the damage in the light of day, they agreed they really were lucky they hadn't broken their necks.

A few moments later, someone knocked on the door.

Colin had no choice but to put on his breeches and talk to Lucas the innkeeper. Rosalyn listened to their conversation from beneath the covers as Lucas said, "The blacksmith says he can fix the wheel, but it will take two days."

"Two days?" Colin repeated.

"Aye, I'm sorry, sir," John answered. "The

room is available to you as long as you want its use."

"Then make it three days, and send up food." Colin shut the door in the man's face. He faced Rosalyn, the devil in his grin. Before she knew what to expect, he took a flying leap and landed right on the bed.

He pretended to gobble her up, and she laughed so hard her jaw ached. Then he made love to her. Sweet, wonderful love . . . and promised three days more of the same.

Rosalyn didn't know when she'd ever been so happy.

However, by the end of the third day, when the phaeton was returned repaired and sat ready for their journey on the morrow, she realized something was missing. Colin had not yet said he loved her. She tried not to let it bother her, but the lack of it worried the back of her mind . . . and caused her to keep her feelings close.

Colin didn't even seem to notice.

They made love that evening, and Colin talked about their return. It was decided they'd go to Maiden Hill first and then he would go, alone, to speak to his brother. "Matt can be funny about some matters," he said. "He's the oldest and so he has definite opinions, and will be a bit put out I didn't say anything to him first."

"You didn't even tell him you were leaving?"

Colin pushed his dark hair back before admitting, "No." Then, apparently realizing how bad it sounded, he said, "I told the children. Boyd will tell them."

"You told the children you were getting married but not your brother?" she asked in disbelief.

"Yes," he replied as if the answer caused him pain.

"Will he be unhappy that we are married?" She feared his response.

He kissed her temple. "No. If anything, he and Val will welcome you with open arms."

Colin made love to her then, a quiet, comfortable love. Over the past days, she'd learned passion in all forms, but this was her favorite. It was the easy acceptance of one another.

Afterward, he fell right to sleep. He liked to curl up around her, his arm across her waist to keep her close. Rosalyn should have fallen asleep easily too, save for the doubts that kept her awake.

She slid out from his arm, rising to go sit by the window a spell. The moon was full and high in the sky. She studied the sleeping man in her bed. Colin had made her a woman and he'd made her a wife . . . but she wanted something more.

Her love for him had quadrupled every day. She was surprised he could not tell. He seemed almost oblivious to anything but the enjoyment of her body. She, on the other hand, could not have given anything without the presence of it.

Was that the difference between men and women? Or was she more like her father than her mother?

The questions haunted her.

In the end, she knew there was nothing she could do. Her pride would not let her confess her deepest-felt emotions first. Better he think she was like him—carefree and unconcerned about such a weighty commitment. After all, he'd been willing to marry her without even knowing her.

No, she'd keep her love a secret, but, *please God, don't let me be like my father.*

With that prayer, she climbed back into bed beside Colin and fell asleep.

Colin opened his eyes. Rosalyn's breathing was slow and rhythmic now. He was certain she was asleep.

The moonlight through the window highlighted the curve of her cheeks. He wondered what was bothering her . . . and why she didn't confide in him.

He feared he knew the answer.

Tomorrow, they would return to the Valley. Tomorrow, he would find out if she resented no longer being *Lady* Rosalyn.

Of course, she must. He understood the power in title. It was the reason he wanted one.

He also understood that of late, Rosalyn had moments of deep introspection like the one she had this night. Moments when he could feel her watch him. The mind that had once been so open to him now seemed closed. He could not divine her thinking at all, not when the subject was himself.

Then again, he feared he knew the directions of her thoughts. She'd married beneath herself. Of course she would have doubts. Why else would she be so quiet?

It was a long time before he went to sleep.

The next morning, Colin woke an hour later than he'd planned. His desirable wife still hugged the pillow.

For the past several mornings, he'd woken her by making love to her. This morning, he didn't.

He needed a little distance between them in case she decided that what had happened between them in Scotland stayed in Scotland.

Colin took the time to shave and dress before he finally woke Rosalyn. She frowned at him groggily. "You're dressed?"

"Yes, I need to go outside and make final arrangements."

She nodded, her thoughts apparently elsewhere.

"Disappointed?" he asked, wanting to know if she missed their morning ritual.

"No, that's fine," she said absently. She pushed her curls back from her face with one hand. "We must go." She smiled, and he couldn't decide if she was happy to be leaving or regretful.

Colin stood a moment, debating whether or not to ask what had kept her up last night.

"Go," she said, waving her hand. "Say hello to Oscar."

Well, there it was—marching orders. He started from the room, but she stopped him. "No kiss good-bye?"

He turned. She looked enchanting, sitting there on the edge of the bed with only the sheets for clothes and her hair curling down around her shoulders.

"Of course there is a kiss," he said, and he dropped one on her lips. He dared not linger because, if he did, he would make love to her. He wanted to. His favorite time to have her was when she was all warm and relaxed from a night's sleep.

He left the room.

A half hour later, his bride joined him for breakfast. She wore the green dress she was married in, and she carried her bonnet. "It's the worse for wear," she said, holding the hat up for him to see what a disaster it was.

Colin shrugged. He didn't care about clothing. Not right now.

Over breakfast, she seemed to lack an appetite. Colin wasn't hungry himself. Women were fickle. Belinda had taught him they could be one way one moment, and another in the next. And what did he really know about Rosalyn? The past few days, they'd barely talked. They'd had more intriguing ways to pass their time.

Oscar was harnessed to the phaeton and was waiting for them when they finished eating. Colin tossed the stable lad a coin, while Rosalyn put on her hat and tied the ribbons into a saucy bow that belied the crooked brim. Offering his hand, he helped her up into the seat and took his place. With a snap of the whip, they were off.

The day was perfect for a drive, and they would have enjoyed themselves . . . except for the subtle tension between them. They were *too* polite to each other. *Too* considerate.

Nor did Rosalyn touch him with the easy familiarity she'd had up in their room at the inn. He sensed she was trying *not* to have contact with him. The vehicle's seat was short and narrow, and yet she placed as much space as possible between them.

At least twice Colin almost said something and then backed away. He wasn't the one who had gotten up in the middle of the night or seemed distant this morning, and he'd be damned before he let her know her quietness bothered him.

The drive was uneventful and miserable.

Half an hour away from Maiden Hill, they heard the bay of the hounds in the distance.

Rosalyn broke the interminable silence that had fallen between them. "Lord Loftus is on the hunt again," she observed, her voice sounding as if she was relieved to finally have a topic of conversation.

"Yes." Colin forced a smile. "The man is mad for it."

"He thinks of little else all year round." She didn't look at him but watched a yeoman's son and a pretty young lass walk past them on the side of the road. Their shy, budding affection for each other was obvious. They must have stolen a few moments away from their chores to be together.

Rosalyn smiled at them—and Colin felt a pang of jealousy.

"The hunt hardly qualifies as sport the way he plays it," Colin said, a trace of the bitterness he was feeling in his voice. It was going to happen again. He saw that now. He was going to give Rosalyn his heart and, like Belinda, she would use it for her own purposes.

Damn, but he was snared in a trap of his own making, only this time, he couldn't run away. Worse, he was starting to fall in love. . . .

The direction of his thoughts shocked him. Here, on the road on a lovely spring afternoon, the realization hit him like a bolt of lightning—*he was falling in love.*

Stunned and horrified, Colin pulled on the reins. Oscar halted but looked back to see what his master was about. After all, he'd stopped the horse in the middle of nowhere, and Oscar was wise enough to know this was not normal.

"Colin, is something wrong?"

Oh, yes, something was very wrong, but he'd not tell her that.

"Your expression is so strange," she said. "Are you taking ill?"

*With the worst malady in the world!* He stared into her gray-green eyes and couldn't decide if he saw a stranger or a lover. The hounds sounded closer, their abandoned howls emphasizing exactly how afraid he was.

Yes, he was scared, frightened out of his wits. What man shouldn't be, when confronted by love?

Oscar spooked, his abrupt movement sending a shake all the way through the phaeton. Colin had to give his attention to the reins even as the reason for the horse's skittish behavior was revealed. The fox crawled out from the thicket by the side of the road. Oscar had sensed he was there, only this wasn't the wily, bold creature Colin had first met.

No, this time, the animal had been run to ground. He was tired. His tongue hung out, and he panted from the exertion of escaping the chase.

He glanced up at the horse as if just realizing Oscar's presence, and then he dropped, too exhausted to go on.

The hounds sounded closer. Colin could hear them crashing through the woods. Loftus was shouting them on, berating them to find him the fox—and Colin knew what he had to do.

He jumped down from his perch on the phaeton and, without a moment's hesitation, scooped the fox up by the nape of the neck. He climbed back up into his seat, settling the beaten animal between himself and Rosalyn.

"What are you doing?" she asked. "You can't take a wild creature like this with us."

"Watch me," he said, and then thought enough to add, "hold on," before cracking the tip of the whip on Oscar's rump.

They took off like a shot, racing toward Maiden Hill.

# Chapter Thirteen

$\mathcal{R}$osalyn held on to the side bar of the phaeton for dear life. Colin was driving so fast that it seemed as if they were flying across the ground. When they took a curve on one wheel, she feared being thrown from the vehicle.

And then there was the matter of the beast on the seat between them. Whoever heard of picking up a fox?

Her bonnet blew off her head. Only the ribbons held it around her neck. The pins flew from her hair. Her husband didn't care. He drove like a man possessed.

They careened off the road onto the drive leading to Maiden Hill. Then, and only then, did Colin make any attempt to slow down.

Rosalyn sat up. Her hair was a mess. She

yanked at what was left of the bow around her neck and removed her bonnet. The poor hat. It had started the journey as her most fashionable article of clothing and ended it looking like a battered rag.

The fox recovered and sat up between them. He acted as if riding beside Colin was the most natural thing in the world.

"What do you think you are doing?" Rosalyn asked.

Colin lifted a quizzical eyebrow. "Cooling down Oscar before I let you off at the front door."

"No, I mean about the fox."

Her husband looked down at the creature, and she swore the animal looked up at him and smiled. "I'm not going to do anything," Colin said.

"You can't have a fox at Maiden Hill," she explained carefully. "Especially this one. This is the fox Lord Loftus has been hunting all season, and if he ever finds out you stole it from him—"

"You can't steal something that doesn't belong to a person in the first place. He can't stake a claim on a fox. Nor will he find out," Colin said firmly. "Unless you tell him."

"I won't tell him, but, Colin, this is a wild creature. It's not a pet."

"I know that, Rosalyn." He glanced at his furry mate and said, "But I couldn't leave him back there to be ripped apart by the dogs while Loftus laughed with glee."

Immediately, she felt contrite. "Oh, Colin, I know. Fox hunting is far from sporting . . . but what are we going to do with a fox?"

"He can live at Maiden Hill."

"Live at Maiden Hill? A fox?"

Her husband nodded, growing pleased with the idea. "Of course. He'll be safe there."

"Yes, but will we?" she wondered.

"Why would we not? He's just a little fox. The only time they are a nuisance is around chickens. We don't have chickens, do we?"

"No, but we have ducks and geese. And think of our neighbors. They have chickens. Colin, what will we do if the fox gets into the neighbor's henhouse?"

"He won't. Rosalyn, look at him. He's as docile as a dog, and more intelligent."

The fox did seem that way. He'd been listening to them argue, his bright eyes going from one to the other.

"But he isn't a pet." Her protests were growing weaker.

"You are right. He deserves his freedom." They'd arrived at Maiden Hill's front door. He reined Oscar to a halt. "He's fought so hard to elude Loftus," he said to Rosalyn. "He was out-numbered, and yet he's put up a valiant chase. I couldn't let the dogs have him. I can't let him fight alone."

"Oh, dear," Rosalyn worried, understanding. She knew what it was like to struggle alone and feel no one was on her side . . . but she didn't re-alize Colin could empathize with that battle, too.

And it made her love him all the more. A love that she wasn't certain he wanted.

"Your fox is welcome here. Of course, you'd best behave yourself," she told the creature.

As if in answer, the fox jumped off the back of the phaeton. He leaped over her flower beds, winding his way past the rosebush they'd planted, and headed for the shrubs that formed the boundary of her yard. Just when she thought he was returning to the wild, the fox stopped. He looked back at them, one foot poised in the air. Silently, he communicated his appreciation be-fore he disappeared into the undergrowth with a flick of his red bushy tale.

Colin faced her. "Thank you."

She searched deep in his eyes, wishing she could tell what he was thinking. "I couldn't see him ripped apart either."

"I know." Colin smiled, and it was as if the world stopped. The connection between them *was* there. It hadn't been something relegated to a single place and time. The early unease between them melted away . . .

The front door opened. "We've been so worried about the two of you!" Covey said. She had Cook and Bridget with her. They helped the older woman down the steps. "I was so surprised when, after days of waiting, I looked out the window and here you were. Where have you been? What has happened?"

Rosalyn's mind went blank. "I wrote a note . . ."

But what had she said? Or had it been nothing more than Colin's announcement he would take care of her?

"I worried," Covey answered as if it explained all. Cook hovered over her, and Rosalyn could see her friend had not been well.

"You shouldn't be standing out here," Rosalyn said. "Let us go inside."

"Nonsense, I've never been better," Covey vowed. "Now what of you? Do you have news?"

Colin had jumped to the ground. He came around to Rosalyn's side of the phaeton and said proudly, "We do. Let me introduce you to my wife." He placed his hands on Rosalyn's waist and swung her down to the ground.

Covey held out her arms to receive Rosalyn. "I had so hoped such would be the case. Come and let me hug you, my child. This is joyous, joyous news!"

Rosalyn accepted the embrace. "Does anyone else know?"

"Lady Loftus has sent a messenger every day to discover if you have returned," Covey said. "We shall send John to her immediately. She will be so happy for the two of you."

"Have you heard from my brother?" Colin asked.

"No," Covey answered, "although I am certain he knows. Information like this never stays a secret long, not in Clitheroe."

Colin made a small groan, and Rosalyn knew he was upset about his brother's reaction. His troubled gaze met hers. "I should have said something before I left. I need to go see him now before he learns of our return through rumor."

"Do you wish me to go with you?" Rosalyn asked.

"No, I think this is one interview I'd best do alone. Matt can be funny about some things." Colin climbed back up in the seat of the phaeton. Oscar's ears flattened. The horse had obviously been hoping their traveling was done.

"I'll return shortly," he said, "and then you can give me a tour of the house. I've yet to have one."

Rosalyn laughed. "I will, and Cook will have a special dinner waiting."

"Good, I'm hungry." With a wave of his hand, he turned Oscar down the drive.

Rosalyn watched them until they were out of sight. She loved him so much. But was congenial companionship enough?

Covey's arm slipped through hers. "Everything will be fine," she promised, and Rosalyn prayed she was right.

Colin drove first to the rectory. Matt wasn't there, but Val was—and her reception was cold.

She answered his knock on the door, took one look at him, and turned away, leaving the door open for him to follow. She walked into the kitchen, where she'd started preparations for dinner.

Emma sat at the kitchen table rolling extra pastry dough into little pies of her own. Val often let her do that. The child looked up at him with big eyes and whispered, "Hello," and Colin knew he was in trouble. He gave Emma a secret wave in return.

"You've heard the news," he guessed as Val picked up a dressed hare by its legs and whacked the meat into pieces on a cutting board for their dinner.

"I've heard rumors," she threw over her shoulder. "Are we to wish you happy?"

"Yes."

Without showing a speck of interest in the news he was married, Val said, "Your brother isn't here. He's at the church."

"Then I'll go find him there." She could have told him this at the door, but he guessed trailing after her was a penance of sorts. He started to re-trace his steps, but her voice stopped him.

"I think it a shame that you cut him out of something so important, Colin. He deserves better."

"I didn't cut him out. I'm here to tell him the news."

"Yes, *finally*," she said sarcastically.

"I'm not a child, Val. I didn't need his permission."

"Oh, Colin." Her eyes softened. "That is the most foolish thing you have ever said."

He wasn't certain what she meant. "I'm going to see Matt." This time when he left, she didn't stop him.

Outside, he went down the street to the church. The late-afternoon shadows were lengthening across the graveyard. A robin eyed him as it hopped across the grass beneath the cherry tree, which was now fully bloomed in all its glory.

Colin opened the church's heavy, narrow door. All was quiet. The air still smelled of the incense used for special ceremonies. Light filtered through thick medieval stained glass, giving the sanctuary the air of another world. The heels of Colin's boots sounded loud on the stone floor.

He expected to find Matt busy fiddling with something or other. Instead, his brother sat in one of the back pews facing the altar. His hands were clasped in his lap, as if he were lost in deep prayer. Colin slipped in beside him.

They sat quietly a moment, and then Matt asked, "So you decided to return home, did you?" There was a beat and then he added, "Again."

This was going to be a difficult conversation.

"Well, I got married and there wasn't anyplace else to go but home," Colin answered, attempting to put a light note on the subject, and failing.

"Nice of you to think of us."

Colin bristled at the implied criticism. "I'm a grown man, Matt. I don't need permission."

His brother faced him. "Don't *need* permission? Is that all I am to you? A substitute for our parents?" He shook his head in disgust. "I had hoped there was more between us. After all, you slept under my roof. You played with my children and ate the food my wife made."

"I didn't meant to slight you, brother," Colin answered, feeling an uncomfortable pang of guilt. "I got caught up in the moment. We were eloping and, since I haven't had to answer to anyone for years, I didn't think of it." Which wasn't completely true. He'd known Matt would not approve of an elopement.

"I didn't expect you to 'answer' to me, Colin. I expected you to *include* me."

His words hit Colin hard.

For a moment, he couldn't speak. His own selfishness stared him in the face, and he was ashamed.

"I should have told you my plans," Colin agreed. "But I feared you would be disappointed, and you know I was never good at handling your disappointment."

"Disappointed? Colin, I was hurt. You didn't want me at your wedding."

"I eloped. There was no wedding."

*"There could have been."* Matt shook his head as if attempting to rein in his anger. "All right," he admitted, "I know you think I'm the fool for answering a calling to the church. I know you feel I failed in your eyes by choosing a country parish life to the politics of the Church. But I never thought you would not invite me to see you wed. Of course, why did I think that?" he said rhetorically. "You've kept me out of most of your life. I'm surprised you even came back to Clitheroe. Or did you want to show me how successful you had become?"

Matt's accusation took Colin by surprise. "I returned because Clitheroe is my home."

"Is it?" Matt snorted his thought on the matter and rose to his feet. He started to push past Colin's legs to get out of the pew.

Colin blocked his exit by placing his hand on the pew in front of them. "Explain yourself," he challenged. "I'm bigger and stronger than you are, Matt. The days when we wrestled and you won because you are the oldest were over long ago, and I'll prove it right here if I must. Now, answer me? What imagined sin have I committed that has you so set against me. Yes, I eloped, but I'm a man full grown. I have that choice."

"Then why are you even here?" Matt returned. "Go. Make your own way. You married the lady, you get the Commons seat, of what importance is family?"

Another direct hit.

Colin pulled his arm back, and his brother exited the pew and walked toward the pulpit to retrieve some papers lying there. Silently, Colin watched him. Matt was not as hard-hearted as he wished to pretend. His hands shook, rattling the papers.

"Family is very important to me," Colin managed at last.

The muscles in Matt's jaw tightened. He did not speak.

Colin rose. "This is about Mother and Father, isn't it?"

"Is it?"

"I sent money."

"Yes, you did," Matt agreed, not looking at him.

Colin gripped the edge of the pew in front of him. "Was it not enough?"

At last his brother confronted him. "Do you think they appreciated the money more than they would have appreciated seeing you?"

"I was away fighting, Matt. I couldn't leave whenever I wished."

"But when you did return, you never came back. We heard you were in London. The Ribble Valley isn't that much of the back country. People write letters, and we knew when you'd come and gone."

"I had commitments. Matters I had to attend to." God, the excuses sounded weak to his own ears! "When I returned—which wasn't often—the War Office usually demanded my time."

"Really?" Matt questioned with quiet disbelief. "You are a brave man, brother, but a coward in what is really important."

Guilt made Colin angry. He came out from the pew. "You're jealous. You chose your calling and your direction, and now you see what I have and you are questioning your decisions."

Matt's fist came down on the pulpit. "Nothing could be further from the truth!"

"Oh, come now. You had a great future ahead, Matt. Father Ruley had plans for both of us. I followed his advice. You chose your own course, and now you are wondering if perhaps you hadn't made the wisest choices. Well, you can't blame me for that. You are the one who fell in love with Val. I had nothing to do with that."

"You believe Val is the reason I'm here?" Matt asked incredulously.

"You were on your way to London before you met her," Colin reminded him.

"I was on the way to a devil of my own making until I met her," Matt lashed back. "I know the dangers of unbridled ambition, Colin. And I've learned Father Ruley was an intelligent man but he didn't know the first thing about life. To him, it was titles and money. He wanted me to dedicate my life to service in the Church but a Church of his own devising. He valued hierarchy and politics. It took Val's love for me to see God and hear Him. I'm in this parish of my own choice. I like my work here. I'm a part of these people's lives. I want to watch my children grow and know their father." He leaned forward on the pulpit. "I would never have wanted my parents to *die alone*. I was even by Father Ruley's side when he passed on. There was no one else there, Colin. He'd helped dozens of lads like us, and none of them were beside him except Father and me."

*Not even Colin.*

"I understand a bit of how you think," Matt continued, "because I knew Father Ruley, and I knew you wanted more than I did. It was always that way between us. I was content and you were restless. So, now, let us bring home to roost some other truths, brother. Has it dawned on you yet that you didn't receive your precious knighthood for service to the Crown during the war not because of your willingness to speak your mind but because the world doesn't always believe the end justifies the means? You run roughshod over people, Colin. You've trampled on your family. You married Lady Rosalyn for the basest of reasons—prestige and fortune. You've done everything without any true conviction other than your own gain. And now, you are here and wanting me to wish you happy?"

Matt shook his head. "I can't. I won't. I would have preferred true and genuine affection. I would have liked the banns to be announced and time taken for the two of you to consider what the vows you would be making before God would mean. But then, it doesn't matter, does it? Because you'll have your life in London and she will be here. Eventually, you'll be too busy on 'important matters' to return to Clitheroe, and so the circle continues."

Colin took a step back. The earth no longer seemed beneath his feet. The truth of his brother's words shook him deeply.

Matt gripped both sides of the pulpit, his face tense from emotion. He stood as Colin's judge, and Colin didn't like it one whit.

"You know, I would like to plant a facer on you right now," Colin confessed.

His words broke the tension a bit. "Why don't you?" Matt asked, the condemnation gone from his voice.

"Because," Colin started, his eyes burning. "Because some of what you said is right."

He didn't wait for a response but turned on his heel and walked out of the church. It would be a cold, dark day before he returned, he silently vowed.

Joseph and Thomas had found Oscar and had led him and the phaeton down to the church. They pulled up grass in the yard and fed it to the starving horse. Colin mumbled something appropriate about their being good lads, and he tousled both their heads before climbing onto the phaeton. He barely remembered driving to Maiden Hill.

And yet, that was where he was going. Nowhere else. Maiden Hill was his home now.

He'd tell Rosalyn what had happened. She'd help him make sense of everything. With her clear, level thinking, she would understand, and she'd sanction his reasons for not returning all these years, not even to see his parents. She'd remind him he wasn't a bad sort . . . just a selfish one.

Colin reined Oscar to a halt. They sat in the middle of the road. He looked around, recognizing this spot of the Valley. As a boy, he'd run and crawled over every field and hillside around Clitheroe. Matt had rarely wandered off, but Colin had always pushed the boundaries. He'd always wanted more.

Was that such a bad thing?

He slapped the reins, and Oscar started off at a trot. What a great heart this horse had. He was loyal to Colin. "Is that not a start?" he asked aloud.

Matt wasn't there to answer.

As Colin pulled up in front of Maiden Hill, he saw they had visitors. John held two fine hunters, one of which was Lord Loftus's horse.

Colin set the brake on the phaeton and jumped down. "We have guests?"

"Aye, you do, sir."

Colin took a moment to unharness Oscar. He

deserved a rest. He'd tend to the horse's other needs in a moment, and he walked toward the door, aware that Oscar was making his way in the direction of Rosalyn's flower beds. Colin wasn't going to worry about it now.

He'd just stepped inside the door and tossed his hat on a side table when Loftus charged into the hallway, his face red with fury. Shellsworth, also dressed in hunting clothes, followed close behind.

"Mandland, I want an answer!" Loftus barked.

"To what question, my lord?" Colin asked, not really in the mood for Loftus's nonsense.

"The fox!" his lordship charged. "You stole my fox! Took him right out from under me! And I want him back!"

# Chapter Fourteen

$\mathcal{C}$onfronted by Lord Loftus's anger, the thought struck Colin that here he had owned Maiden Hill for a little over three weeks and he'd yet been able to sit in front of the fire and put his feet up.

Behind Loftus and Shellsworth stood a very scattered Mrs. Covington and a tall, confident Rosalyn, who said proudly, "I told Lord Loftus his charges are silly."

Colin smiled. Damn if she wouldn't brazen it out and get away with it, too. She had more pride than a queen.

"They aren't silly!" Loftus returned. "A young lad and his girl saw Mandland pick the fox up off the road and put him in his rig. They saw it! And I'd just about run him to ground! He was mine."

Rosalyn opened her mouth, ready to defend Colin's actions, but he couldn't let her. His brother's words still echoed in his ears. What did he care that Loftus was upset over the fox?

"My lord, you are right. I did pick up the fox," he said. "The creature appeared injured and, since I value all God's creatures, I rescued it."

"Do you expect me to believe that horny toad nonsense?" his lordship shot back. "'All God's creatures.' What a farce!"

"Farce or not, it is what happened." Colin dared Loftus to take the matter a step further and call him a liar. He'd stared down better men, and he was not afraid to put steel behind his words.

The portly lord didn't want to back down. His temper had the better of him, and, yet, his sense of self-preservation was starting to doubt the wisdom of a challenge.

Shellsworth took this moment to interject himself. "My lord, may I make a suggestion? It's admirable and noble of Colonel Mandland to rescue a woodland creature, but now he knows it is your fox, and therefore should hand it over to us."

"Yes! That's right!" Loftus quickly seconded. "Give me back my fox, and all will rest easy between us."

"No." Colin didn't even weigh the consequences before he gave his succinct, definite answer. He'd not turn the fox over to be destroyed.

Lord Loftus's response was something to behold. His face grew redder, his eyes crossed, and his whole body shook. He sputtered out, "You would tell me no?"

Colin flicked his glance to the lawyer, who shrugged with an apologetic smile. "I would tell you no," Colin affirmed.

For a moment, Lord Loftus's mouth opened and shut like a fish gasping for air as if no one had ever dared to defy him.

Rosalyn came forward. "Lord Loftus, you look as if you could use a glass of a . . . um . . . what do we have, Covey?"

"We have some sherry," Covey answered. "Perhaps two glasses—?" she suggested hopefully.

"Yes, Covey, two glasses of sherry is a brilliant idea," Rosalyn was saying. "Lord Loftus will feel better in a moment. Here, I'll pour." She started for the sitting room, presumably to fetch sherry, which no man worth his salt would ever drink, when Lord Loftus's voice stopped her in her tracks.

"If you believe I will give the Commons seat to

a man who would defy me, you are wrong," Loftus said. "Now, give me that fox."

There it was. The gauntlet had been thrown down between them. What man would be fool enough to toss away his future for the life of a miserable little fox?

What was it his brother had accused him of? Believing the ends justified the means? Of running roughshod over others for what he wanted?

Apparently not when it came to a fox.

"I will not give you the fox," Colin said.

Loftus stumbled back, as if he had not expected Colin to defy him. "You have made an error. A grave, grave error." He looked to Shellsworth. "You want the Commons seat."

"I would be honored to accept the position, your lordship," the lawyer responded promptly.

"And you know your place, too," Loftus practically growled out. "Come, let us discuss the matter." He stomped past Colin and out of the house.

Shellsworth had to scurry to keep up.

Colin watched the two of them mount their horses and ride off. It wasn't until the dust of their leaving had settled that he realized what he had just done.

He knew the Valley. Everyone knew better

than to offend Lord Loftus. The man wielded real power, passed down through his family from one generation to another. He was the feudal lord, the law. His power in the Valley rivaled the king's.

And he was furious with Colin.

Shutting the door, he turned to find Rosalyn and Mrs. Covington looking at him, each in a state of shock.

"Sherry? Right?" he said, not expecting an answer. He walked into the sitting room, where he didn't have any trouble identifying the liquor cabinet.

Rosalyn couldn't gauge Colin's mood. She exchanged a glance with Covey, who was even more confused than she was. The barely controlled violence in Lord Loftus's temper had been disconcerting, as was Colin's silence following the scene.

With a nod, she silently asked Covey to give her a moment alone with her husband. Her companion didn't even miss a beat. "I'll see to supper," she said.

The sitting room was dark enough now that a candle would not be inappropriate. Colin had the liquor cabinet open. In his hand he held a bottle of whiskey three-quarters full. He acknowledged her presence by saying, "There's sherry, but also this bottle of aged whiskey here. Do you think Mrs. Covington has been holding out on us?" He poured himself a glass.

"She probably didn't know it was there. She rarely goes into the cabinet. It may be years old."

"Perfect. That is the best whiskey." He toasted her and downed the glass.

"You didn't do anything wrong," Rosalyn said. "I wouldn't have let him have the fox either."

Colin didn't answer, save for a self-deprecating smile. He refilled his glass.

"Colin, drinking yourself into a stupor solves nothing."

He shook his head. "Do you think I give a damn what that petty little tyrant thinks?"

"Yes."

At last he looked at her, and what she saw in his expression tore at her heart. "You know me better than I know myself," he admitted. He drew a deep breath and released it slowly. "Rosalyn, let me have some time alone. I fear I'm not going to be good company."

He grabbed the bottle in one hand and walked over to the upholstered chair in front of the hearth. He set the glass and bottle on a side table and, propping his booted heels on a footstool, sat down as if settling in for the night.

Rosalyn didn't know what to do. She'd been shut out. Their early camaraderie, the connection between the two of them, had vanished as if it had never existed. She sensed his distance. He wanted nothing to do with her right now. He preferred his bottle.

"I'll see you at dinner," she said uncertainly.

He didn't answer, his attention on the drink in his hand. She had no choice but to leave the room. She shut the door, needing a physical barrier to symbolize the emotional one between them.

An hour later, she met Covey in the dining room. "Is the colonel coming?" Covey asked. Bridget and Cook had gone to great pains for this dinner. The table was set as if for the most respected company. Rosalyn hated disappointing them.

"I don't think so," she said slowly and braced herself for the questions that would be asked and for which she had no answers.

But Covey surprised her. "Ah, well, sometimes men have to work out their frustrations in their own ways. Let us enjoy the meal."

Bridget served, and then Covey excused her so that she and Rosalyn could be alone. Rosalyn was thankful her dear companion had taken charge. Personally, she had little appetite.

"I don't understand it," she said finally, setting aside her fork and giving up all pretense of eating.

"He wanted the Commons seat," Covey answered.

Yes, Rosalyn knew that. He'd married her for it . . . and right now, with her heart involved, the knowledge that it had meant more to him than herself hurt in ways she could never have imagined.

Covey leaned across to her and covered Rosalyn's hand with her own. "Don't think it."

"Think what?" Rosalyn challenged.

"You are wondering what you mean to him. You are equating his behavior now to his feelings for you."

She was right. "How did you know?"

Her companion smiled sympathetically. "You are in love with him. I could tell the moment I saw the two of you together this afternoon."

"More the fool I," Rosalyn confessed.

"Why? Because he's feeling sorry for himself in the other room?"

"Because he doesn't love me," Rosalyn answered. There, she'd said it. "It's the story of my father and my mother all over again. Covey, I told myself I would never let such a thing happen, and here I have gone off and fallen in love with a man who married me for political gain. And now he isn't going to get what he wants. . . ." She put her elbow on the table and pressed her fist to her lips, struggling to not break down.

"My dear, he's disappointed—and, yes, in a bit of a pout—but I don't believe he blames you," Covey said stoutly.

"Who else is there to blame?"

"Himself." Her friend leaned forward. "The colonel is a fair man. He made his own choices."

"You and your 'choices,'" Rosalyn said in frustration. She shook her head. "He doesn't love me," she repeated, the words still having the power to hurt.

"Then make him love you." Covey pushed back her chair with an exasperated sound. "You don't try, Rosalyn. You've never tried."

"Tried what?"

"Tried to make yourself loveable. It's as if you can't trust anyone. You assume the only reason any of us near you is for our own gain. You think I'm here because I have nowhere else to go.

You organize routs and parties because it gives you power and from power comes respect and need. You've never once entertained the idea that we enjoyed your company, that *you* mattered to us."

That was true. Covey was the only person Rosalyn trusted, and only after she'd secretly tested the depths of that friendship.

"The irony, of course," Covey continued, "is that now that I am a member of the tight sphere of your friends, I was so valuable you would have sacrificed yourself to marriage for me. Rosalyn, please, you must not always be so afraid. I haven't let you down, others won't either."

"But Colin isn't you," Rosalyn protested.

"No, and he could leave. My dear, he didn't *have* to marry you—"

"He wanted the seat—"

"He tossed it aside for a fox!" Covey shook her head. "Rosalyn, Rosalyn, Rosalyn. Please, don't be so hard. Be forgiving. None of us is perfect. Let your husband have his 'pity' time . . . but don't be so stiff and unyielding that he can't turn to you."

"I'm not that hard," Rosalyn said, hurt and a bit embarrassed over Covey's characterization.

"You are hard," Covey answered without sentiment. "I know about the letters your mother has sent. You've never answered one, and I imagine she has begged you for some small word of forgiveness or understanding."

"You know she has written me?" Rosalyn thought this her secret alone.

"Who do you think gave her your address?"

"You?"

"Yes." Covey folded her hands on the table.

"She abandoned me," Rosalyn said, her temper rising.

"She made a mistake—a grave one—but she is trying to make amends."

*"She can't!"*

Covey didn't flinch in the face of Rosalyn's flat rejection. "No, she can't," she agreed. "Not unless you are willing to unbend."

"My pride is all I have," Rosalyn reiterated.

"Your pride is leading you around by the nose," Covey corrected.

If her friend had slapped her in the face, Rosalyn would not have been more surprised—until the truth of Covey's words sank in.

The older woman must have sensed she was making progress. She leaned forward again and took Rosalyn's hand. "You spend too much time trying to please the wrong people. My dear, there is so much to life, but not if you hide behind hurt feelings. I don't ask you to write your mother. That is between the two of you. But that man in the other room is your one chance for a happiness greater than any you have known."

Tears filled Rosalyn's eyes. She looked away. "What if he never loves me?"

"How can he *not* love you? See? It's a matter of changing the perspective. And there is something between you. I could sense it from the moment you met. Go to him, Rosalyn. Make him share his feelings. Men sometimes have to be coaxed a bit."

"I don't know if I can do that," Rosalyn said, the words tight in her throat.

"Yes, you can," Covey said firmly. "Rosalyn, you are a woman now. You weren't away for nearly a week in Scotland looking at the sights. You could already be carrying his child in your womb. There is so much that awaits the two of you, but first you must conquer your doubts."

"I don't even know what to say to him. I tried. He wasn't in the mood to talk."

"Then try again."

Rosalyn looked into her friend's face and wondered how she could make something so hard sound so simple. "Where do I begin?"

"You begin by being a wife. You can fix a plate of dinner for him and take it to him. If he's drinking Alfred's whiskey, he is going to need something in his stomach."

"You knew about the whiskey?"

"In the liquor cabinet? Yes. Alfred always had a wee dram before dinner."

"But you didn't offer any to Lord Loftus."

"Of course not," Covey said dismissively. "He isn't worthy of Alfred's Single Malt. I've always feared it would go to waste, but now that we have the colonel under our roof, it won't."

"Especially if he drinks it all tonight," Rosalyn said more to herself than Covey. She pushed away from the table. "You're right," she said decisively. "You are right about everything." She stood, took the plate from Colin's place at the table, and started heaping food on it. "I will go to him. He should talk to me, even to say he is angry he married me and now he won't have the Commons seat."

"He won't say that," Covey predicted.

Rosalyn stuck the serving spoon back in the peas. "He might, Covey. We don't know each other well. He is ambitious."

"As you are yourself."

"You keep telling me that."

"That's true."

Rosalyn looked down at the plate of food she held. "I'm afraid," she stated.

"Be bold," Covey advised her. "Your marriage depends on it."

For a second, Rosalyn hesitated. It would be easier to blame Colin for everything and shut him out of her life. But then she thought of what Covey had said. She could be pregnant . . . and were aloof, distant parents what she wanted for her child?

She picked up a candle and started for the door.

"I'll see the table is cleared," Covey called. "Don't worry about anything this evening. Think only of your husband."

Rosalyn gave her a nervous smile and left the room.

The hallway was dark. She knew her way, gracefully skirting the chair by the stairs. The door to the sitting room was still closed. She set the candle down on the side table, next to his hat, and opened the door.

Colin was sitting where she'd left him before dinner, his legs stretched out and the heel of one boot propped on the toe of his other. He'd not bothered to light a candle, nor did he turn to greet her.

She lifted the candle, juggling it with the plate of food as she entered the room. The whiskey bottle was now halfway empty.

Striving for a light tone, she said, "Are you going to save some of that for me, or down it all yourself?"

He looked up at her then, his expression lazy. "Damn me, but my wife surprises me again. I'd not known you had a taste for hard spirits."

"I'm developing many new tastes of late," she said. "Here is your supper."

"I'm not hungry."

"That may be true," she said with the patience one saved for a child, "but Cook went to a great effort on your behalf and you owe it to her to take a bite or two."

As she anticipated, appealing to his sense of honor worked. He took the plate and set it in his lap. He made no move to pick up the fork, because that would mean he'd have to put his whiskey glass on the side table. He acted as if it were permanently attached to his hand.

Rosalyn started lighting candles on either side

of the hearth. She usually didn't light these unless they had company.

"What are you doing?" he demanded, his voice husky from drink.

"Being a wife." She went over to the door and shut it before returning to him. "Eat."

His eyes glittered, and a muscle tightened in his jaw. She was certain few people ordered him around. Well, that was one of the things a wife did, she reminded herself, and she sat on the edge of the footstool, forcing him to move his feet.

"Here, let me help you remove your boots," she offered.

For a moment, he looked as if he'd like to wish her to the devil. She returned his stare with a level one of her own.

A corner of his mouth turned up reluctantly. "All right, *wife*." Holding the plate with one hand, his drink with the other, he unceremoniously put his right foot in her lap.

Rosalyn looked down at the scuffed boot with mud on its heel and bit back a sharp retort. Instead, she took firm hold and pulled it off. She reached for his other boot and did the same, setting both boots aside.

"Go on, eat your dinner," she ordered softly and began massaging his feet.

Of course he didn't do as she asked. Instead, he watched her under veiled eyes—and she was struck by a memory of once seeing her parents sit together just like this.

"What is it?" he asked, always attuned to the nuances of her thinking.

"I had recalled something I'd forgotten," she said, kneading the ball of his foot with more purpose. "My mother used to massage my father's feet. It was a ritual of theirs. I'd forgotten."

Or had she deliberately put it out of her mind? An attempt to erase all the good memories along with the bad?

Covey's accusation of shutting people out returned twofold.

He set down his glass and lifted the fork. He took a bite of his dinner. Leaving his feet in her lap, she reached for the whiskey and took a sip. The smoky burn of the liquor tasted good. It gave her courage. "Alfred had good taste. He was Covey's husband, and she said he always had a nip at night."

"I'm glad she wouldn't share it with Loftus."

Rosalyn nodded and took another sip. He moved his plate to the table and held his hand out for the glass. She gave it to him, and as their fingers brushed, she felt the same strong simmer of desire that always seemed to be between them.

For a long moment, they sat in silence, he staring at the fireplace, she out the window.

And then he said, "Did you ever want something so much you would have sold your soul for it?" He shifted his gaze to meet hers. "You knew you deserved it. It should be yours . . . and yet, it kept eluding you?"

She swallowed, afraid of the topic and yet knowing it had to be discussed. "Are you talking about the Commons seat?"

He sat up, bringing his feet to the floor, his expression more serious than she'd ever seen him. "I'm talking about a knighthood." He rolled the glass between his hands. "It sounds silly, doesn't it? Colin Mandland, son of the local cobbler, dreams of being knighted. When I was younger, I used to want to be a knight like the days of old. A jousting knight. I'd pretend to have a horse, and I'd harass Matt to joust me until he'd get irritated and wrestle me to the ground. That was before I grew bigger than he was."

"You saw him this afternoon."

"Yes." He polished off the whiskey in the glass and set it on the floor. "He's not happy with me."

There was pain, and confusion, in his words. "It is the banns? Does he believe we should have a church wedding? We can." *Anything so that Colin would not be sorry he married her.*

"It's not the elopement. It's something else . . . something more personal."

"Like what?" she had to ask.

His gaze met hers. He smiled. "You are relentless."

"I'm a wife," she said, the words sounding good.

"A wife," he repeated, reaching out to brush the pad of his thumb over her cheek. "A lovely wife."

Rosalyn turned her head and kissed his hand. "What bothers you?" she asked. "I know now it is not Lord Loftus."

"That blustering fool?" Colin snorted an opinion. He rose to his feet and took a slightly unsteady step away from her. The hardest part was waiting for him to speak. Just when she feared he was not going to confide in her, he said, "Matt accused me of ignoring our parents. He believes I look down on him for what he has chosen to do with his life." There was a pause.

"It's true. All of it. I did ignore my parents when they were alive. Well, not ignore—worse. I took them for granted."

Rosalyn thought of her cousins and the many households she had lived in. "How you behaved is not uncommon. Many children assume their parents will always be there."

He stabbed his fingers through his hair. "But I wasn't a child, Rosalyn. I was a man full grown. I found out this afternoon from Matt that Mother and Father had known those times I'd been in London during the war. They had hoped I would come see them. I didn't make the time because I was involved in military politics."

"And trying to earn a knighthood."

"Yes," he agreed, "one that was denied me." He came back around to sit in the chair, leaning forward as if needing to talk to *her*, to make *her* understand. "You see, I always believed I was destined for greater things. I was always over-reaching myself—such as my desire to win Belinda Lovejoyce. I wanted the best, Rosalyn. Nothing less would do. My parents were like millstones around my neck. They were humble and kind and far from what I wanted to be."

Rosalyn didn't say anything. She was afraid.

Colin continued. "My father could have been

anything he wanted to be. He had a fine mind, much like Matt's. But he met a milkmaid named Mary and chose to be a cobbler in Clitheroe instead. He wanted to stay close to her and hers. So his mentor became ours. I've mentioned Father Ruley?"

She shook her head.

"He was the headmaster at Stoneyhurst. He'd been Father's patron, too. He used to tell Matt and me how disappointed he was in what Father had thrown aside for love."

"Is he the one who urged you to go in the military?"

"He found me a sponsor," Colin said, remembering. "Matt was the smart one and Father Ruley chose the Church for him, which made sense. Matt always had a serious frame of mind. I was relegated to the military, and I've done well to rise through the ranks."

"Why was he so interested in your family?" Rosalyn asked.

"All men like power," he said. "I think Father Ruley would have liked to be a bishop. Instead, he was sent to Northern England, and it had to be a disappointment for such an ambitious man. So, he transferred his ambition to students he thought worthy. Matt and I weren't the only boys he pushed. He sponsored several."

"Where is he now?"

"He died. You know, after I left Lancashire, I never came back, but I did write him once. I thanked him for all he'd done."

"Did he write back?"

"Yes, to complain about Matt and his lack of ambition. Father Ruley blamed Val. He was a priest," Colin said with a small smile. "They are all somewhat suspicious of women."

"Your brother seems very happy."

"He is . . . with everyone but me."

Rosalyn leaned forward. "What did he say this afternoon, Colin?"

"Nothing that wasn't true. Funny how a man whom I have dismissed most of my life because he *is* my brother and *is* always supposed to be there whether he wishes to or not, can turn out to be the one person who knows me well enough to make me see the truth. I have been a fool, Rosalyn. I've wasted my life . . . and I don't know what to do about it."

She took her husband's hands. "Colin, it is not bad to have people in our lives who see our faults clearly and care for us anyway."

"I don't know if he does care or not," he answered. "I discovered too late the one person I should have been impressing knows me too well."

There was true pain in his words. Pain that made Rosalyn's heart ache in response. Especially when he added, "It's too late to make amends with my parents, Rosalyn. I should have been here. I was too wrapped up in my own greed to think of anyone but myself. Now I have nothing, and it is exactly what I deserve."

*You have me.*

She didn't say the words, though. She was afraid to. Instead, she did what she was beginning to do every time words failed her. She kissed him.

# Chapter Fifteen

*R*osalyn's kiss was the blessing Colin needed. It soothed him as no balm could.

Dear God, he wanted to believe he wasn't as selfish as he'd acted. He wanted someone to make the pain of self-realization go away—and was there any better way to find comfort than in her body?

He didn't know until their lips met just exactly how much he had counted on her understanding, how he'd needed it. Her kiss tasted of smoky whiskey and acceptance.

Wonderful, freeing acceptance.

Colin cupped her face with his hands and took the kiss deeper. He drank her as a thirsty man drinks water. She didn't shy away. For the first time, he recognized the deeper meaning behind these moments between a man and a woman.

He slid his hands down to her shoulders, his fingers moving to unlace her dress. His need for her was building. He was hungry and anxious to relieve the pain. He wanted to matter to someone, to prove he wasn't a wastrel.

And here was Rosalyn, offering herself.

Matt was right. Colin was a selfish bastard— because right now, he wanted the solace his wife offered. The whiskey had given him nothing. His memory was still too sharp, his sins too obvious. He had regrets his brother didn't even know. He'd watched men die, many of whom he'd killed with his own hands, in battle. He'd made hard choices, and what did he have to show for it?

Nothing.

But Rosalyn would help him forget, if even for a few hours. And, perhaps, he would regain his equilibrium, ignore his brother's charges, go on his way.

"We should go upstairs," she whispered.

No, he wanted her right here. "I'll not make it," he murmured, kissing her neck. He licked a line up to her ear. "You taste like honey."

She practically melted against him, and Colin

knew she was his. He could do anything with her. Anything.

He lowered her to the floor. He knew her secret places. He knew what she liked, where she needed to be touched and exactly how. He'd taught her those things. *See, Matt?* He wasn't entirely a self-centered bore. He made his wife happy. He slid his fingers up her thigh beneath her petticoats and touched her intimately.

She broke off the kiss and glanced at the closed door. "We mustn't. What if someone walks in?"

"They won't," he promised and took a moment to blow out the candle. "They'll think we've gone to bed." No moonlight came through the window, and Colin found he liked it this way.

He lifted her skirts as he nuzzled her loosened neckline down. Finding her breast, he sucked, and she caught her breath.

Deeper, she was already hot and wet to his touch, and he could wait no longer. Not even bothering to pull down his breeches, he unbuttoned and freed himself. Rolling on his back, he brought his beautiful wife to sit on him.

They'd not done this. Her gasp of surprise and then pleasure added to his own enjoyment. He lifted his hips, thrusting deeper.

Her bodice was around her waist. He placed his hands on her hips and he showed her what to do, what they both wanted her to do.

What pins were left in Rosalyn's hair fell on the floor around them. She tilted back her head, her neck a pale line in the darkness, and she sighed her enjoyment.

Colin thrust up, the weight of her body taking him deeper than he had ever been before. "Ride me," he ordered. *Make me forget.*

Rosalyn understood. She began moving, slow at first, but with building momentum. She leaned forward, her hands on his chest. He pushed deeper, reaching up to capture her glorious curls in his fist.

They made love with an abandon he'd never known before. She gave her all to him. She held nothing back. Her release was quick and powerful.

Her body tightened around his. She cried out his name, the sound triumphant.

This woman was magic.

Colin rolled her onto her back. She followed him easily, her arms round his neck, her face buried in his shoulder. Her teeth rubbed his skin over his scar, as if to mark it. He thrust once, twice, a third time, going to the very center of her before finding his own release. He claimed her with all he had. She was his . . . and the outside world ceased to exist.

In this moment, buried to the hilt inside her, Rosalyn was his universe.

They lay on the floor, so exhausted they couldn't move for what seemed forever. Their lovemaking had been hard, and Rosalyn had barely recognized herself as the pagan woman who had demanded everything she'd wanted from her lover.

In the aftermath, the weight of his body felt good. The taste of his skin was on her lips, and all should be right, except it wasn't.

He moved off her, and she was aware that she was fully dressed. She even had her shoes on.

Colin sat up. She heard him buttoning his breeches in the darkness. He leaned close. "Are you all right?"

She heard the embarrassment in his voice. Was it because they had been so uninhibited? Only now did she realize she'd not been as quiet as would have been prudent.

"I'm fine," she said and didn't add that she'd been completely surprised by herself. The habit of feeling guilty was hard to break—and yet she also enjoyed this newly discovered freedom.

He raised her hand to his lips and pressed his mouth in the palm a second before placing a kiss there. "I did hurt you. I should have held back—"

She silenced him with a kiss. "No, I don't ever want you to hold back. In fact, I'm thinking of asking you to make love to me on every floor of this house."

His teeth flashed white in the dark. He ran a finger up the bare skin of her arm. "We could start tonight, or we could find our bedroom, which I've yet to see."

*Our bedroom.* "Help me up," she said.

He came to his feet, pulling her up at the same time. She slipped her arms into her dress but didn't bother with the lacing. All was dark outside the doorway. Bridget and Cook had gone to bed, as had Covey.

She took his hand and led him up the stairs to her room. The moon was rising, providing light that came through the familiar windows of her personal haven.

Suddenly, Rosalyn wavered.

He stood behind her. "Are you afraid demons will follow you?" he asked, reminding her of the story his mother had told. He didn't wait for her answer but lifted her in his arms and carried her over the threshold.

Her room was of a good size, but his presence took up every inch. He carried her to the bed, laid her down, and then stretched down beside her, both of them fully clothed.

For long moments, he did nothing but hold her, and slowly she relaxed, accepting him here, too. Her love grew even deeper as she realized how completely he seemed to understand her. And wasn't that what she'd always longed for—someone who cared enough to notice her needs?

"How is it you sometimes know me better than I know myself?" she whispered.

He drew her closer. "Rosalyn, every thought you have is expressed in your eyes. I wish everyone was as honest."

She sat up and looked down at him, her hand on his chest. "Colin, why did you want the Commons seat? Why is a knighthood so important? Is it for the prestige? After all, you are the owner of Maiden Hill. In the Ribble valley, that carries a great deal of weight. Is London so important?"

"I don't know, Rosalyn. Sometimes, I don't know myself. I've always wanted to go as far as I could . . . and yet, Matt's words, and now your question, make me wonder why." He shook his head. "I don't know the answers."

"So you just wanted to be Sir Colin."

He laughed at that. "Sounds ridiculous, doesn't it?"

"Not really. I think it is a fine name."

Colin rose from the bed and began undressing. She did the same. They didn't bother with night-clothes. The rules that had guided them in the inn now applied here. Nakedness was good between a man and a woman, she decided. Nothing could be hidden.

Climbing back into bed beside him, she caught herself wondering if her parents had ever been this honest between themselves. She remembered her mother having a room separate from her father's. Did her mother now, after all these years, share the same room with the riding instructor?

Colin snuggled her close, his legs intertwined with hers. "What are you thinking?"

She didn't want to confess her thoughts had veered toward her mother. He was too astute and she, too vulnerable.

Instead, she turned the subject back to him. "You and your brother will find common ground," she promised.

"No, we'll go on as we have before, both of us slightly disapproving of each other."

"But you don't want it to be that way."

His lips brushed her hair. "You of all people should know that sometimes there are chasms between people that can't be crossed."

She knew he referred to her mother. He'd known she was on her mind. He'd known.

Did he know she'd fallen in love?

Rosalyn picked up his hand and studied it in the dark, tracing the lines and shape with her fingers. "I used to play a game where I would pretend I had what I wanted. So, let's pretend you are Sir Colin."

"And you are Lady Rosalyn?"

She laughed. "No, I'm Lady Mandland." The name sounded full and good.

He must have agreed, because he repeated it. "Lady Mandland." He gave her a kiss.

"So, Sir Colin, what are you going to do now that you are a member of the House of Commons?"

Colin didn't miss a beat. "My first act would be to propose we abolish the House of Lords."

Rosalyn turned to him, shocked. "You can't be serious."

"I can. There is a growing democratic sentiment in the world. Power in the hands of a few is no longer acceptable. Look at this Commons seat. There should be a vote, but there isn't. Loftus decides because his ancestors settled here centuries ago and intimidated everyone. Even if he were to authorize a vote, it would go his way. He's the major landowner. We are all such sheep, but the world beyond the Valley, beyond England, is changing. The war is done and now it's time for men of ideas to step forward."

"Yes, but, Colin, there are men of ideas in the House of Lords."

"True, but I'd wager there is a larger share of idiots."

His verdict was an affront to everything Rosalyn had been taught. "My cousin George is a member of the House of Lords."

"Ummmhmmmm."

"Very well, so he isn't the best example. But there are good men there, men whose families have been governing England for generations."

"Men whose brains have been addled by marrying in the same circles. Sometimes I think the

French had it right. Power in the hands of a few leads to tyranny."

Rosalyn almost fell off the bed. "You would support a revolution like in France?" she demanded incredulously.

"No, but I believe I have a right to my say as a free man."

"That's what the House of Commons is about," she said with relief.

"Not if there is no vote for the seats," he answered. "Too many peers like Loftus own the seats. Trust me, if any man could run for the Commons, laws like the Corn Laws would not have passed."

Rosalyn didn't understand. "The Corn Laws are good. Otherwise, cheap grain from France would undermine our farmers."

"No, cheaper grain means cheaper prices for bread and less money for landowners like Loftus. So now we have expensive grain and expensive bread. Rosalyn, there are people angry to be used in this manner." He sat up now, crossing his legs and speaking earnestly. "Listen, there are those who believe the expectations of the Commons carry more weight than the House of Lords."

"But everything is fine the way it is," she whispered.

"Is it? Do you realize how little wages people earn working at a loom all day, while Loftus gallops over the countryside chasing a fox? And if a man speaks up, he says what is true and right, if he demands his government listens, then he can be thrown into jail or transported."

Rosalyn didn't want to give credibility to what he was saying. "Those people are radicals. You aren't radical . . . are you?"

"I'm not." He pushed a hand through his hair. "Or I didn't think I was. Matt is making me realize how far I'd strayed from my own beliefs." He stopped, as if struck by a new thought. Then he reached out, took Rosalyn by both arms, and kissed her hard on the mouth.

"Why did you do that?"

"Because I had almost forgotten," he said. "You and Matt are making me think. I *had* lost sight."

"Lost sight of what?" she demanded with growing alarm.

"With why Father Ruley had singled us out. He singled us out, tutored us privately because he had a vision of how the world should be. He wanted us to be men of importance."

"I don't understand."

"No, you wouldn't," Colin agreed. "Because you were a part of that old order. You were never expected to question. But I'd forgotten one of Father Ruley's maxims—Change is good. It's necessary. It defies evil."

"I don't want you to *change* anything."

He kissed her again, laughing. "I know. And I also know how frightening what I'm saying is for you. Ah, Rosalyn, rest easy. In the end it doesn't matter. I wasn't offered a peerage or knighted in the army, but I did fight the good fight. I stood up for my men and I didn't let anyone run roughshod over them."

She placed her hand on the side of his face, feeling the growth of his whiskers beneath her palm. "Colin, you are frightening me. I don't understand what you are saying."

He drew her close, his presence comforting. "It's fine, Rosalyn. Everything is fine."

"Are you going to have radical meetings at Maiden Hill?" she asked, fearful that he would say yes.

"I'm going to stand up for what I believe," he answered. "As every good Englishman should." He shook his head. "I can't believe I spent so much money on that silly phaeton. Oscar looks ridiculous pulling it, but a rig like that was all the rage. I just couldn't bring myself to sell Oscar."

Colin kissed her neck and pulled her close. "Don't worry. I turned out not to be the man I should be." There was a heaviness in his voice. "I failed."

Her body spooned to his, she said, "But you were a good officer."

"I was. My conscience is clear of that. But I wasn't a good son, and I am not a good brother. I am going to be a better man, Rosalyn. I vow I will be."

"I think you are a wonderful man." His talk about change was frightening, and yet, when he held her like this, she felt safe.

He rubbed his nose in her curls. "Violets?" he whispered. "Or is it lilies?"

"Is what?" she wondered.

"The scent in your hair." He cuddled her closer. She could feel his arousal. "What would I do without you?" he asked. "You make it easy for me to start anew. And I will find my way again. I will."

His weren't whispered words of love . . . but they were enough. He needed her. Was that not a start?

She thought of what Covey had warned her of over dinner. Her husband's hands cupped her breasts. He entered her from behind. His breath was hot against her ear as he teased her into responding. Colin knew how to slip past her defenses. He had been the only person who had cared enough to do so.

And she would do anything for him. Anything. She loved him so much that his dreams had become hers.

Amazingly, this time was more satisfying than the last. She wondered if he felt the same, but she lacked the courage to ask him.

Her husband gathered her in his arms and fell asleep, but Rosalyn lay awake.

What he'd said tonight challenged beliefs so deep-seated she hadn't even realized they were there. The idea that every man, regardless of whether he owned land or not, should vote was beyond her imagination. She knew what George would have to say!

But the more she mulled over the idea, the more it made sense. She wouldn't mind laws being made by men like Colin or his brother. George and his ilk couldn't care less.

And she remembered all too well the shock of learning that George had sold Maiden Hill out from under her. In that moment, she'd wanted to be a man, to have rank and privilege—and she began to understand Colin's ambition.

A woman had no expectation of anything. But what must it be like to be a man and be powerless?

In that moment, Rosalyn identified with those who needed a voice most. She thought of other concerns that had bothered her over the years, like the fact that she was not allowed to inherit anything out of her father's estate, especially since her mother was alive, while an oaf like George received it all.

But there were other things that bothered her, matters she'd seen in London, such as the chimney sweep who'd been no older than six and had burned to death because his master had forced him into a chute that had not quite cooled. Or the women who begged on the streets because they didn't have money for food and there wasn't enough charity to go around.

George often said there were those who had and those who wished they had. He'd been pleased to be part of the former group. Rosalyn wondered if he would be so self-satisfied if he were in the latter?

Indignation filled her soul, coupled with a growing sense of responsibility—Colin *could* fight for those people. Had he not changed her life? Forget the title. He *was* like the knight of his childhood games. He could lead the battle for justice . . . if he had a seat in the Commons.

Staring up at the ceiling, Rosalyn set her agile mind to work. There had to be a way to reclaim the seat. She'd learned how to get most people to do her bidding. Aunt Agatha had been difficult, but those outside the family were fairly pliable if one knew what influence to use.

It didn't take long for her to realize there was only one person with enough control over Lord Loftus to make him change his mind—Lady Loftus.

She rolled over, shaking his arm to wake him. "Colin," she said softly.

He mumbled her name and tried to turn over. In the short time they had been married, she'd learned he liked his sleep.

"Colin, I think I have an idea of how you can gain the Commons seat."

"Thasss good," he sighed and patted her shoulder.

Rosalyn didn't bother him anymore. It was

enough that he knew she was taking up his cause. And she would succeed. She had no choice. Maybe once he saw her faith in him, he'd realize she loved him and he'd love her in return.

When she finally fell asleep, she dreamed of babies. Beautiful, bubbly babies who looked just like Colin and herself.

She woke late the next morning full of energy, her hopes high.

Colin was already up and had had his breakfast. He was being given a tour of the property by John.

Covey said slyly, "It appears today the two of you are doing well."

Rosalyn felt her cheeks burn with hot color, but she didn't deny it. "We are doing *very* well." She pulled on her gloves. "Covey, I need for you to give a message to my husband. Tell him I've gone to pay a call on Lady Loftus, and one which I hope will bring us good news."

"What sort of news?"

"He'll find out when I return," Rosalyn said happily and slipped out the door before another question could be asked.

She harnessed the pony cart herself and started

down the drive. She'd not gone far when she felt someone watching her. She turned and saw the fox sitting in the shade of her garden, a big grin on his face.

She smiled back.

# Chapter Sixteen

"*Y*ou've arranged *what*?" Colin asked,
stunned by Rosalyn's news. He'd met
her in the hallway just as she'd returned.

He was excited about prospects for the farm-
land. Rosalyn had always known Maiden Hill
could be a profitable estate, but from the ideas
Colin tossed out, she also learned that money
was not a problem for him, something that had
been a question to her nearly a week ago and
meant nothing now.

She was too full of her own news. "I've
arranged for you to have another chance to earn
the Commons seat," she repeated patiently.

"How did you do that?" her husband demanded. "When did you see Loftus?"

"I didn't see *him*," Rosalyn said. "Well, not at

first. I called on his wife and explained her husband was about to break his word to my husband. It's a matter of honor, Colin. I assure you, we women have just as much honor as men."

He took her arm and led her into the sitting room. "Rosalyn, what have you done?"

He didn't sound very happy. She drew a deep breath and, taking a moment to remove her straw bonnet and gloves, said, "I discussed the matter of the Commons seat with my *friend* Lady Loftus, and we both agreed his lordship was being high-handed."

"She thinks her husband is high-handed?"

"Well, that isn't exactly the way she phrased it, but she does want to please me. You must understand, Colin, I have a certain amount of power, too."

"Rosalyn, why did you do this?" He wasn't pleased. In fact, he acted irritated.

She sat on the edge of the settee, trying to look composed. "I spoke on your behalf," she said, wanting to correct any misimpression he might have. "I didn't beg. I didn't whine."

He frowned. "What did you do . . . on my behalf?"

"Nothing terrible," she answered. "Really, Colin, you don't seem happy at all."

"I don't know if I should be. Rosalyn, I don't want you pleading my case. Loftus won't respect me."

"He doesn't respect anyone. Besides, it isn't quite what you think. You don't have the seat. At least, not yet."

Colin pulled the upholstered chair around to sit in. He leaned forward, a sign he was interested. "Tell me exactly what you've done."

"As I said, I explained to Lady Loftus what happened yesterday. I left out the story of the fox. She knows her husband well and can imagine him losing his temper for a hundred different reasons, and I didn't think she would be sympathetic to a tale about the animal."

He motioned that he wished her to move on with her story. "You told her he refused me the seat?"

"I told her he was going to give it to Mr. Shellsworth. Colin, Lady Loftus cannot abide Lavonia Shellsworth. She is not quite—what is it Lady Loftus says all the time? Polished. Lavonia lacks polish. We both agreed she would not be a good choice for the role of an MP's wife. In fact, the reason Lord Loftus has not given the seat to Mr. Shellsworth before now is that Lady Loftus would disapprove."

Colin frowned with interest. "This is fascinating. All my life I thought men held the power."

"We women have had to create our power. You see, I've always known how Lady Loftus felt about Lavonia. That knowledge gave me great power. Anyway, today, I commiserated with her over how *boring* London will be with Lavonia there. Lord Loftus doesn't go to London any more than he must, but there are times he can't escape, and his wife, who preferred London until I made her the queen of society in the Valley, panicked at the thought of introducing Lavonia amongst her set. She would have to invite the Shellsworths upon occasion, something she only does here because I force her to."

"So she persuaded her husband to reconsider me?"

"Not quite," Rosalyn was sorry to say. "He's very angry, Colin. He wanted that fox."

"He has no right to him."

"Exactly," Rosalyn agreed, falling a little bit more in love with him. Was there ever a man so principled? "But for some reason, he didn't explain the situation to his wife. Instead, he made a terrible error in judgment."

"Which was?" Colin said, his elbow on his

knee and his chin resting in his hand, like a child fascinated by a bedtime tale.

"Right there in front of me, he told his wife he did as he pleased."

"Why was that so terrible?"

Rosalyn almost felt sorry for him. "Colin, a wise man never verbalizes such a thing in public. Without realizing it, he challenged her to prove him wrong, especially since he said those words in front of me, another social hostess. A wife's authority comes from her husband, and if she has no influence over him, she has no authority."

"Like being one of a general's aides?" he suggested. "One is only as important as his officer?"

Rosalyn laughed. "I don't know. Do they feel incumbent upon themselves to prove their sway?"

"All the time. It's imperative."

"Then it *is* the same. I hadn't planned on that turn of events, so he has no one to blame but himself." She ticked off on her fingers the abuses. "He contradicted his wife, refused to hear what she had to say, and walked out on her in front of a guest. Three things a sensible man shouldn't do."

"I shall remember that in the future," Colin murmured.

"I pray you do," she answered, pleased.

"So what happened next?" he asked.

"Lady Loftus followed him out of the room. I don't know where they went. I could hear angry words being exchanged." She leaned closer. "I heard threats about going to London mentioned numerous times."

"It's the reason he wanted me to marry you," Colin agreed. "If you left the Valley, his wife would drag him back to town, and he couldn't abide the thought."

"The next thing I know, she returns and announces that she has convinced her husband to reconsider both you and Mr. Shellsworth for the seat. It was the best I could do, Colin. Lord Loftus is being very stubborn. He claims there are many who already know he is putting Mr. Shellsworth in the Commons seat and there are those who think he is a bit brain-addled—his words, not mine—for not picking his man and staying with him."

"So what is he going to do?"

Now came the part that made her a bit nervous. She hoped he liked this next bit of news. She had her doubts. "Lady Loftus wondered how we could present the two of you in a way her husband could save face."

"And—?"

"And I suggested an oratory contest."

"A what?" Colin came to his feet. "What are Shellsworth and I to do? Stake a side in Loftus's dining room and bore him through dinner?"

"No, actually, I talked to the owner of the White Lion, and he said the contest could be held there." The White Lion was a public house located at the crossroads in the center of Clitheroe.

Colin slowly sat down. "Rosalyn, you have been busy."

"I fear so." Misgivings assailed her. "Colin, you aren't frightfully angry, are you? Once I made the suggestion, Lady Loftus said it was perfect, and after she told his lordship, he came out of hiding and agreed. In fact, he was enthused about the idea. He said there have been those encouraging him to be more republican."

"I'm not surprised." Colin leaned back in the chair and shook his head. "Go on. What else?"

How did he know? It was hard to look at him as she said this next bit. "Mr. Botherton, the owner of the White Lion, was overjoyed at the idea of having an oratory contest on his premises. The day should be nice tomorrow—"

"Tomorrow?" He seemed numb to her surprises by now.

She nodded. "Lady Loftus and I got caught up in the excitement of the thing, and his lordship did not want to string this all out."

Colin gave a heavy sigh. "Tomorrow," he agreed.

"In the afternoon, at half past two, or at least that is what the handbills say."

"Handbills?" he asked, incredulous. "You and Lady Loftus have been giving out handbills?"

"No, um, Mr. Botherton had his children draw them up. He's excited about the business. You know, he purchased the Lion last year, and people have taken their time warming up to him. He's a Manchester man."

"Well, if he is a Manchester man, then he would be keen on political speeches."

"He is," Rosalyn agreed, somewhat amazed that Colin would know this.

"So, tomorrow at half past two, I am to speak before a crowd of people—"

"Hopefully, and Lord Loftus, too, of course."

"Of course," he agreed patently, as if it was silly of him to forget his patron. "Anyway, Shellsworth and I will give speeches and Loftus will be our judge?"

"Yes, but Lady Loftus will be there too, and,

Colin, she likes you very much. Everyone likes you better than Mr. Shellsworth. Even, I suspect, Lord Loftus."

"So the words of the oration don't matter. What is important is how many people like us?"

"Well, yes," Rosalyn agreed, puzzled by his lack of enthusiasm. "I mean, isn't that the way of everything?"

He stared at her a moment and then, to her relief, smiled. "As a matter of fact, yes."

"But—?" she prompted. "Don't you want the seat?"

Colin drew a breath and released it slowly, his gaze on some point beyond Rosalyn. "I did. I *do*." He shook his head. "It all changes so fast. I thought of myself one way, discovered a frightening shallowness, and now, I'm being tempted again."

"I don't think you are shallow," she asserted. "Mr. Shellsworth is shallow. You are certainly more deserving of the seat."

"What I don't know if I deserve is your trust in me," he said slowly.

Rosalyn froze, afraid to move, not understanding what he was saying. Did he mean that he didn't want her to be involved in his life? Did she do something wrong and he was angry with her? She didn't have the courage to ask.

Instead, she said faintly, "Everyone will be at the White Lion on the morrow. I admit I may have become a bit too excited. I know how to do these things and now, Colin, this contest is all anyone in the Valley can talk about. It escalated before I realized I'd not truly discussed the matter with you."

Rosalyn had been so elated to have Lord Loftus reconsider his decision, and, with Lady Loftus's encouragement, she'd taken much on herself. Perhaps too much?

"Colin, I'm sorry. I didn't think. I wanted you to be happy."

He reached for her hand. "Rosalyn, being denied the seat was a bitter pill, but yesterday, I was more upset about the words my brother threw at me."

"So you didn't mind losing the seat?"

Colin looked down at her hand. "Or is it you are disappointed that I'll not have the seat?"

His question caught her by surprise. She hadn't been thinking about herself . . . or so she had thought. . . .

"Good God, it's Shellsworth," Colin said.

Rosalyn looked up and saw her husband staring out the window. Sure enough, the lawyer was galloping up their drive. He yanked his horse to a stop and leaped off it. John had seen him coming and was there to take the reins, which Mr. Shellsworth threw at him.

"You stay here," Colin ordered as he rose to go to the door. Rosalyn immediately came to her feet and followed him.

Mr. Shellsworth was just getting ready to pound on the door when Colin opened it. The expression on the lawyer's face at seeing Colin was almost comical.

"Have you come to pay a call?" Colin asked.

"I've come to wish you to the devil," Mr. Shellsworth ground out, his hat low on his head, as if he'd jerked it on.

"Well, if that is all," Colin said pleasantly, "then good day." He would have shut the door in the man's face except Mr. Shellsworth pushed his way in with astounding strength.

"How did you do it?" he asked. "That Commons seat was mine—*twice*! And each time, you are behind my losing it."

"You haven't lost it," Colin answered. "My understanding is that Loftus will make his decision after our speeches. You are a lawyer. Do you have such little faith in your own talent?"

If he'd threatened the man, his words could not have had more impact. Mr. Shellsworth's eyes almost popped out of his head. His chipmunk cheeks turned red. "I will *bury* you with my speech!" he promised. "What does an upstart like you know about governing? If you were really worth your salt, you would have been knighted, but then, they don't give titles to cobbler's sons, do they?"

Colin laughed. "Is this an insult? We all know what my father did. I was raised in this Valley, Shellsworth. Here, the name Mandland means something."

The implied insult was not lost on Mr. Shellsworth. He had to know he was not well liked. Why else would he be so upset about having to give a speech?

"We'll see, won't we?" the lawyer said tightly. "Your true colors will be found out then, Mandland. I've been asking questions. I've heard about some of your stances during the war, how you wanted to eat with your men the night before a battle and not in the officers' mess. There are those of good name and family who do not trust you. I know you were almost cashiered for countermanding the order of your superior!" he finished triumphantly, "cashiered" referring to an officer being dishonorably discharged.

"I rescinded an order from a fellow officer that would have led to the needless slaughter of a company of men," Colin returned evenly. "The duke himself stepped in on my behalf. I don't think you or Rawlins will go far on that piece of nonsense."

"Rawlins?" Mr. Shellsworth said, pretending to not know the name.

"Brice Rawlins, Varny's youngest son, and a lazier, stupider name never walked the earth," Colin answered. "You can tell him exactly what I said. And, if he ever attempts to smear my name again, he'll meet my steel."

Mr. Shellsworth backed out the door. His gaze darted to Colin's side as if looking to see if he was armed. Out on the step, he turned and walked toward his horse. Waiting until he was safely in the saddle, he addressed Colin, his face contorted in disgust. "You'll not win," he vowed. "Loftus has more sense than to choose you."

He slapped the animal, urging it to go as quickly as he'd arrived.

Rosalyn stepped out on the step by Colin's

side. She was deeply disturbed by the venom in the man's nature.

"Don't worry, he's gone," Colin said, putting his arm around her waist.

However, a quarter of the way down the drive, Mr. Shellsworth jerked his horse to a stop. He looked over at the woods bordering the drive. Rosalyn followed the direction of his gaze and saw the fox, watching.

Colin saw the animal, too.

However, neither of them anticipated Mr. Shellsworth's next action. He reached inside his coat and then straightened his arm in the direction of the fox. Too late she realized he held a gun in his hand. A shot rang out.

Mr. Shellsworth swung his horse around to face them, the triumph in his eyes frightening. He put heels to horse and rode off.

Colin was already running to where the fox had been. Rosalyn picked up her skirts and went after him. John followed. Of course, Colin reached the animal first. The fox was not where they thought he would be.

Rosalyn dared to hope he had escaped unharmed, until she saw the blood on the ground.

Her husband went down on one knee and climbed into the underbrush. Rosalyn caught sight of the animal. The fox watched him with wary eyes, and there was no mistaking the blood staining his red coat.

"Easy," Colin whispered.

The fox seemed to understand. He laid his head down on the damp ground and let Colin gently probe the wound. "I don't think he is badly hurt," he said. "That pistol of Shellsworth's is more a toy than a gun."

Rosalyn knelt beside him. "What are we going to do with him, though? Look at the way it bleeds."

Colin removed his jacket. "We'll take him in the house and put him by Cook's hearth in the kitchen. He'll get better."

"You'll take him into the house?" repeated John, who had come up behind them. "A wild creature like a fox?"

"Yes," Colin answered decisively. "We'll take him in and nurse him to health." He gathered the fox in his arms and stood. To his credit, the animal understood Colin meant no harm. He trusted Colin enough to let himself be carried.

Cook was not overly pleased about having a fox in her kitchen. To her way of thinking, foxes were little better than vermin, but she was not about to gainsay Colin.

Rosalyn found a basket and put some rags in it for a bed. John brought to the kitchen a salve he used on the cart horse's cuts. Together, they made the fox feel welcome.

"Mr. Shellsworth had no business firing a gun this close to the house," Cook said. She looked right in Colin's eyes and added, "I hope you talk the breeches off the man tomorrow. We'll all be there to cheer you on."

"Thank you, Cook," Colin answered. "I plan on destroying him."

He turned on his heel and walked out of the kitchen, leaving a fearful Rosalyn behind. She was afraid of what might happen on the morrow . . . and knew whatever it was would be all her fault.

# Chapter Seventeen

$C$olin had seen destruction in his life. He'd witnessed whole villages being razed in India, watched men beside him blown to pieces in Portugal, seen the senselessness of war. But nothing had ever made him as angry as Shellsworth shooting the fox.

And he didn't know why, except, perhaps, coming on the heels of his brother's words, it crystallized just how insane his world had become. Nothing was as it should have been.

It never would be. He seemed destined to never amount to anything, but he was too ambitious to give up. And he didn't want to be bested by a bastard like Shellsworth.

Colin looked down at the blank paper on the desk in front of him. Matt's charges against him echoed in his ears, except he had his own questions.

Was it senseless ambition to know he was a better man and wanted his due? Why must he accept his class status? Matt had, whether he realized it or not. He'd turned his back on ambition and felt Colin should too, and every fiber in Colin's being rebelled at the idea.

He'd beat Shellsworth at his own game. He knew what Loftus wanted to hear, and he'd give it to him.

Colin picked up the pen and started writing. He was so involved that Rosalyn must have been standing at the door for some time before he registered her presence.

"Yes?" he asked.

She didn't step in the room but lingered in the hall. "The fox is going to be all right."

"Good." He frowned at the phrase he had just written and crossed it out.

"Colin, I'm sorry."

He was impatient with the interruption, but he took a moment to focus his attention on her. That's when he noticed how pale she was. "Sorry? Rosalyn, this isn't your fault."

"I'm the one who talked Lord Loftus into the oratory contest."

Colin shook his head. "No, you gave me another opportunity to do Shellsworth in, and I shall."

"I thought you were angry with me earlier."

He set aside his pen and spoke the truth. "Rosalyn, I don't know what I am anymore, but I'm not angry with you."

She nodded absently.

"Why did he shoot a defenseless creature?"

"Because he couldn't shoot us. Frightening, isn't it? It tells you how far some men will go unless someone stops them."

"Colin, I'm afraid. What if you win the contest? Then what will he do?"

"Are you asking if he has the nerve to challenge me?" Colin laughed. "Did you see how fast he galloped away after he shot the fox? He was afraid I *would* challenge him. No, I'll publicly beat him on the morrow, and it will be shame enough."

"Are you going to talk about the ideas you shared with me last night? The ones about all men having the right to a vote?"

So. That was it. She feared he would speak his mind.

All his past failures rolled back to him.

Colin pushed back from the desk, uncertain. Of course, he shouldn't have spoken his mind to Rosalyn last night. He thought of Belinda Lovejoyce, whom he had loved so much and who had betrayed his love.

But Rosalyn had gone to Loftus for him. Rosalyn had wanted him to have another chance, even after she knew his deepest thoughts.

The two of them watched each other, and he knew she was as wary as he.

"What if I do discuss my deepest convictions?" he asked.

Rosalyn's gray-green gaze focused on the floor. "I don't know much about politics, Colin. I just want to make everything right."

He stood and crossed over to her. "Rosalyn, would you leave with me right now? Would you walk out the door with me and leave Clitheroe, the Valley, everyone?"

"Even Covey?"

This was a hard test. "Yes."

She leaned back. "You are angry."

"No, I'm not, I'm just—" He stopped. He'd been about to say he wasn't sure of her love. But to do that would be to confess his own.

For a moment, Colin struggled with himself.

His brother was right. He was a coward. He wasn't about to expose his heart again. It had taken too long to heal from that last time.

"I think," she said slowly, "it would be easier if you had challenged Mr. Shellsworth to a duel."

Her observation surprised a laugh out of him. "You're right." The tension between them eased.

"You will come to bed?" she asked.

"As soon as I'm done."

Rosalyn took a step back, and he found himself thinking of how beautiful she had become. "I'll be waiting," she whispered.

He nodded, words unnecessary. She turned, lifted her hem, and climbed the stairs, but then she stopped. "Colin, it may be best if you keep your more radical ideas a secret."

There, she'd finally said it.

"You believe it unwise to speak out?"

The lines of her mouth flattened, and there was that delightful dimple that intrigued him so much. He liked seeing it better when she was smiling. "I think you must be careful if you want the Commons seat," she replied. She released her breath, as if she feared she'd already said too much. "Good night." She hurried to their room.

Colin watched her and then returned to his

work. Suddenly the rights of men paled in the face of caring for this young woman. He looked down at what he'd written, a hodgepodge of what he thought Loftus wanted to hear, married to some of his own beliefs.

If he won the seat, Loftus would expect him to represent his interests. Colin would not receive it any other way. If he really spoke his mind, he could be ostracized by the gentry.

And that might cost him this new and very fragile love.

He sat at the desk and looked out the window into the night, caught in the devil's own dilemma.

Rosalyn wished she was more experienced in life. Then perhaps she would know how best to counsel him. The moment her warning had left her lips, she had felt guilty.

She undressed, putting on a thin cotton night rail. Sleep didn't come quickly, nor did she search for it. Colin's distance bothered her more than his earlier anger.

The candle had burned itself out before she heard him come to bed. She lay there, listening to him remove his boots, unbutton his breeches, pull his shirt over his head. The mattress gave as he climbed in beside her . . . and she realized that if he had wanted distance between them, he could have had a separate bedroom. That was the way her parents had been, the way her aunts and uncles had lived.

But Colin had not once suggested such a thing. The insight gave her courage. She turned to him. He was naked, and she smiled. This was the way she liked him.

Without words, she began kissing him—his shoulder, his neck, working her way to his lips.

Colin was hard and ready for her. Soundlessly, they made love. Words would have been super-fluous. They laced their fingers together as he pulled her beneath him. When he entered her, she knew she would follow him anywhere.

For him, she would give up her home, her friends, her very identity.

Afterwards, he fell asleep, still inside her. She cradled his head against her chest and said the one thing she was so afraid to speak aloud—"I love you."

And the truth of those words filled her with hope.

When Colin woke the next morning, he discov-ered Rosalyn was already up. He found her out digging in her flower beds. She wore a faded blue dress and a wide-brimmed straw hat. Curls peeked out from beneath her bonnet and made his heart ache with love for her.

He knelt down and picked up a hand shovel from her basket of tools. "You were up early."

She smiled. "I didn't want to wake you."

"You've had less sleep than I."

"I had compensations." The light dancing in her eyes made him laugh.

"We both have." He dug in the soil a bit. Rosalyn's hands moved with purpose, while he was merely filling time. The speech was on his mind. "You helped me sleep well last night. I was so tense I might not have slept otherwise."

She looked up at him through her lashes. "We helped each other. Did you check on the fox?" she asked. "I forgot to."

"Yes. John's salve is a cure-all, and wild creatures hate confinement. The fox was ready to leave, and so I let it go."

Rosalyn sat back. "You what?"

He met her gaze. "I let him go. He was anxious to be where he belonged." The meaning of his words were not lost on him. "Of course, Cook was anxious to have him gone, too." He dug back into the earth. "It seemed the right thing to do."

She looked to the line of trees where the fox used to sit. He wasn't there. "Do you think he'll be back, or will he go off on his own?"

"Rosalyn, he had to leave sooner or later."

"I suppose." She rested her hands in her lap. "And this way, we can tell Lord Loftus we don't have the fox."

"I prefer not talking to him on the subject at all. Besides, Shellsworth has probably already had his say."

She rose to her feet. "I think I'd best get ready." She turned and left, and Colin found himself sitting alone. She'd not asked after his speech. He knew she must have doubts. He tossed the spade into the basket and got to his feet. He'd best see to their transportation into town.

They did leave earlier than Colin thought they should, but then, they both had a bit of nerves. Covey came with Cook and John in the pony cart. Bridget had made plans to attend with some friends.

That Bridget and her friends wanted to go was the first inkling they had that the event might be larger than Rosalyn and Lady Loftus had anticipated.

They knew by the time they reached the ruins of the old Norman keep at the top of the street that this was an event. The roads were packed. The streets of Clitheroe were busier than if it had been a market day.

As they rode down toward the White Lion, all around them came the call for good wishes. Colin recognized many faces from his childhood. He remembered that, at the time, there had been a good number of them who'd wanted to see him in the stocks. They all seemed pleased with him now.

A podium and stand had been set up outside the public house to take advantage of the spring afternoon, and to allow Botherton to sell more ale and cider. Everyone was there.

"Oh, dear," Rosalyn said on the phaeton's seat beside him. "I wasn't expecting this."

Lord Loftus had already arrived. He and his wife sat in an open carriage close to the podium. They nodded their heads and waved like visiting royalty. Mr. and Mrs. Blair, the mill owner and his wife, as well as the Lovejoyces and their daughter, Belinda, were also part of their party. Colin could feel Belinda watching him. Funny that a woman who had once meant so much to him was little better than a stranger now.

Shellsworth and his wife were in a carriage, pulled up as close as possible to the Loftus'. The lawyer appeared tense, which made Colin all the more relaxed.

He set the brake and jumped down. Immediately, men held out their hands to him. He was a local lad, and they'd come to give him support.

Colin's heart swelled at the good wishes, but the person he wanted to see—his brother—was not there.

Botherton called the meeting to order. He enjoyed having the White Lion be the center of attention. "We're here to hear two good men speak," he shouted in a commanding voice. "As you may or may not know, one will fill our Commons seat."

No one said anything. What was there to say? A man close to Colin grumbled, "The decision is nowhere close to ours."

"Loftus buying the ale if he wants our vote?" another man wondered aloud, and those who overheard him laughed.

Colin stood next to Oscar's nose. The warhorse nuzzled his neck. Rosalyn sat on the phaeton with her hands in her lap. She wore the wide-brimmed straw hat she'd had on earlier that morning and the dress of marine blue that brought out the green in her eyes and the gold in her hair. She'd never looked prettier.

Botherton looked to Loftus. "How do you wish to proceed, my lord? Do you have a choice, or shall we draw straws to see which should go first?"

"Draw straws," Loftus said airily, relishing his role of lord.

Colin and Shellsworth were called forward. The short straw would go first, and that was drawn by Shellsworth. Colin returned to the phaeton and stood by the side, where his wife was sitting.

Shellsworth was a good orator for the first forty minutes. He stood up to the podium with a confidence that said he did not know everyone didn't like him. He spoke exactly as Colin predicted he would. He talked about Loftus's generosity and the power of the conservative Tory party. He went on about British victory and British power in the world.

It was obvious that, in preparation for the speech, he'd been giving it to his wife, who knew it so well that she mouthed the words with him. Someone caught her doing it and nudged a companion, who quietly laughed and tapped another to look. Pretty soon, people weren't watching Shellsworth but his wife.

However, after the first hour passed, and

Shellsworth gave no sign of abating, the crowd grew restless. Even Loftus started looking at his fingernails. The lawyer kept talking.

Rosalyn tapped Colin on the shoulder. "He will be difficult to follow if everyone is tired of hearing speeches."

He noticed for the first time she'd brought a handkerchief, which she had wrung into threads with worry. "All the better for me," he assured her.

Rosalyn didn't say anything.

At last the lawyer finished. His final words were greeted by a smattering of applause. "I clap because I'm glad he's done," said a man standing next to Colin, and all around them laughed.

Botherton used the moment between orators as a chance to encourage everyone to refill their tankards, which many did. The mood of the crowd was still festive but definitely more fidgety than it had been at the beginning.

Botherton called Colin down. As he walked through the crowd, many clapped him on the back.

They expected much out of him, he realized. He was one of them. Shellsworth represented the gentry. Colin was the upstart.

As he climbed the makeshift stage to take his

place at the podium, he still wasn't certain what he would say. Inside his jacket was his carefully written speech. At this height above the crowd, he could feel the clear, fresh spring wind. The air was ripe with the promise of new life.

The people settled in. Surprisingly, there were as many women there as men. When he'd left years ago, such would not have been the case.

Loftus watched Colin with suspicious eyes. He stroked his upper lip with a finger. Lady Loftus beamed at him. There was no doubt she was on his side. The Lovejoyces prepared to listen with benevolent tolerance. At one time, Mr. Lovejoyce had thrown Colin out of their home for daring to call on his daughter. That same daughter now ran her tongue over her lips, slowly, so that he would not mistake the message.

Colin looked away. He put his hand on the podium—and then he saw his brother.

Matt stood in the back of the crowd, baby Sarah in his arms and Val at his side. The children were probably off playing elsewhere. Colin understood without words that Matt was here to support him. He might not approve of red wheels on sporty phaetons. He might think Colin's goals wrongheaded. But he was present as a brother.

The connection between them spanned years and ideology. They had been birthed by the same parents, trained by the same disciplined tutor, and Colin realized they were not so far apart after all. Even if Matt could sing and he couldn't.

The one difference between them was the fact that Matt had the courage of his convictions, the courage he believed Colin lacked.

And then Colin's gaze turned toward Rosalyn. She sat on the phaeton's perch with her hands in her lap and her eyes shining with pride. She alone had the most to lose if he spoke his mind.

She alone was the one encouraging him to do so. As if a blindfold had been lifted from his eyes, he saw what he should have seen all along—she loved him.

The knowledge struck him like a bolt of lightning.

Rosalyn hadn't been attempting to sway his decision. She had been trying to let him know that it was his to make, and she would be there come what may.

He remembered her touch last night in bed. The way she had offered herself to him. Love had been in every movement.

Yes, she loved him. Her love was there for all

to see, provided the person wasn't a duffle-headed husband.

Colin looked right at his wife and began speaking. He didn't even bother to pull out the pages of the speech he had prepared the night before. He knew what he wanted to say. He'd yearned to say these things so many times over the years.

He started with the usual homage to God and King, but from there he diverged. "But what I've come to discuss with you," he said, looking at these people who had been a part of his youth and would now be players in his future, "is the question of Parliamentary reform."

The moment the words left his lips, there was a reaction. Loftus dropped his hand and sat straighter. Shellsworth grinned.

But the crowd listened.

Colin spoke of the necessity for representation for all men. He talked about the vote and the need for a strong House of Commons to represent Britain's future for all. He mentioned the importance of education and taxes going to support not the landlords but those who earned the wages.

He spoke out against injustice and shared his vision of a new Britain, one where all men could be safe from the threat of habeas corpus being suspended, or being imprisoned without legal protection. He said the time had come to end corruption at the very highest levels of government and in the military. He'd witnessed how class distinctions had benefited a few while keeping good men from achieving. "I have achieved what I have in my life," he said, "because I had a man like Father Ruley, whom many of you knew and trusted. He gave me an education, one that should be available for all. I want the Commons seat. I wish it could be put to a vote *as it should be.* But if I don't receive it, I want all who hear my voice to know that a new time is dawning in England. The ways of the hierarchy are changing. The individual is important. We are standing with one foot in the old ways of feudalism, and another in the modern world. What happened in France will not happen here. We are Englishmen. We don't behead tyrants, but *neither do we tolerate them.*"

With those words, he'd finished.

In all, he'd spoken for only ten minutes. The crowd had gone silent. Even the children had stopped laughing during their play, as if picking up the mood of the adults.

Colin didn't look to Loftus's carriage. Instead, he looked at the crowd, uncertain of their response.

And then Rosalyn stood. All eyes turned immediately to her, and Colin felt people hold their breath, wondering what drama was about to unfold.

She began clapping.

At first, she clapped alone, but then Matt joined her, then Val and even little Sarah, mimicking her parents. There was laughter then and a groundswell of applause. Shouts went up, congratulating him on the courage to speak what they'd all been thinking.

Shellsworth stood, calling for quiet. His shrill voice charged, "Mandland speaks insurrection against the government!"

Botherton took the podium from Colin. "Sit down, man!" he shouted back. "He said no such thing!"

"Yes, and if your head wasn't so far up someone's arse," a wag yelled at Shellsworth, "you'd know he spoke truth!"

Everyone laughed at that—save for Shellsworth and his wife, who threw her hands up over her ears in a ridiculously childish gesture. To show his anger, Shellsworth picked up his whip and lashed out at those in the crowd closest to him.

For a moment, chaos was in danger of overtaking the assembly. Angry hands reached out to pull the whip and the lawyer out of the carriage, but Colin cried out, "No! Leave him be. He has the right to his opinion."

Several heads nodded, and there were acknowledgements of agreement.

The moment was interrupted by Loftus's coachman backing his carriage out. The matched pair of bays, which also served as hunters, pushed their way toward Downham Manor, the crowd stepping aside to let them pass. Colin noticed that some men even removed their hats while Loftus passed, a sign of respect, while others stood silent and sullen.

Shellsworth wasted no time in turning his vehicle around and trailing in Loftus's wake.

Colin saw exactly what his speech had done.

The powerful of the parish would no longer welcome him with open arms. He truly would be making his own way now. And Loftus would never give him the Commons seat.

There was a step on the stage, and Colin turned to see his brother climbing up to join him. Matt threw his arms around Colin's shoulders.

"That took courage," he said. "I'd not dared voice those thoughts, even from the pulpit, but now, brother, I know I can't keep silent."

Botherton led the cheer for the Mandland brothers. Colin knew the nature of men. Today they would cheer; tomorrow, when there was hell to pay, half of them would deny having even been present . . . or would they?

Could not the seeds of change that had swept the Colonies in America and led the French to revolt find root here?

And if so, what role would he end up playing?

He looked to his wife, to the woman who had given him the freedom to say what he believed . . .

She was gone.

The phaeton was still there with young Boyd holding Oscar's harness. But his wife was nowhere to be seen.

# Chapter Eighteen

$\mathcal{R}$osalyn was beside herself. If she didn't catch up with her patrons, Lord and Lady Loftus, Colin was going to lose the Commons seat. She knew she could make them see right.

It would have been impossible for her to drive the phaeton out of the crowd. She'd asked her husband's nephew Boyd to watch Oscar, and then she'd made her way up to the top of the hill by the Norman keep, where Covey, John, and Cook waited.

"John, you must take me to Downham Manor," Rosalyn said.

Covey asked, "Is that wise? Lord Loftus is not pleased."

"But I can calm him down," Rosalyn said. "He must see that Colin speaks what people are thinking. He must understand that Colin didn't direct his comments at him."

"He certainly did," John said stoutly. "And about time. I say the colonel is a rum one. He should be in the Commons seat."

Rosalyn was taken aback by her usually reserved gardener being so forthcoming.

Covey stepped in. "Yes, John, you drive her. Cook and I will find a ride home with friends."

John had no choice then but to do Rosalyn's bidding. In the end, it was all for naught. The pony cart could never catch up with a carriage, and at Downham Manor both Lord and Lady Loftus refused to see her.

Rosalyn stood on the step, slightly stunned. She had expected her cachet with the two of them to carry some weight. She had wanted to protect Colin.

And she couldn't.

She came down off the steps and walked to the cart. "I think we'd best go home, John."

He grumbled something about the rude manners of the gentry. Rosalyn barely heard him. Instead, she was struggling with her own doubts.

Had Colin gone too far? Had she encouraged him?

However, for the first time in their acquaintance, John talked all the way back to Maiden Hill. He discussed the parish and the people he felt needed more concern.

Rosalyn was surprised, to say the least. When the house was in sight, she gathered her wits enough to place her hand on his arm. "John, why are you telling me this?"

"Because you are the colonel's wife. You are the one who can see justice done."

*See justice done.*

The words didn't make sense to her. "But I founded the Borough Charity League."

"That's nothing, my lady. What good did they do except pay a pittance and sit around preening for each other? I and most of the lads at the pub, lads who had families with mouths to feed, thought that your Charity League was more for planning dances for Lady Loftus and her kind. That's all the gentry want—opportunities to la-di-da over each other. They pay you a pittance, expect your hard work, and look right through you as if you don't even exist. I thought you were one of them, but now I know you are different." He looked her in the eye. "I'm proud to be working for you, Mrs. Mandland."

"Why, thank you, John," Rosalyn said uncertainly. Had she been that selfish?

Well, of course she had. She knew firsthand how John felt because it had been the way her father's family had made her feel.

And so she had brought her knowledge of social order to the Valley, which was not to say it hadn't already existed; she'd just managed to escalate the stakes a bit and had been very proud of herself—until now.

John brought the cart to a halt. "Here you are, Mrs. Mandland. I'll take the cart to the stable."

"Thank you," she murmured and stepped out. John drove off, but Rosalyn stood in the drive looking at the house. By right of marriage, this was her house now. Maiden Hill. She wondered if her husband waited inside and what she would tell him. He must know that Lord Loftus would never give him the Commons seat.

She entered the house. Colin was not in the sitting room, although the desk still had papers and the inkwell and pens from last night. She walked to the back of the house. Cook was busy with dinner. Covey was sitting in a chair in the kitchen doing her needlework.

"Have you seen my husband?" Rosalyn asked.

"No," Covey answered. "I'm not certain he has returned yet. There was quite a celebration going on at the White Lion. Apparently there were gentlemen there who wished Colin to go into politics."

"What does that mean?" Rosalyn said, removing her straw hat.

"I don't know," Covey answered. "How were Lord and Lady Loftus?"

"They refused to see me," she confessed.

"It is not such a great loss, Rosalyn," Covey answered. "They are not your friends."

No, but they were of her class. Where did one go when one threw off all that was expected and accepted?

The front door opened. "Excuse me," she murmured and went down the hall. She took only a few steps, however, before she stopped.

Colin was there, standing in the doorway, and she was reminded of the first moment they'd met.

Only, he was no longer a stranger . . . or the confident man who had come to take over her home. He removed his hat. "Did I go too far, Rosalyn?"

"You won't have the Commons seat."

"I don't want the damn thing."

She nodded, and then, taking courage in hand, said, "It means we will be here together." She glanced around the hallway. "No separate lives, you in London, and I in Clitheroe."

"No." He was watching her closely now, and there was something in his expression that was different from the way he had looked at her even this morning.

Rosalyn feared to hope. He'd been so quiet this morning. . . .

"A great deal has changed," she admitted.

"Yes." He drew a breath and released it. "Rosalyn, I've made a muddle of everything. I don't believe we will be on anyone's guest list."

She understood that by "anyone" he referred to the gentry.

"Even my brother is in danger of being ostracized," he continued.

"Val will like that."

Her words sparked a reluctant smile. "Yes, she will. She's a bit of a republican."

"I expect the sermons will be fiery from the pulpit from now on."

"They may be," he said. "He was proud of me, Rosalyn. He told me so."

There was a wealth of unspoken emotion in his last sentence. She, who had no family that cared, understood what he meant.

"The question is," he continued, "can *you* live with what I've done?"

For a second, Rosalyn was stunned. Now she understood her husband's quiet mood. "You fear I disapprove?"

No one had truly ever cared what she thought about anything other than a dinner invitation or a dress hem. The significance of his question set her heart beating in her chest.

"You left," he said. "I looked and you were gone."

"I went after Lord Loftus." Rosalyn caught her breath, fearful that he might not mean what she thought. "I wanted the Commons seat because I believed that was what *you* wanted. I thought I could help, but he will have nothing to do with me."

A muscle hardened in Colin's jaw. "How dare he refuse my wife."

Rosalyn hurried to his side. She placed her hand on his chest lest he turn and walk out the door to avenge her honor. His heart beat as rapidly as hers. He looked down at her. Their faces were mere inches apart. "Colin, I don't care about him."

"You don't understand. He may never speak to you again."

"Then it will be his loss." She dared to move closer, feeling the familiar pattern of his body, which fit so well with hers. "I was proud of you today. Yes, I'm fearful. The crowd, their reaction . . . Lord Loftus . . ."

He covered her hand with his. "I'm no radical, but I can't stay silent any longer. I used to believe that I had to join their ranks. The truth be known, I'm worse at pretending to be a snob than I am at singing."

Dear God, she loved him so much. "I was the snob," she confessed. "I'd worked so hard to become someone of importance, I'd forgotten what is important. *You* are important."

"Rosalyn, are you saying—?" he started cautiously.

"Yes, Colin, I love you to distraction." There, she'd said it. She'd taken all of her pride and placed it in front of him.

It was not misplaced.

Colin gave a glad whoop, swept her up in his arms, and twirled her right there in the front hall until she was dizzy. "And I love you," he practically crowed. He spun her around again. "Ah, Rosalyn, you have made me the happiest of men."

When she could gather her wits, she dared to ask, "When did you know?"

"That I loved you? I don't recall. It seems to have been living inside me, a constant companion waiting for me to notice." He kissed her hand joined with his. "Last night, when you stood in the doorway, I realized my one fear in speaking what I truly felt was of losing you. When I looked out in the crowd and you were gone . . ." He shook his head. "But I knew you hadn't left. Deep in my soul, I knew."

"I could never leave you," she said. "And I think I started to love you from the moment you butted your head into my life."

His eyes danced with mock offense. "I never butted into your life."

"You walked right into my house."

"*Whose* house?" he dared to ask, and she laughed.

Colin swung her up in his arms and started up the stairs. "It will be time for dinner soon," she weakly protested.

"I'm not hungry," he answered. "At least not for food."

She didn't argue. She couldn't. Her appetite was for something decidedly different too.

Colin carried her into their room so no demons could follow . . . and none did.

Oh, no, none at all.

Matt insisted that they remarry "decently," as he put it.

Colin and Rosalyn made no protest. They even went through the formalities of having the banns announced. Everyone in the congregation took great delight in teasing them. Everyone, that is, save for the Lovejoyces and Lord and Lady Loftus. They no longer patronized St. Mary Magdalene's Church. Neither did Mrs. Sheffield and her husband, although Mr. and Mrs. Blair still came.

Mr. and Mrs. Shellsworth left in a month's time for London, so they didn't have the opportunity to wish Colin and Rosalyn happiness.

The wedding itself was held on a Tuesday afternoon with the wedding "breakfast" at the White Lion. Colin spared no expense, and Rosalyn found herself married to a wealthy man. No more worrying about candle stubs.

She'd discovered over the past few weeks he'd been talking to John about improvements to Maiden Hill. What she learned at the wedding was that she wasn't the only one who had noticed. Their farming neighbors had been wondering what "Young Mandland" was up to, and they had questions about new farming methods.

They drove home in the phaeton, which Matt's children had decorated with colorful bits of paper and ribbon.

On the way to the house, they passed a stretch of woods. Rosalyn saw a flash of color in the border of the field. She put her hand on Colin's arm.

"Please stop."

He did, and she pointed to the fox sitting in the shadows. It was *their* fox, and sitting by him was a vixen. "Is it my imagination, or is he grinning at us?" Rosalyn asked.

"He's grinning," Colin agreed before their bold little friend disappeared back into the shadows. His mate followed in his steps.

Colin and Rosalyn sat for a moment in the middle of the road. "Once I wondered where in the world I would find a place to fit in," she said.

"Do you know now?" he asked.

She nodded. "In your arms."

"Let's go home," he whispered.

"Yes."

And together they drove off.

Yes, life was good.

Very good indeed.

# Epilogue

$C$olin and Rosalyn decided to change the name of their estate from Maiden Hill to Fox Hill.

The move was enough to set Lord Loftus's teeth on edge. To everyone he could, he told the story of how Mandland had denied him his fox.

Most people sympathized with the fox.

Of course, Lord Loftus's hunting days were over. Lady Loftus discovered she and her friends didn't have the wherewithal to create a society in the Valley without Rosalyn. They could have their routs and soirees, but they lacked the special "extra" Rosalyn had brought to these functions. Hers had been interesting; theirs were boring.

There was nothing left to do but return to where society reigned, and so Lady Loftus packed up her household and her husband and moved all to town.

The Valley heaved a sigh of relief. Most people liked Lord Loftus but agreed with Colin that a new age was arriving. Loftus was part of the old order. The Mandland brothers were the new.

Fortunately, Colin's viewpoints were those of a Moderate. There were those with more radical opinions, and he was instrumental in cooling down hot tempers. Not to say he didn't relish the role of loyal opposition and having the power to badger Mr. Shellsworth at every opportunity.

Very quickly the people in the Valley started talking about what steps could be taken to send Colin to the Commons. After all, not every seat was "owned" by a peer.

In December, Rosalyn realized she was pregnant. What's more, she'd grown very close to her sister-in-law, Val. Still, there was something missing from her life. She couldn't decide what . . . or, rather, she was afraid to face it.

On a sunny day the following May, Covey helped her discover what it was.

Rosalyn was scattering seeds in her front flower bed, the one that was her pride and joy and Oscar's favorite snack.

"A letter has arrived for you," Covey said.

"I don't remember seeing the post."

"It didn't come that way." Covey held out the envelope.

Rosalyn recognized the writing and the seal. Heedless of her serviceable gray dress, she sat on the lawn and broke the wax.

The letter was from her mother.

For a moment, Rosalyn couldn't breathe. Covey was watching her with concern, and Rosalyn didn't want to show emotion. She forced herself to focus on the words:

*My dear Rosalyn—*

*It has been my fondest dream to someday see you again. Mrs. Covington has told me of your marriage and the impending birth of a child. I have always prayed for your happiness and take great joy in knowing you are married to a good and honest man.*

*I have decided to take a great risk. I have journeyed from our home in Glasgow to see you. I am staying at the home of a friend of Mrs. Covington's. I will be there until Monday. I hope you will have time to see me.*

*Your mother*

For a moment, Rosalyn couldn't think. Now she knew why Covey watched her so anxiously.

"Should I not have given you the letter?" Covey asked.

"No, it's fine." Rosalyn raised her hands to her temples and rubbed them. She got to her feet. "I need to find Colin."

She found him in the barn. Without a word, she handed him the letter. He read it. Except for when they were first married, she'd not mentioned her mother again.

"Do you want to see her?" he asked.

"I don't know." She fanned her hot face with the envelope.

"Rosalyn, how would you feel if our child had this decision to make?"

"Our child will never have this decision to make."

Colin put his arms around her waist. "The world changes every day. You don't know what the future holds. How would you feel if our child had this decision to make?" he repeated.

"I'd want her to see me," she said. She leaned against his strong chest. "And yet, I'm afraid."

"I'll go with you," he said, and he did. They went that very afternoon.

Rosalyn was nervous—until they arrived in

front of Mrs. Howell's cottage. There was no mistaking the identity of the woman sitting on a bench in the sun there.

This woman was a far cry from the mother of Rosalyn's memory. This mother was older, sadder, rounder. She came to her feet, and for a moment the two women stared at each other as strangers—and then her mother opened her arms and said, "Rosalyn."

Rosalyn could not have stayed away if she'd wanted to.

That afternoon was bittersweet. The rift between her and her mother would never be completely bridged, and yet, at last, they could understand each other better.

Charles Mandland was born September second. He came into the world screaming with the healthiest set of lungs anyone had ever heard. Matt predicted he certainly had the makings of a bishop and told everyone so during Charles's christening.

Colin didn't care what his son had the makings of. He'd learned it made no matter if a man was a cobbler or a vicar or a farmer.

What was really important in life was whether or not a man had learned to love and to love well.

Wasn't that what Val had once tried to tell him?

He stood in the church, his son in his arms, his wife by his side, and felt his parents' blessings.

"No demons," he whispered when they retook their seats.

Rosalyn smiled. She knew he referred to the threshold and his mother's tale.

"No," she agreed, "not now or ever."

And so it was.

# Acknowledgments

I had the best time researching this book.

If you ever find yourself in the Ribble Valley, you must visit the Old Post House Hotel on King Street in Clitheroe, John and Janet Spedding, innkeepers. Order John's toffee cake and cream. I tell you, I wake up in the middle of the night dreaming of it. John promised me the recipe, which he then *never shared*. You have my permission to badger him for it—and if you get it, I can be reached at *cathy@cathymaxwell.com*.

Truly, John and Janet are delightful hosts and well worth a visit.

I'd also like to express my appreciation to Mr. Simon Entwistle, local historian, raconteur, delightful traveling companion. He gave us a tour of the Valley unlike any other and patiently answered my questions. What a day we had.

Let me advise you now that any errors are my own and cannot be credited to that good man, who did his best to set me straight.

Also, if you are in the mood for a good story, Simon is easy to find. He conducts ghost tours for tourists like us, and the local tourism offices have his name. But see if you can share a few minutes over a pint alone with him. He knows the rumors behind every murder and bit of skullduggery in the Valley for the past eight hundred years and has the talent for telling a tale.

> *Exit, pursued by a bear.*
> Stage direction in
> ***The Winter's Tale***
> Wm. Shakespeare